THE GOLDFINGER BITE

Colin Roberts

Two men, one woman
And someone has crabs

Yersinia Press

Published by: Yersinia Press

ISBN: 978 0 9563340 0 8

First Edition 2009

Typeset, printed and bound by:
Lazarus Press
Unit 7 Caddsdown Business Park
Bideford
Devon EX39 3DX
www.lazaruspress.com

For Mum and, obviously, Dad.

Yersinia Press

Chapter 1

Danny Benton slumped forward, out of breath and strength, almost out of ammo and terminally out of luck. Outnumbered, pinned down, there was nowhere left to run. His face was an inch from the dirt behind some flimsy piece of machinery, his only cover. It wouldn't stop their bullets but at least they couldn't see him if he kept his head down.

Sirens wailed and the machinery of battle rumbled and rattled incessantly, near and far. Danny felt the sweat break through his forehead as he gasped and panted, catching up on oxygen before the final push. Because he would push on, he knew it, and it would be for the final time. He couldn't stay cowed in this Hell-hole forever, and he swore by St Butch and St Sundance that he'd take with him every last one that he could.

He risked a glance. Flickers of movement in the waste-land gave away their positions at once, and Danny already had clear shots at two bobbing heads, maybe three. But they didn't need to hide. They weren't the ones low on ammo. Checking his pockets, he felt the reassuring shape of his cell radio, but enemy fighters swooped low in tight formation and he knew that a call for reinforcements would be useless.

He'd never even have had time. The enemy weren't waiting. They were coming for him, now, but they were coming in their own sweet time, like they knew his last bullets weren't silver.

He heard them first, low, snarling growls rising up from their hiding places, the gnashing of wet fangs and the hiss of needle-sharp bristles piercing leather hide, and when he dared look out, and saw the first scythe-clawed hand closing over Joan's computer monitor he. . .

'*Noooo!*' He wailed and leapt to his feet. 'Mondays don't have werewolves!'

Danny blinked and looked around. Most of the office was looking back. A few of the typists had even stopped machine-gunning their keyboards but the telesales slaves just stared their contempt without once breaking stride on their scripts.

Now they'd all think he'd spent the weekend on mushrooms. Danny sat down, a little irritated but not embarrassed. What did he care what they thought? The cowards, slogging away nine to five every day, without one word of thanks for all the Nazis and monsters he was fighting off. It was worrying, though. Early werewolves was a sure sign that the coming working week would be a dull one, dull even by the standards of *Barum Fixings & Attachments*, where you didn't have to be brain-dead to get the job; it was the first thing they trained into you.

He stared at the papers in his in-box, realigned the pencils in the holder, then began to count the pixels on his computer screen before realising he had a pen in urgent need of chewing. Very early werewolves, come to that. He rarely had to resort to even wartime slaughter fantasies until Wednesday at the earliest, and he always saved delusions of werewolves and vampires for Fridays. Something to look forward to, wasn't it? But now, Friday would have to be zombie hordes, or there'd be no getting through the week. Danny slumped low in his chair. Zombies were supposedly reserved for special Fridays, those pre-holiday ones or the eve of the staff Christmas party.

'No werewolves on Mondays,' Joan Lobb murmured to no one, barely heard. Danny watched her greying head rise slowly as she frowned into the distance. 'Are there?'

Danny loosened his tie again. The damned thing always felt like a garotte, however slack the knot. He sighed, got up and went to the window. A low ceiling of charcoal cloud was April-showering Barnstaple with everything it had, and for a moment he considered jumping, ending the nightmare once and for all.

He would almost certainly survive the one-storey drop, which would be nice, especially if he judged the wind right. A good bullseye, right at the top of Jocelyn Mullacott's spine, where she stood outside, chain-smoking in the partial shelter of the porch, would go a long way toward ending the nightmare in one fell splat. He would have aimed for her head but feared impaling himself on the point of her witch's hat. Danny snorted drily. Fantasy, maybe, but with the *Obergruppensupervisor* permanently out of the way, at least life at Barum Fixings would be bearable.

But they'd had their taste of freedom, and now it was being cruelly snatched away from them again. It was Jocelyn's first day back at work after a couple of weeks off sick, which had been ten working days of milk and honey for all other employees. Probably having her lungs de-tarred, Jim had speculated, though Danny had thought it far more likely she was away on a secret mission, supervising genocide or the corruption of innocents, or dubbing vocals for a death metal band.

Look at her, he thought, the soulless sow, hunched over that cigarette like a vampire sucking a midget. And desperate enough to stand out in the mother of all downpours. Crazy. He caught the sneer in his reflection, rolled his eyes and looked away, across town. In the distance, the River Taw estuary meandered away, flat silver under the blackening sky. Tiny with distance, a small formation of birds rode the breeze seaward along the shoreline, tracking the *Tarka Trail* aerially, and Danny was suddenly desperate to be standing there instead of in the office, mother of all downpours or not.

The rain's patter was soon over-dubbed with the white-noise tapping of keyboards. Danny rested his forehead against the glass and raindrops burst a double-glazing's width from his eyeballs, blurring in the fake hot wind blowing up from the wall heater. Why hadn't he found himself a job outdoors? Recently, he had been seriously considering running amok in a shoplifting or graffiti-spraying spree, then turning himself in, in the hope of getting community service order and spending his days picking up litter in the park. Jim, though, had pulled him up short with three timely pieces of wisdom. One, his community service might be blanket-bathing the elderly; two, the pay was less than poor; and three, that they were both far, *far* too drunk at the time to be making serious career path decisions like that. Sometimes, Jim Molton was a very wise man.

Others didn't think so, though. Lithium Jim, a lot of them called him, although never to his face. Danny wasn't quite sure why. They always said it with a snigger, almost like there was a story behind it, perhaps something that happened before Danny had joined the company and was never spoken of openly again. Danny had never asked his friend about it, and probably never would.

'Busy, Mr Benton?'

Danny jumped out of his skin, barely avoiding head butting the window. 'Yes, yes. Just. . . warming my pen, Mr Slade.'

Warming my pen?

But Slade, the branch manager, was already gone. It was always the same, whenever he slithered out of his lair and crossed the sales floor. When he did get up on his hind legs he was quite tall, and looked like he'd once been a big bloke, muscle-wise, too. Well gone to seed now, though, and with his long arms, fledgling paunch and the hint of an all-new extra chin, he always reminded Danny of a bored, caged orang utan, especially with the red tinge to his straggly, self-cut hair.

Slade didn't believe in speaking to his staff, ever, but he was more than happy to shout, hiss or scoff at them in an effort to display authority. And he never listened to excuses, just in case he ever came across someone doing something right and might actually have to praise them. Jim had a great way of mumbling nonsense back at him in a way that sounded like real speech, but Danny just tended to say the first thing that came into his head. He sniffed. It didn't really matter, did it? Who's boss ever listens, anyway?

Danny went back to his desk and sat down, blowing out a sigh that sent a ripple across the sea of Post-it notes flooding the space around the base of his computer monitor. He glanced around, caught Joan still staring at him, then realised she was just off in one of her usual waking comas and just happened to be facing his way. Joan, grey and unkempt, was the oldest in the room, and always seemed to be resisting a permanent out-of-body experience. She struck Danny as just a random redundancy away from a future on the streets, a bag-lady in waiting but who hadn't yet made the break with society. Danny grinned weakly. It was all too easy to see into the future where Joan was concerned. He closed his eyes and there she was, with crazy Don King hair and her world in a shopping trolley, screaming bible quotes at traffic lights.

Joan's phone rang, and rang, and Danny watched her sitting there so impervious to it that he started to wonder if she might be dead. He was wondering, too, how long it would take anyone to notice, as long as her corpse didn't topple and stayed vulture-free, when he realised that the unanswered call would soon trip across to his own phone, so he snatched up the receiver and dialled Jim's extension.

'Whassup, man?'

'Hahahaha. Dan the Man! What's going on?'

Danny grinned. 'Nearly had to take a customer call.'

'Ooh, nasty. Busy?'

'Nah. You?'

'Yeah, sending e-mails. You should have yours by now.'

Danny pulled a face of horror, pointless while on the phone. 'You're not doing. . . *work*, are you, Jimmy?'

'How dare you, you dirty-!' Jim slammed down the phone.

Danny chuckled and sat back and stretched out, hands behind his head. Amazingly, the customer call had dragged Joan back to the land of the living and she was prodding at her keyboard with both index fingers. *Hmmm*, thought Danny, impressed. *She's been practising*.

Chappell, the accounts guy who he'd never heard speak, glanced at him as he walked past Danny's desk, clutching papers to his chest and letting his gaze linger just long enough to throw in a look of disapproval.

Jerk, thought Danny, but realised the old slap-head might just have a point and took down his feet from his desk. Danny decided to bury his face into his computer, to look busy to anyone not able to see him surfing the Internet, a million miles from Barum - fixings, attachments and all.

He blew another long sigh. A whole wide world of World Wide Web and all of it a waste of space. He was bored of other people's blogs, of lists of jokes and wacky pics, and browsing the crashes, explosions and pratfalls of *YouTube* just wasn't the same on a computer not wired for sound. He wasn't much in the mood for funnies, anyway, so he settled on the local news web site to see how Plymouth Argyle had got on, the night before. They'd won, four-nil.

Immediately even more depressed, Danny flicked on through the headlines. It was just the usual stuff: thrilling village hall refurbishment updates, threats of hospital closure, a derelict barn burning down, someone doing a charity walk dressed as a carrot.

Sad. Very sad. This looked better, though. At least, it was just a good, eye-catching photograph: grinning trawlermen landing a catch. Danny clicked on the link to get the enlarged picture and article. And what a catch it was, too! Three men in coloured, padded suits stood on a dockside to the rear of the picture, with their net tipped out toward the camera. Dozens of fish, gleaming silver slabs around three feet in length, were spilled into a low, slippery stack, filling the foreground.

> '*Southwest Fishing Boats Strike Silver!*'
> 'Fish of unprecedented size are being landed by commercial fishermen in the region. These jubilant men, of the Cornish fishing boat *Marie De Madadd*, are shown unloading a catch of bass - a common enough fish in our waters, but these are fish of distinctly uncommon size!'

Danny yawned and leant back. He was bored with the news, bored with everything, but when he saw Mr Slade returning through the office he ducked back down and busily read the end of the article:

> 'Scientists have been quick to blame manmade climate change for the phenomenon and government ministers have already called for heavier taxation on all fishing vessels operating within two hundred miles of the shore.
> 'Our science correspondent asked Lionel Worsel, captain of the *Marie De Madadd* and a man with more than forty years' knowledge of Cornish waters, for his opinions on the climatological influences affecting patterns of marine migration, and on the environmental and moral implications of his trade.

"Yarrrr," he told our reporter. "What does I care, my beauty? Do you have any idea how much a twenty pound plus bass'll fetch down market? An' I got dozens of the beggars! Yarrrr."

Danny slid open a drawer and took out one of the last few glacier mints mixed in with his paperclips. He used to go fishing with his father when he was a kid - not out to sea like Dad had used to, but just chasing the tiddlers in rivers and ponds - but the vague memory of the feel of a fish on the line returned for the first time in two decades, and he wondered what the *Hell* it would feel like to have one of those silver monsters on there! Somewhere approaching. . . *awesome*, probably. For a little while, the dream of that feeling just wouldn't go away.

It did, though. He hadn't fished in twenty years and their rods, packed away in his parents' attic, were probably just mouldy sticks by now.

He peered over his computer screen. Janice Bodley was holding the door open for Mr Slade, beaming inanely and sticking her chest out at him as he passed. Janice, early twenties, was a drab girl most of the time, mostly down to her fixed expression of gloom. She was an impenetrable mixture of painfully shy meets obstinately sullen - most of the time - with the exception of whenever the boss, or anyone senior within the company, came within ten feet of her. Janice's brown-nosing was instinctive, immediate and impressive, with the merest glimpse of a manager instantly bringing life and colour into bloom across her barren, stony face like a drought-ending downpour in the desert. The worst thing for Danny was that it did, really, make her briefly more attractive, which made seeing her blatantly crawling all the more annoying. Not that Danny had anything against seeing an attractive woman crawling, just. . . Oh god, no. Not Janice!

He hid a long, deep yawn, then discretely slid back his cuff. How could it still be that early? If time ran any slower, nothing would happen at all! Then again, wasn't that Danny's problem all along? He shook and tapped his wristwatch, hoping it had been taking a quiet nap for a while and would quickly leap forward an hour or two to catch up.

No such luck, not even when he shook it harder. He noticed that some stapled-together sheets of paper had arrived on the desk beside him while he had been engrossed in the local news. He eyed them suspiciously. With luck, it would just be another memo to ignore, but they were usually single pages. Danny leant closer, sniffing. No, this was starting to look dangerously like work, work that *someone* was expecting him to do. He crunched his mint like chewing gum. A shiver ran across his shoulders and he felt himself pale, his breathing quicken and his heartbeat start battering his breastbone. He reached out cautiously, his fingertips damp with perspiration and trembling finely as they closed in on the paperwork. He shut his eyes.

And then it was gone! Breath and relief whooshed out of him and he clenched a fist in triumph before flopping back into his seat. He had barely made contact with it: one quick, firm shove and the paperwork had sailed like a puck over ice across the vacant work-space beside his own, then glided silently down into the gap between that desk and an unused filing cabinet.

The danger had passed. Danny drew several calming breaths. *Steady, boy*, he told himself, *it's over*. Work had been avoided and he had survived unscathed. He just didn't know how much longer he could handle the stress. To add to it, his phone rang.

He groaned when he saw the incoming number. Slade, always the boss-at-a-loss, lately, since his last PA walked out and the agency refused to supply temps. He's a nice man, see, Mr Slade.

'Yes, Mr Slade?'

On the telephone, the boss always sounded like a retired gangster, slow and gruff, and every word he spoke sounded like a threat.

'What are you. . . *doing*, right now, Benton?' The question, dripping with accusation, slipped from his lips on a fog of heavy breathing. Danny just knew that Mr Slade made a lot of mostly-silent, private calls at night.

'I'm, um, just about to —'

'I've had whatshername,' Slade interrupted, spitting out words one at a time. 'The personnel girl, she has left the branch transfer figures on your desk. Beside you. I would be. . . more than grateful, to receive your revisions by this evening.'

'Sure, I'll do what I can, Mr—'

'That is, if your pen is fully warmed.'

There was a long silence. Slade waited, long enough for Danny to chuckle weakly and begin blustering an excuse, then immediately hung up.

Danny waited to make sure that Slade really had gone, then slammed the phone onto its cradle and swore. Now he'd have to find those papers he'd so carefully lost. But Joe Stibb, the computer kid, was looking up from the unit he was servicing on *Printer Central*, the table at the far end of the room where everyone's computer sent their documents for creation. Or rather, Stibby was looking up from the cleavage of Charlotte Langtree, one of the general secretaries, who he'd been chatting up for the last fifteen minutes while he should have been pushing more mechanical buttons. Annoyingly, Charlotte always insisted on being called Charlie, which Danny, satisfyingly, always ignored. He thought *Charlie* was better used for what she'd made of most men in the company as she'd worked her way through them. She just hadn't got around to Charlie-ing him yet, Danny rationalised. Must be doing it alphabetically. And backwards.

Joe Stibb stared back at him without a flicker of expression. Stupid git, with his eyebrow stud and never the same black, obscure-band sweatshirt. He couldn't have been more than five years younger than Danny, but trying to look like he wasn't even out of his teens.

Jim hated him, truly, madly and deeply. On the quiet, Jim was something of a computer whizz and knew everything about them, even that the giant one on *Family Fortunes* was called Mr Babbage. Jim only used his powers for evil, of course, or for a bit of a laugh when things were quiet. At the last staff Christmas party, Jim had been particularly busy with his digital camera, and the results - inventively and pornographically *Paintshop*-doctored pictures of assorted colleagues - had been filtering onto the e-mail system, via hacked-into accounts, ever since. Everyone knew that Jim was the only one in the office who knew how to do all this stuff, but he never liked leaving a trail, actual evidence, and Jim hated Stibb because he was sure that Mr Slade was onto him, and had the geek on a bonus to track down enough evidence to fire him. Some days, Jim could be as paranoid as a midget nun at a penguin cull.

Others, though, he just didn't give a damn. Danny wondered, sometimes, why Jim worried about keeping his lowly pen-pusher job at BF&A. The company car might help a little but was it really worth all the suffering? It still peeved Danny that Jim's job had come with a car, just because it was in a different department. He wasn't on a higher rank than Danny, or had any use for the car in the working day. Only management got cars, as a rule, and management - Slade - was not famed for its giving spirit. It wasn't jealousy, though, not of Jim. Not with the state of the car, a battered old red estate, long enough to carry a coffin in the back if only the rear suspension didn't look so close to death already. But how he'd wangled wheels as part of the deal remained a mystery. Perhaps he had more photos of Slade, non-*Paintshopped* but just as bizarre and incriminating.

But why didn't Jim go freelance and set up his own computer business? He knew his IT well enough, that was certain. But, within a few short hours, Jim would always do something like swapping the sugar for salt in the staffroom or signing some or other co-worker up to an Internet marriage bureau or online cult, and Danny would have his answer.

And now Charlie-otte was looking at him, too, her barely visible sigh and rolled eyes the kind of look that schoolboys got from girls in the years above. Danny pretended not to notice.

The phone rang again, an outside call on his direct line. Damn! He would have to try sabotaging the socket again. But when he'd done that before he'd ended up sitting on the vacant space across from Joan for the five working days it had taken for an engineer to turn up and replace it, and that had been about as much fun as visiting time in the old folk's home after the sedative trolley had been around. *And* he'd still had a working phone!

Danny sighed and lifted the receiver. 'Barum Fixings & Attachments. Sales office. Danny speaking.'

'Hello. Hello?'

'Hello!' said Danny, with a bright and convincing tone of fake cheeriness. 'How can I help you?'

The man's voice was slightly effeminate, shaky, old and foreign, though Danny couldn't quite place the accent.

'Hello, would that please be the selling department, please?'

'It would, Sir!' Silently, Danny sighed. 'And would you like to place an order?'

Danny didn't usually place orders on the system. That was down to the vipers' nest, the coven of alcopop-sucking witches in the sales department, but having the grand title of *technical* sales' meant he had the computer access to do so, and was expected to help out whenever things got busy. Although it wasn't busy at all now, calls from foreigners, the befuddled or downright weirdos were often amusing releases from boredom, and dealing with this one would, at least, postpone having to crawl around like a fool on the floor, searching for Slade's figures.

'My name is Mr Crowley,' snapped the receiver, 'and I would please like to place an order for some size three reverse attachments, please. In orange, if you have them. And just the one box. I'm DIY-ing it myself, you know?'

Danny inhaled, closed his eyes tight and pinched the bridge of his nose. One tiny box of size threes, orange. Well, that was the pension fund and retirement palace sorted at a stroke. Might as well go home now. Might as well really lash out and throw a wild, free party in Rock Park, book Led Zep on stage and hire a thousand body-glittered serving-wenches to——

'Can I please pay you now, please? Hello?'

'Hello!' said Danny. 'Er. . . yes. Over the phone? Sure, if you have an account, or a credit card. That will be a grand total of four pounds and thirty five pence.'

'Very good. Let's see. . . One, two, three, three-fifty. . .'

Danny gritted his teeth, listening to loose change being drag-counted.

'Sir? Excuse me, Sir.' Danny had to repeat himself, louder. 'We can't take cash, I'm afraid. Not over the phone.'

'Oh, oh, I'm sorry,' the old man said, a little flustered. 'Credit card, you say?'

'A credit card will be fine. Do you have one?'

'Well, I er. . .No. No, I don't have one. Should I have?'

It took many long, unprofessional seconds for Danny to compose himself enough to reply politely. 'If you want to pay by credit card, then yes, it would help if you—'

'My wife has one.'

'Can we use that?' There was hope. Danny even managed a friendly laugh. 'Would she mind?'

'I-I-I shouldn't think so. Shall I ask her?'

Danny nodded. 'Perhaps you'd better.'

'One moment please.' He rested the receiver down with a clunk and cleared his throat.

'Martha! Martha? I need to know if it's all right to use your credit card.

'Martha?'

Danny listened patiently. There wasn't a sound from Mrs Oldgit. The old man's voice slowed and got quieter.

'Martha, can you hear me Martha? It's Reginald, your little Reggikins. Can you hear me?'

Silence.

'Martha?' Mr Crowley continued. 'Come back to me, Martha. Come back, please. It's been so lonely here.'

'Mr Crowley? Mr Crowley, is your wife. . . is she actually there with you?'

Gentler now, Mr Crowley chuckled. 'Of course she is, young man. She is always with me. But some days are worse than others, connecting to the world of spirit.'

Danny nearly choked. 'The world of spirit?! Your wife's not . . . she is, isn't she? She's f—'

'I've got a debit card. Will that do?'

It took two full, slow breaths before Danny could answer. 'Yes, Mr Crowley, as long as it's yours and it's current.'

'Good. And I'll have thirty pounds cash back as well, please.'

'Sir, for Chr. . . for goodness sake, this is a telephone order!'

Silence fell, the old man thinking. 'Right. . .' he said slowly, 'so can I have fries with that?'

'Can. . . *what*?'

'And extra anchovies.'

Danny was completely lost for words that can be used to a customer. Then a din of jeering, cheering, whooping and applause burst from his earpiece.

'Yaaaa! BFA tossers!'

The cheers decayed into obscenities, chanted. Realisation dawned, and it stung. Danny slammed down the phone and whirled around his swivel chair.

The Pasty Boys!

Danny knew he shouldn't look, shouldn't give them the satisfaction, but however hard he fought, he could not stop rage twisting his face slowly toward the double glazing. He knew they'd be smiling.

They weren't exactly smiling.

Three floors up in the block across the junction, all the way along the windows of The Pasty Boys' regional head-quarters, paired, bared buttocks bloomed in sequence.

It wasn't only the business headquarters of a chain of hot pastry take-aways. To Danny, it was a pustule on the beauty of glorious Barnstaple. Well, a pustule on Barnstaple, anyway. It was the base of operations for a vile and insidious campaign of sabotage and subversion, a tiny piece of stolen, occupied territory from which the first shots were being fired in a war which would surely split the nation.

That was Jim's theory, anyway. The two of them had been at war with The Pasty Boys for what seemed like forever. Weeks, at least, had passed since Jim had first been spot-lit by someone reflecting the sun with a mirror. Danny had immediately started to search for something to signal back with, to make contact with another lost soul in the world of work, but the shiniest thing he could find was Chappell the accountant's scalp, and he'd never have cooperated.

Jim, though, played it differently, and was soon stagger-ing around, screaming discretely, with his hands clamped over his face.

'My eyes! My eyes!'

'Take it easy, man, or you'll wake Slade.'

But Jim wouldn't have it. 'I could have been *blinded!* Or worse!'

He'd snatched up a large padded envelope and a marker pen from Danny's pot, scrawled, 'Manager - The Pasty Boys' on the front, then dashed out of the office. Some minutes later, Danny had spotted him from the window, dodging between the traffic and heading for their building. He had no idea what was inside, but the envelope had clearly been bulging fit to burst.

The Pasty Boys' response was of middle-Eastern proportions. Over the next week, Barum Fixings sales office had been peppered with more sun-flashes, abusive crank calls, laser-pointer dots and, by Friday morning, eggs. The stains were still visible and the battle was, and remained, well and truly on.

According to Jim, there was an all-out invasion underway and it was a fight for survival. He was convinced. It wasn't only the arrival of a Cornish pasty company in town, it was the Cornish Carbuncle, too. Supposedly representing the jagged bits of the nearby coast, this prominent traffic-roundabout sculpture consists of jagged lumps of stone slumped on girders. Rumour had it that, on the day of the official opening, the council's telephone system had been jammed with calls reporting fly-tipped building rubble.

'But it's *Art*,' said the council, so everyone was content and respectful for the next year, until it leaked out that it wasn't the commemoration of nine-eleven, ground zero, that it appeared to be. Respect lessened more when the costs were made public, and hit rock bottom when it was revealed that the stones weren't even from Devon. They were Cornish.

'Alien,' Jim had called them, and was convinced they'd been planted by Cornish invaders who'd seen the red weed colonisation of Earth in *War of the Worlds*.

That was Jim, through and through, though. For Danny, the fun part was that a mooning from a *Cornish* office meant Jimmy would go ballistic.

Still annoyed but with a growing sense of evil, Danny lifted the phone again, punched in Jim's number and waited, staring out beyond the invaders' outpost and watching clouds of pinpoint birds wheeling over the distant river estuary. So peaceful.

The calm before the storm.

'Wassaaaaap!?'

'A problem, mate,' Danny said, teeth gritted. 'A big one.'

They spat it together.

'The Cornish!'

Chapter 2

'Yeah, Jimbo, we've got trouble. Pasty Boys. They got me. Must have had the call on speaker, too. They were loving it.'

The phone to his ear, Danny tapped his desk with a pen. The window blinds behind him were closed. 'Yeah, hook, line and sinker, my friend. Fake order. . . Yep, full row of moons in the windows, the lot. . . Awful. Flabby. That's what a high-turnip diet does to you. . .'

'Yeah, and if it does it to them, think what it would do to human beings.' Abruptly, Jim had to go, but he promised to be along when the danger of being seen not working had passed. Danny hung up, blew the sea of Post-it notes again and returned to his computer screen. He knew what he should be doing. He should be plotting revenge on the scumbags at *The Pasty Boys,* but he was still seething inside and, knowing revenge was a dish best served cold, decided to put it out of his mind until after lunch. He turned to his e-mail in-box for distraction, but only because Jim had said he was sending something.

He scanned the senders' names in the short list of fresh e-mails. There was nothing from Jim, but one from Jocelyn caught his eye. That was unexpected. She must have learned to read and write. Danny opened it, read, and his jaw dropped.

'For anyone wondering about my recent absence from work and spell in hospital, I wanted to let you know that the surgery was a complete success and I look forward to standing next to all you men in the urinals. Please amend your address books and do not refer to me by my former name any more.
Love & XXXs
Butch Mullacott
Office Supervisor, Barnstaple.'

The recipients line listed every employee, not just of the Barnstaple branch but everyone across the southwest. Danny placed a mint on his tongue, raised his jaw and smiled.

Jimmy! It had to be! This was what 'sending e-mails' had meant - sending other people's from their accounts!

At once, Danny was buzzing. There would be Hell to pay when Jocelyn found out, and as everyone at a computer had now received the e-mail, the Devil wouldn't have long to wait for the cash. He looked toward the door. No sign of Jim yet. Maybe Jocelyn already knew, maybe she'd caught him, and maybe he would never make into the room alive! But. . .

There was nothing happening.

Nothing ever did.

The clock ticked on. Danny was right on the verge of doing some work when he realised he hadn't planned his week-end yet, and there were only four and seven-eighths working days to go!

With a yawn of enthusiasm, his thoughts turned to yet more wild nights of DVDs and single-portion takeaways. Then again, he was word-perfect on the scripts of anything with the undead in it, so that was eighty percent of his collection ruled out for the rest of the month. Also, the last time he'd taken home a curry it had almost put him in hospital. The sewage police were probably still looking for him over that little affair, staking out Indian restaurants and checking suppliers for any suspicious bulk orders of toilet rolls.

Danny banged his forehead down onto his desk and stayed there with his eyes screwed tight. God, was that all he could think of to do? Weekends are supposed to be looked forward to. They're only there to stop mass week-day suicides! And all he had to get excited about was being just as bored within a different set of walls.

He could always go out. Oh yeah, he had a lot of choices there. Lately, though, Danny had found he just couldn't raise enthusiasm for any pub, not like he used to. He had thought about it before but it still struck him as odd. His whole circle of friends had changed in recent times, without any change in Danny himself, not that he was aware of. They were good lads in that circle, every one, all up for a good drink and a laugh and a good drink and a chat and a good drink, but with very little to chat about after the first gallon.

Was he getting old? Danny had hoped to reach his forties, at least, before starting to crumble but at this rate it would be pipe and slippers time by the end of the year!

He sighed again, louder, and sat up. Lacing his fingers behind his head, cracked his knuckles and moaned, loud and pained, knowing no one around would take the slightest bit of notice. It wasn't that he was getting old, just stagnating. God, that was Old with a capital O, and not much to do with how many years he had lived.

Chappell from accounts came back through clutching even more papers and the same disapproval on his face. Danny just tried to blend in with the others, lolling his head to one side, open mouth drooling, and staring off into infinity. Chappell's sniff of criticism hung in the air as he passed.

Baldy git, thought Danny. Who does he think he is, just cos he's got extra buttons on his calculator? He watched Chappell all the way out, fascinated by the curved reflections of the overhead strip-lights on his polished scalp. He no longer had enough left for a comb-over, which was a shame, as his attempts in the past had been superb. And Jim bellowed 'Gotcha!' right in Danny's ear.

Danny swore.

'I've been doing some research, mate,' Jim said, clapping him on both shoulders from behind. 'And I gotcha-ed those pasty bummers, too. Big time. We've won already. I'm telling you, when this gets out, they're going to have to close down.'

Danny spun his seat around. 'Tell me more.'

Jim rubbed his palms together. 'The Pasty Boys, the *Cornish* pasty boys. . . they're total fakes. The whole company is a lie. It's criminal that they even exist, a crime against humanity!'

There was little he could say. 'Go on, then. Why?'

'Fact one,' said Jim. 'Cornish pasties, invented in Devon. First recorded in Plymouth, fifteen-o-nine. And fact two, Devon still makes the best so-called Cornish pasties.'

'Obviously,' Danny agreed, 'but that's just a matter of-'

'And that was the opinion, my friend, of *The* British Pie Awards. It's all straight from the BBC web site, this stuff, and you can't argue with the BBC. If you do, they send people around.'

Danny rubbed his chin slowly. 'Well. . .'

'What do you mean, 'well'? This is gold dust!'

'Well,' Danny repeated, 'it's all good info but how are we going to use it? It's not *really* going to shut them down, is it. It's not like they'll let cold, hard facts get in the way of a good sales pitch.'

Jim, disappointed, agreed. He was a couple of inches shorter than Danny, and a couple of years short of his age, but they got on like they'd grown up together. They weren't like brothers, though. Jim's hair was very pale brown, just a surfer's soak in lemon juice from blonde, while Danny's was the other end of brown, close to black. Jim was a bit of a scarecrow, too, a little too gaunt in the face and always looking in need of a good meal. He was always neatly turned out, though, unlike Danny. Jim's tie, for example, was immaculately tied, even if it was the thickest, fattest, seventies-est kippers that he could find on the rails in charity shops. Today's offering was relatively restrained, somewhere between lime-stained beige and the high-visibility orange of a road-digger's jacket. The knot was the size of a cooking apple. Danny couldn't help but snigger.

'Changing the subject ' he said, 'that Jocelyn e-mail. Total classic, man. Total classic.'

Jim tried to hold in his smile. 'We aim to please. There's not a soul more deserving, though, is there?'

'I'll tell you what she deserves, mate,' Jim grunted, 'a chain around her neck.'

Danny laughed. 'You can't go hanging employees in the office! Or was that a dog lead?'

Jim shook his head. 'No way! I mean a proper, chunky gold chain. Maybe even a posh black car. Everyone knows she's the mare of Barnstaple.'

'Sure, more riders that Uncle Tom Cobley's grey one. But she's gonna rip you some new ventilation, Jimbo, when she reads this. And, no question, she's gonna read it.'

Jim shrugged. 'Ach, what's the worst she could do?'

'Ha! Get you fired, maybe? Haul you in on sexual discrimination charges or something, for definite!'

'How dare you?' Jim faked shock. 'I said she was *both* sexes. Well, first one then the other. But how can that be discrimination?'

'Harassment, then.'

Jim shrugged again. 'I can live with harassment. Gives you street cred, don't it, like snatching laundry off washing lines. So tell me about those toe-rags at The Pasty Boys. Let the side down a bit there didn't you me old son? Bet it still stings.'

Danny looked away. 'Too right it still stings.'

'Revenge?'

'It's in hand. I'm putting my best man on it.'

Jim rolled his eyes. 'Yourself.'

Danny raised an eyebrow. 'Very observant, mate. But after that e-mail you sent, for now, it's your self.'

'Me? *Me?*' Jim clutched his hands to his chest. 'I-I just don't know what to say! Obviously, I'd like to thank my agent, my Mum and Dad, and of course, the big feller up in the sky. Y'all know who I'm talking about.' He sniffed, dabbed the corner of an eye and gazed sorrowfully skywards. 'Yes, rest in peace, King Kong, rest in peace.'

'Come on, Jimbo, this is serious.'

Jim's normal voice returned. 'I know it is, I know. Seven bums of serious. Can't let them get away with pulling cracks like that. What do you want me to do?'

Danny screwed up his face. 'Dunno yet. That e-mail, you sent it through her account, right?'

'Hey, I ain't admitting to nothing, man!'

'Sure, sure. But maybe you could hack into The Pasty Boys' computers or e-mails or something? And you could, couldn't you, Jimmy.'

Jim half-nodded, staring out at the rival office, the muscle in his jaw twitching a slow pulse. 'Oh, I'll come up with something,' he growled. 'I like a challenge.'

Danny knew he did and was sure he would. When it came to warfare in the workplace, Jim was the perfect attack dog. Any excuse for a wind-up and Jim was there, taking any joke played on him as a personal slight and tenfold-revenge as a matter of honour. Sometimes, Danny was grateful they were on the same side.

And Jim would could come up with something special. He knew the computer system inside out, and could print off anything 'sensitive' from any machine in the building, under anyone's name. He'd laid many a trap for the IT department, disabling his and Danny's computers or crashing the whole system whenever they decided they were overworked and underpaid. Like, most Mondays.

'Or what about writing them a letter. . . a letter of complaint! Threaten to take them to court over something, or . . . . no-no-no, scribble all kinds of like, Devil-worship symbols in the margins and say you will exact a terrible revenge upon them if your complaint is not addressed immediately.'

Jim laughed. 'That's pretty good, you know.' He fell silent, thinking, automatically digging out his car keys to jingle, as though it helped his brain to function. Danny had often seen him do it, usually at the start of a plan to do something they both knew they shouldn't. At first, Danny had thought Jim was rubbing his nose in having a company car but, anyway, the fob on the ring was better than the car itself, and probably worth more. It was a small, chrome and plastic sniper's rifle with a button trigger, that shone a red laser pointer from the barrel, just like the gunsight on the real thing. Ok, he thought, perhaps the car was worth more, in cash money, but it wasn't nearly as much fun to play with in the office.

Jim surfaced from deep thought, disappointingly. 'Hey, they're your ideas, man,' he said. 'You do it.'

'I can't,' said Danny quickly, groaning inside. 'No time. Got to get these figures in to Slade, today.'

'It's late anyway,' said Jim. 'Do it tomorrow.'

It was still only ten in the morning. Danny remained reluctant. Jim had that touch of *Crazy*, didn't he, that blind-to-all-consequence mix of daring and stupidity that meant anything good for a laugh was a good thing to do. It wasn't that he didn't know the boundaries of rational behaviour, just that he seemed to get his kicks from hopping back and forth across them. And Danny really wanted payback on The Pasty Boys. He needed Jim in.

'Tomorrow's no good either, mate.' Danny tapped his leather-look desk diary. 'Fully booked.'

Jim's face fell. 'That sounds suspiciously like honest graft.'

Without expression, Danny held Jim's eye and opened the diary. 'There.'

'Slade PA interviews,' Jim read aloud. 'They let you do *interviews*?'

Danny shook his head. 'But you don't think Slade's going to interview here, do you, when he can do it in style and get a free lunch on expenses?'

'How come?'

'He's got a room booked at *The Saunton Sands*, all day. And you don't think that's coming out of his own pocket, do you? Anyway, point is, he's out all day. Not here, with mine the first face he sees whenever he looks out of his lair.'

'Ideal,' said Jim, grinning. 'So why can't you do the letter then?'

'Because I, my old son,' said Danny, 'will be putting my feet up.' He put his hands behind his head and went to demonstrate but quickly had second thoughts. 'Better not,' he said, nodding to Slade's door. 'He's still in there today.'

'You're a class act, you are,' said Jim, starting to leave, 'but if he's in there, I'd better shift. I'll see what I can do about, you know.' He nodded at Pasty Boy Central, shaking imaginary coffee beans in one hand.

Danny nodded and waved him away.

'But it ain't gonna be easy,' Jim continued. 'Bad fish. Swallow you whole.'

'You what?'

'Got any mints left?' Jim asked.

Danny slid open his drawer. 'Only three.'

'I'll find 'em for three but I'll catch 'em, and kill 'em, for ten. For that you get the head, the tail. . .' Jim checked his watch. 'Oh forget it, I'm off.'

Danny laughed. 'What's the hurry? Stick around! If Slade sees us, we. . . could be discussing work?'

Jim cocked his head to one side. 'Could you say that to his face, Dan? With a straight face yourself? And do you think he could keep a straight face? And, more important-ly, what if he's in there, reading his incoming e-mails? Or *she* is?'

'Jocelyn!' Danny rubbed his hands eagerly. 'Yeah, sure. Go, go, mate. Get out of here.'

Jim started for the exit but stopped again. He pressed a palm onto his forehead and sighed.

'Look, if we are gonna get back at those Cornish moon-bandits, I mean properly, we need to know who they are! We know the company, yeah, but we nothing about who owns the arses. You should have taken a picture, man.'

Oh sure, Jim, like we could identify them from their cheeks! What would we be supposed to do, blow up the snapshot and fly-post Barnstaple with *Wanted* posters? Bug public toilets with tiny cameras until we get a match? You try explaining that one to the magistrates if you're caught, with or without a straight face.'

Jim curled up his nose and thought. 'If you had a picture, you could show the Police.'

'Indecent exposure? You think Old Bill would really go for that?'

Jim looked thoughtful. 'We could tell them it was a crack house. But really, if we knew who these blokes were we could, I don't know, put calls in to them personally. More convincing, see? Either that or look them up in the phone book and burn their houses to the ground. I mean, surely somebody knows someone who works there?'

The Pasty Boys' offices were on the third floor of a block six high. A security desk overlooked the street door, manned by a guard with a toilet seat collar size and no vowels in his surname. Danny or Jim could have stood out-side and watched workers come and go but how could they tell who worked for which company?

'Well, we do know a little more now,' said Danny through gritted teeth. 'There's seven of them, at least.'

'Seven!' squealed Jim. 'Them's high odds, man. How do you know?'

Danny closed his eyes and sighed. 'I counted the but-tocks.'

'Seven?' Jim shook his head in disbelief. 'Seven buttocks!'

'Fourteen, mate. All gleaming up against the glass. Looked like the front bench of the House of Commons, it did.'

'They're gonna try and top this,' said Jim. 'You know that, don't you.'

Jim lifted the edge of the blind with one finger and peered through the window. 'All they need to do is rope in the floors above and below to do the same and they'll have a twenty-one bum salute.'

Danny stared at Jim, disappointedly, for a long, long time. Jim hung his head.

'Sorry,' he muttered, stuck out his lower lip and shuffled from the room like a schoolboy sent from class.

When no one was looking, Danny quickly checked over the figures for Mr Slade. Battling with branch transfers took all the mental power and concentration that his calculator-finger could muster, and he set down his pen, panting and shaking, six minutes later, after the longest, hardest spell of work he could remember. To recover, he spent the next twenty idly looking for new ways to amuse himself on-line, eventually reading the longest list of blonde jokes he had ever found.

Few were good. He could post a better list himself, he thought, apart from, maybe, the one about the blonde, the vicar and the electric screwdriver, which was immediately copied on an e-mail to Jim. Posting on-line, that was an idea! He considered joining a chat room somewhere, some place to meet other, like-minded, slave-driven, semi-comatose office drones, but that just made the pub much more appealing again.

Wasn't it time for a coffee yet? Surely there had to be better ways to pass time. He'd have to look into getting a *Gameboy*, or *DS*, or whatever they were calling those hand-helds, these days. Or just bite the bullet and get a new job.

Closing down some browsers, he caught sight again of the giant fish and those beaming trawler men. Outdoors . . . no ties worn. . . no Jocelyn. Now, that would be the job for him - at sea!

Naah. He didn't have the stomach for it. He'd been sick making the crossing to the Isle of Wight a few years back, and that was just in the queue to board the ferry. But it was the second time today that he'd thought about fishing, he realised, and he daydreamed for a while about minnows in streams, memories the colour of faded Polaroids.

But, wait, those rods stored away in his parents' attic. . . they weren't in his parents' attic, were they? It was all coming back, now. . .

Yes! Danny had been carrying those rods around with him for years, in amongst all the other never-opened-since junk that his parents packed him off with when he left home for college up in London. He'd taken the lot at the time, thinking they were being over-fussy to their baby boy leaving the nest, but now he realised just how canny they had been, clearing their whole house of a skip-load of crap without paying a penny for disposal. He smiled. But he might just dig those rods out when he got home, check them over.

Yeah, he might just do that.

And, come to that, hadn't he been at a loss for something to do to fill the empty weekend?

A small, cartoonish lightbulb appeared in midair above Danny's head, glowing brightly.

Chapter 3

'It's Monday morning - again - I've just turned myself in to this voluntary prison for another five sevenths of my week, there's a pile of paperwork in front of me, so I have decided to do something constructive for once and start a blog. It's not that I'm bored - I am, but I like being bored - but I did something different, even interesting, yesterday, and I should make a permanent note of it so I can avoid unexpected fun interrupting my routine ever again. Plus, of course, anyone watching my typing fingers fly is going to think 'Look at that company dynamo go!'

So: Sunday, and doing something I hadn't done since I was ten or eleven - I went fishing! In the sea! Straight up!

When I left this hole at five on Friday I thought I was in for a weekend of the same old same old, but two things happened: First, my cash card got swallowed on the way to the pub. I had enough in my pocket, though, to ensure that on Saturday morning I couldn't remember why it got swallowed, or where, but it meant I was going to be pretty strapped for cash until today and gave me an even better reason than 'Never again!' to stay sober.

Secondly, the resulting boredom drove me into the attic, where I found my and my father's ancient freshwater rods. To my surprise, I found one of Dad's sea rods in there, too. It was a red, two-piece, fibreglass beauty, still in very good condition, that could still be a top-range rod today, for all I know! So what could I do. . . but go fishing!

It really was as spur of the moment as that. The decision, I mean. Obviously, I didn't just, like, drop everything there and then and leg it to the seaside. I had to find out what sea fishing tackle the old man had packed for me, and just finding that in the black hole of my attic, amongst the rest of the ton of unused junk, took nearly an hour on its own.

To cut to the chase, I had pretty much everything I needed. . . I thought at the time. I needed bait, of course, and had the good sense to get some new line for the reel while I was in the tackle shop, because when I went to strip the original stuff off, it was so old that it fell away like Tutankhamun's hair.

But. . . to the point. I went fishing for the first time yesterday. First time in the sea, with a rod from the shore, anyway. I may have sounded pretty up before but that was just because anything beats the old routine. Actually, I'm still kinda thinking it over but, if I have any sense, it could be my last time fishing, too.

Anyway, I decided on Woolacombe. Never fished it before, of course, but I know the place fairly well from childhood. All days were unendingly sunny, of course, splashing about learning back-stroke, then gallons of ice cream; followed by nights learning all about heatstroke, and splashing on gallons of after-sun cream. Good memories, even the napalmed skin, but especially Woolacombe itself, and the beautiful, long, clear sweep of sand left behind by the ebbing tide. It's so popular with tourists, you just know there aren't going to be any sharp rocks out there, not within paddling depth.

And that's at low tide. I went to fish the high water, safe in the knowledge that 'Oh yes, you'll definitely get some big bass there,' plus every other line, sinker and hook that the Devonshire Del-Boy in that big, new out-of-town tackle shop talked me into buying.

Me, bitter? Whatever gave you that idea? But you've probably guessed that I definitely didn't get some big bass there, or any bass, or any fish at all of any size! So there, you can skip the rest, unless you're stupid enough to want to wait for the catch photos.

Bitter?

All right, bitter. But I just had the worst of first nights, that's all. And it wasn't as if I lost my fishing virginity in an earth-moving anticlimax of nothing happening. I could have handled that. As a newbie, I was expecting that. What I wasn't expecting, though, was the sudden and totally unexpected discovery that I was a changeling, a cruel genetic experiment switched at birth with the real Danny Benton.

Well, that's the only rational explanation I can come up with. You see, pretty much the moment my boots hit the sand, something altered in my DNA and long-hidden genes emerged, battling for control of my hands whenever they reached for anything fishing-related. Chaplin, Keaton, Squarepants, Scottish goalkeepers; all the great clowns of ages past had clearly had their twigs somewhere in my family tree, and the sight of a rod was like a magic wand, summoning them up to make everything that could go wrong, go wrong, then go even wronger. Except it wasn't funny. None of it.

For starters, how was I supposed to know that, on the way there, I'd coast merrily along with the radio up high until all the dual carriageway was behind me, then immediately find myself bumper to bumper behind Mother Teresa of Calcutta in a Nissan Micra. I began drumming angry rock tunes on the steering wheel.

It wasn't really Mother Teresa, of course, despite the strong resemblance. The real Mother Teresa had been dead since nineteen ninety-seven, roundabout when the driver in front's brain had also turned to dust.

Then he - Oh yes, 'He'. Little old men can look and drive like deceased nuns, too - he spotted me in his mirror, adjusted his flat cap and gradually dropped ten miles an hour, drifting left to right as if to disguise it.

He was determined to drive me crazy. My drumming grew increasingly Keith Moonish in response. In my head, Roger Daltrey chimed in:

Hope I die before I get old, I mouthed along with him. Finally, I understood what Pete Townshend had meant with those lyrics. It made me feel ancient, myself, remembering the song from childhood, and the way my old man would always roll his eyes and say, '*That one was out when I was a lad*'.

Even with the dead nun's hundred or so years of motoring experience, though, I knew one thing that he didn't: my car could kick his car's arse.

Talkin' bout my generation.

Oh, well. We would reach the straight bit on the way up Mullacott Cross soon enough, I thought. Then I thought, no, not soon enough, generated all the revs I could and got around him on one of the broad, long bends.

In the rear-view, Mother Teresa was hunched forward over his steering wheel, shaking a feeble fist at me and toothlessly mouthing ancient swears. So it's true, then:

People try to put us d-down,
Just because we g-g-get around.

I'd have mooned him, too, if I hadn't had a headrest on my seat. And if I hadn't run over that rabbit. Poor sod, but then again, it's up to them to watch the road and to stop when the driver isn't. Keeping a better eye out ahead, I watched the old git *f-f-f-f-fade away*. God, that song is older than I am! I chewed my lip, hoping it wasn't Pete, driving the Micra.

Anyway, I'm wandering. The upshot was I got there later than planned, with what turned out to be only an hour and a bit of useable daylight left for fishing. That wasn't too bad, I thought, to begin with. First time out alone, I was only there to give it a try, get a taster. And if I was enjoying myself, the torch I'd packed would let me stay a little longer. I was quite chuffed at myself, thinking to bring that torch. At least I was, then, to begin with.

I had little trouble parking within sight of the sea. However, by the time I had changed into my Wellingtons, extra jumper and leather jacket, unpacked the car, unpacked and re-packed my rucksack full of kit to check I had everything I'd need, and unpacked and re-packed it a second time to recover the car keys from the very bottom, it was half an hour before I set foot on sand.

It was beautiful down there, though, and I have to admit wasting a couple more minutes just standing there, soaking up the scenery as afternoon faded through dusk. The deep blue sky was already laced with night, and a just-cool, refreshing breeze carried in the sounds and scents of the breakers and the open sea. With the twinkle of the last lights in town adding a little coloured glitter to the wave tops as they broke, it felt more like the scenery was soaking me up, sucking me into the perfect night-shot seaside picture postcard.

A single car was winding its way above the rocks toward Mortehoe but, otherwise, there wasn't a soul in sight; not on the beach, the car parks, not even the small town centre. The holiday season isn't long away, though, so I doubt that dusks will stay so quiet for very long. Or so amazingly, refreshingly empty! I thought of this airless office, the crush in the tea room and the battle for parking outside, and I laughed. Then I did it again, roaring and hooting at full lung-power, knowing no one was going to hear me.

I noticed the time, then, and how it had been slipping by, wasted, as I'd stood like an entranced tourist watching their first ever sunset over something that wasn't concrete, slate or the car in front. It would be dark before my first cast, at this rate!

The two sections of rod slipped easily from the cotton case. I fitted them together, slid the reel into place and screwed it tight as expertly as though I did it every week. Finding the free end of the line, to thread up through the rod's six rings, I allowed myself a little smirk at how smoothly things were going. Although I hadn't caught a fish yet, I was feeling just a little like a pro.

Of course, I only found out how wrong this feeling was once I had pulled a yard or so of line through the last ring at the tip, retuned to the reel to wind in the slack and thought, in the gloom, that its handle had fallen off.

I'd put the reel on upside down, so the handle was backward, on the left (Right-handers wind a fixed spool reel left handed, I remembered that much from my freshwater days). I unscrewed it, tipped it over and tightened it on again, then, finally, let out a lot of loose line and threaded it up through the rings. Adding a weight, a bead and a hook on two feet of finer line; I was ready to bait up, ready to go.

No I wasn't.

I'd picked up the rod to tighten the slack and found the reel would hardly turn. Failing daylight and gross inexperience meant I wasted another five minutes loosening various screws and attachments before discovering the cause was the line spiralling twice around the rod and winding tight.

Why hadn't I checked when I'd turned the reel over? Because I am an idiot. How can I be sure? Because I spent another five minutes unscrewing, removing, un-spiralling, replacing and re-screwing the damned thing before I realised that I could have just loosened it and twisted it around the rod.

And then, more or less, it was dark, and my mood was even blacker. So much for this being a relaxing sport. I looked around the beach, grateful, at least, that I could see no one else on the beach, watching the steam coming out of my ears. It had taken me so long setting up that a fair crowd of gigglers would have had plenty of time to assemble. Then again, who would be out in the middle of a beach in the dark? Only idiots.

At least I had my torch, and a hefty and bright one at that. Surprisingly, perhaps, and at that point, worryingly, I found a lot of comfort in that big, blinding beam and the heaviness of the lamp in my hand. Having a switchable light was like being at home, where, although I didn't want to admit it, I was starting to wish that I had stayed.

So, bait. Like a scene from the Devil's Christmas, I unwrapped the flat, newspaper parcel from the tackle shop and stared at the slowly writhing mass of lugworm inside. Wow, they were bigger than I'd thought. And messier. Each was as thick as my index finger, as long as my entire hand, and the mass of purplish and dull crimson worms slid slowly, wetly, over one another like the contents of a disembowelled teen in a slasher movie. Now, don't get me wrong, I've watched the *Discovery Health Channel*, and more than once, so there's no way you could call me squeamish, but these worms were something else.

Cautiously, I prodded the mass. They barely reacted, and weren't *quite* as awful to the touch as I'd expected. I teased one free, picked it up and moved to the shiny, sharp hook, swinging free from the end of my rod, propped on the sand spike. And this, as I'd read on-line, was what you're supposed to do: put the point into the hole in the fat end, then slide the whole worm up and around the hook.

Don't break off the thinner tail; just keep shoving, impaling until the point comes out of the poor beast's vent.

I needed both hands for this so I put down the torch and stood up. You're ahead of me here, now, I'll bet. How was I supposed to accomplish this in pitch blackness, by Braille? I retrieved it and tried holding the end in my mouth but it was such a big torch that it wouldn't fit, not without at least partial dislocation of my jaw. I tried it under my chin but that just lit the sand at my feet. Finally, awkwardly and uncomfortably, I clamped it between my shoulder and ear, and just about got the edge of the beam onto the hook.

The worm felt the sharpness of the point, recoiled and . . . gritted my teeth and. . .

Frozen calamari squid, now there's a good idea if ever there was one! I placed the world's luckiest lugworm on the sand, patted its head and folded the rest back inside their newspaper prison. Long-deceased squid was far easier to handle than a live worm fighting to stay that way and, although pushing the hook through was a little tougher, it was a lot less tough on yours truly. Glancing down at the lugworm as it nuzzled its way into the sand, I could see that it agreed, wholeheartedly.

The squid, suspended tentacles-down with the hook out of sight amongst its thawing innards and the point jammed clean through its head, didn't look quite so enthusiastic. Then again, I'd remembered to peel off the skin and it did look like a fantastic bait! Its body alone was a good five inches long so I knew I wouldn't be pestered by whatever the sea's equivalent of minnows were. This was a big-fish-only bait and, finally, I was ready to catch them. I turned off the torch, stuffed it into my pocket, carefully lifted the rod from the rest and approached the sea.

The sound of the low surf was amazing; not loud, just completely entrancing, hypnotic. Maybe it was pitch blackness, focussing my ears, or the absence of the usual ten-thousand laughing, crying and screaming kids, even the gulls, that had come as standard whenever I'd visited a beach before. Then I realised that I'd *never* visited a beach before at night, never had the whole place entirely to myself, two miles of pristine sand and not another light in sight, bar the glitter of Woolacombe's streetlights some distance behind my right shoulder. Still holding the rod I stretched my arms wide and turned full circle, sucking in the feeling of freedom, revelling in it. *Dork*, you're thinking, aren't you, but no one was there to see me so what did it matter?

It mattered because of the six-ounce lead weight that smacked me in the back of the head when I stopped, but at least that brought me back to my senses and about an hour later than planned, I readied myself for my first cast. This. . . went just fine! I'd fished rivers and canals as a kid so I had the basic idea of how to do it, when to release the line and so on, so although this was heavy-duty kit compared to pea-sized weights and hooks no bigger than a bent staple, my squid sailed off into the night a good fifty-plus yards!

Yesss! I think I even punched the air. I couldn't get the rod back into the rest fast enough, knowing nothing further was left to go wrong. All I needed now was a touch of beginner's luck. And a quick dash back to the water's edge, to sluice the last, mortal remains of Lucky the lugworm off the heel of my boot.

Lucky? Well, kinda. . . I actually got a bite! *Definitely* a fish because I felt it, yanking, fighting, alive on the end of the line!

I was watching the rod at the time. No great surprise as, by then, I was getting a bit bored with the scenery and I was hunched against the cold as still as one of those iron Anthony Gormley figures that Scousers have on their beaches. Well, that's Scousers for you. They'd go mad if they went down there and had no one to get excitable at.

Anyway. Rod: bang, BANG. No question! The second time that tip went down the whole rod nearly tipped onto the sand. I snatched back at it, backpedalling furiously up the beach and winding like mad and *Wallop*, there it was on the end, fighting back like its life depended on it! You've never felt anything like it, I'm telling you, if you haven't done this before. When you have to actually pull, and hard, to stop your rod being dragged into the sea, that kick, really it's just. . . scary! Good-scary, though, when you wonder what's out there, and how big it is, how angry, and if it's got teeth, and Pop. Hook's out and fish has gone.

Barely started but it's over.
You feel. . . you feel really crap but that's not all there is.
It. . . It does something.
Cos even though it's gone your heart's still racing.

Well, this beginner was, on balance, out of luck. Looking back, I'd probably used up my day's luck quota by not breaking my neck on the way down the steps to the beach, by not being mugged, not drowning in a freak tsunami and/or not being eaten by off-course salt-water crocodiles (we get enough Australians serving in our pubs, so what's so improbable about their reptiles swimming in our seas?)

It was a long, cold night, all ninety minutes or so of it that I could bear, holding my clumsy great torch to see if the rod tip was moving, then holding the rod when the torch batteries died just after my second cast. I was badly underdressed in just a sweatshirt and leather jacket, badly kitted out and very badly mistaken in thinking I knew enough to get by in sea fishing because I once caught a perch in a canal.

Damn. Gotta go. Slade's making his way over here, he's just caught my eye and he doesn't do that to say good morning. Doesn't catch your eye at all - he targets you and tries to psyche you out. One more thing, though. Writing it all down like this, remembering exactly what that tugging, yanking on the line did to me, it just don't seem quite so bad any more.

Nope. Not half bad at all.

Chapter 4

Slade had read Jim's e-mail. The look in his eyes gave it away, as he scanned the office from the entrance of his private dungeon. Intrigued and a little unnerved, Danny did his best to look busy.

The explosion came when Slade took his first step forward. Not from Slade himself but from the swing door, right beside him. Without warning, Jim flew in backwards, a foot clear of the ground and landed on his backside against the base of the vacant desk just outside Slade's lair. He rolled to one side, his face screwed up in that agonized way that says one thing: *I'm a eunuch!*

Slade didn't look back and reached Danny's desk just as Jocelyn followed her victim through the door. She looked down her nose at the writhing Jim, then stepped on his fingers for good measure as she left.

'Butch enough for you, Lithium?' She almost danced out of the room.

Danny looked over. He watched Jim for a while then asked the boss, 'Do you think we should call a priest?'

The slightest change in the stony folds on Slade's face was enough to give away the smile he was trying to hide. 'Well,' he said coldly. 'Never hack into a female's e-mails.' He paused, forcing a smile far less genuine than the first. 'I think we've all learned a lesson there, haven't we, Mr Benton.'

'He could report her for that,' said Danny. 'He could report her to the Police.'

Another little shift in Slade's wrinkles warned, *Don't even think about it, boy!* Danny let it wash over him and waited patiently for whatever criticism it was that warranted the boss delivering it personally.

'Good work on the transfer figures.' He said it slowly, scowling. Clearly, words of praise came sour to his thin lips. 'Saved us all an evening's overtime, there.'

Praise? Danny was shocked. Slade must have won the lottery or something. Or, he was on a masochist high over Jim's pain. There had to be something else. There was no way Slade was just. . . being nice!

Maybe it was just the saving in wages. Danny shrugged. 'We aim to please.'

'Some of us have better things to do at night than work.'

That really took Danny aback. Slade with a life outside of Barum Fixings? He'd always assumed the man was on day-release from the circus.

As the boss slithered back into his hole, Danny watched Jim pulling himself upright again and looking around, and all the gigglers and sneerers resuming conversations or pretending to look busy. Gingerly, Jim jiggled the mass of bruised flesh and chewing pain in his trousers, tightened his massive tie-knot and headed for the staff room, walking like John Wayne astride an invisible mule. Danny gave him long enough to fill the kettle, then followed.

Even prison cells had windows. The staff room didn't, just an extractor fan behind a painted-over grill. It ran noisily whenever the light was on, which was always, as the staff room had no window. The walls were painted and bare, apart from a graffitied year planner and the tar stains of a thousand bored employees of the past, from the days long before nicotine was declared a Class A drug if smoked indoors.

There were also a sink, a yellowed fridge, a scattering of chairs and someone's old settee, and Jim, staring at the kettle.

'It's not true,' said Danny from the doorway. 'Watched pots do boil.'

'Everyone knows that.' Jim didn't turn. His voice was still hoarse. 'But has anyone ever thought to try it with kettles?'

'Jocelyn. . . guessed who sent the e-mail, then?' Danny put a second cup beside the kettle and dropped in a tea bag. 'How are the twins?'

Jim readjusted his trousers. *'They'll survive,'* he squeaked, pretending, then winced as he tried smiling at his own joke. 'Like two apples that fell off a very high tree, actually. I'm thinking of giving up the ballet lessons, but apart from that. . .'

Danny pulled a face. 'There's always The Nutcracker. Anyway, at least Slade can't do a disciplinary on you now. Or you could take Jocelyn down with you for assault. That's probably why he was so happy. Case closed. No paperwork.'

Jim turned. 'Slade was *happy*? I thought he was doing something similar to you.'

'No, mate. Get this: *Your figures were excellent, Mr Benton. Very well done!* Word for word, I'm telling you. Grinning from ear to ear, he was, too. Looked like a bloke who'd grown an inch, length and girth.'

Jim was impressed. 'Ah, but you know why that is. The new PA's been appointed. Starts a week today. He's been pulling his greasy hair out since Monica left. Had a taste of the W-word himself, for a change, instead of sitting up in his coffin and watching the rest of us doing it.'

Danny nodded sincerely. 'Too right. And we have work to do, my brother. The true and honest work of restoring our honour with those bottom-waving bandits over the road. I've been thinking. How do you fancy coming up with another fake letter? Catch them out in some way, show 'em up.'

'Me?' asked Jim. 'I couldn't possibly come up with anything like that! Apart from, maybe, I dunno, say. . . this customer of theirs who turns out to be a crazed Satanist. . . All he wants to do is complain about, I don't know, something trivial. . . or maybe he's just writing to ask what the dates of the summer sale are, but he writes the letter in blood with all these, you know, Satanic symbols and stuff all down the margins. A real polite letter but it finishes, *RSVP in the envelope provided or suffer the wrath of the Dark Lord.* And the envelope's soaked in blood, too, of course.'

Danny looked at Jim sidelong. 'Of course, mate,' he said slowly. 'Of course.'

'And to make it authentic,' Jim continued straight-faced, not even reacting as the door clicked open, 'we're going to have to find a virgin to murder. For the blood.'

From the doorway, Joan Lobb gasped and started to back away.

'Not you, obviously, Joanie,' said Jim, not for her to hear. 'I didn't mean vergin' on the unconscious.'

Danny doubled up with laughter. Recovering, he picked up a chair and started swinging it. 'So when do we make our first kill?'

Charlotte Langtree, still trailing the geek Stibb, stopped in the doorway and looked at Danny like he were something better scraped off and left outside. Danny tried to think of another wisecrack about virgins, but couldn't.

'Still here are ya, Stibby?' he said. *You tool.*

'Ignore him, Joseph,' said Charlotte - *Joseph!* - 'we have more important things to discuss.' She led him to the sofa by the fingers.

'What's that then?' Danny grunted. 'Chlamydia? Foot and mouth?'

Jim, who'd stayed silent, nodded Danny toward the door. They left before Charlotte could string together enough crude words for a response.

'Seriously, I like the idea of a fake letter. Those Pasty Boy bandits are still laughing at us, you know? They're going to expect us to try and beat their phone call, maybe they won't suspect the post. Just. . . a letter without any murder would be good. Reckon you can come up with something?'

'I don't know, man,' Jim sighed, leaning against the wall in the short passageway back to the office. 'I think I really ought to keep my head down today.'

'Yeah, maybe rest it on a cushion.'

'You're loving this, Dan, aren't you.'

'Of course not,' said Danny. 'Yes.'

'Shut up.'

Danny shrugged, then saw Jim glance past him.

Jim's eyes widened. 'Got to go.'

'Jussst a moment, Mister Molton!'

Slade. Danny clapped Jim on the arm and scuttled away, head down, back to his desk.

'A quick word in my office, Mr Molton,' - *said the spider to the fly* - 'IF I'm not interrupting anything. . .'

Abandoning Jim to his fate, Danny opened his word processor and settled down to plot.

Chapter 5

Danny looked over the top of his monitor. His alarm, the clock that made time fly, ticked a full hour on from the time it had woken him, early. 'Time-for-work time in twenty minutes,' it told him now. 'Course, I'll make it feel less than ten.'

Many days had passed since Jim's near-gelding. Although he had taken a blow to crack coconuts, he'd made a full and fairly quick recovery. Even so, he'd taken the rest of the day off - 'to get them checked and counted at the hospital' - and that was the last anyone had seen of him for the rest of the week. Danny was surprised that Slade let him get away with it, until Jim phoned in once from his sickbed, a sickbed in a bar somewhere, from the sound of chat and clinking glasses in the background.

'Amazing what reporting staff members to the cops can get you,' Jim had told him. 'Or threatening to, anyway.' Danny had urged him not to push his luck too far, but how do you tell a man he's doing the wrong thing, if he's got a pint and pork scratchings when he knows that he ought to be at work?

Danny felt like he'd spent every waking hour of the last few days on line, both at home and work. From the numb tingling in the tips of his middle three fingers on each hand, it also felt like he'd asked the computer more questions on sea fishing than there were fish in the sea.

He hadn't been able to fish the last weekend. One of the first things he'd learned, from an on-line angling web site, was that dusk and dawn were great times to fish from the shore. Unfortunately, though, it had been just about low tide at dusk, not high, and Danny was pretty sure high tide was the only time for fish from the beach. When the tide was out, they had no water, did they? Shame, though, as the weather had been perfect, a taste of a good summer to come, and down there on the beach, even at night, would have been perfect. And dawn? Well, the suggestion of fishing at dawn was clearly just there to catch out the gullible. Like the very existence of mornings on Saturdays or Sundays was anything more than an urban myth!

Computers had revolutionised fishing, he realised. The learning process, anyway. When he'd fished as a kid, there had been one or two angling mags and papers available but, otherwise, it was all father-to-son stuff, or meant joining the local library. Libraries - buildings like miniature Internets but much, much smaller and heavier - were rumoured to have become extinct in the late twentieth century. A good thing, too, Danny thought, as it was saving him a fortune in petrol and shoe leather and, anyway, all he had to do now was type in his questions and Internetland would, without fail, spout answers. If he wanted to know what was being caught, he didn't have to read fading hardbacks, listing what *ought* to be caught at certain times of year; now, he could simply log on and see photos of what was *caught* last night!

He'd spent hours reading articles, especially those recounting fishing expeditions, the better ones making him virtually feel he was there. He was becoming quite the armchair. . . no, quite the swivel-chair angler! Amazing what you can learn on line, he thought. He could probably even find out why only high tides were worth fishing.

The phrases 'best tide', 'beach fishing' and 'N Devon' went into the search engine and sure enough, seconds later, Danny was scowling and kicking the metal bin under the desk. Most of the links were to catch reports from the recent past, where people lied publically about how well they had got on. Others, perhaps more useful, were the small, local fishing web sites where small angling clubs or experienced hobbyists threw out everything they knew on catching nearby fish. Local knowledge had to be better than general principles, didn't it?

And that was what had annoyed him. Almost everyone recommending a particular state of the tide for the beaches said that low water was the best. Several said that dusk put the icing on the cake. And Danny had just spent a weekend's perfect evenings' fishing sat right in this spot, typing the opportunity away. He shut down the computer, kicked the bin again and left for work.

Some way up ahead, traffic lights went red.

The journey was depressingly slow, so much so that, by the time the car reached the tailback into the town square, Danny was ready to shoot himself. He decided to wait until he was at the head of the queue, then stop and wait for the lights to go green before blowing out his brains, just so he could see the look on everyone's faces when his corpse didn't drive off. He scratched at the wheel with a thumbnail. Just as the critical flaw in his plan began to dawn on him, he realised he hadn't come armed. The lights up ahead went green and he sighed. He could be dead now, if only he'd brought a Colt .45 instead of just his sandwiches.

He tapped the sun visor down and opened the window. The day was cold but a good cold, crisp, the kind that April has little trouble thawing when it's sunny. Actually, he thought, the congestion was nothing compared to how it used to be before the town's new downstream bridge, was opened a few years back but it was still chockablock enough with four wheel drives that his car was in neutral fifty percent of the time. What did he expect, though, leaving the house late and getting stuck in the school run?

Danny gripped the steering wheel tightly and felt his shoulders knotting up. If anyone argued with humankind being, by nature, incredibly stupid, why was nobody yet selling mass-market jet packs?

Maybe the traffic was no worse than usual and it was just him, wound up. He felt like he hadn't been away from work, or rested, like he'd wasted the weekend so completely that he'd blanked it from his mind. He hadn't felt like that until fifteen minutes ago, though. Not until discovering how completely he'd wasted a perfect weekend's fishing.

It was bad. He could deny it no longer. One trip out and already, he had the bug, had it big-time. He decided to put all things fishing-related entirely out of his mind for the next few minutes, to concentrate of getting there and parked, scrape-free.

The Cornish Stones came into view and Danny scowled. He'd be stuck staring at those for the next few changes of the traffic lights. Protruding smack in the middle of the view of the town on the Taw, the roundabout looked like a great green zit now, he decided, with the stones a ragged, crusty scab, just aching to be picked off. The green lights were merciful and he drove past them, concentrating on nothing but not hitting the number plate in front.

So, why the heck should low tide be a better time to fish beaches? Permanent water, perhaps. Beyond the furthest the tide ever goes out, would there be a different environment, more and different creepy-crawlies for the fish to eat? More food, more fish? Deeper water as the tide comes in? The number plate in front real close and someone stepping out?

'LOOK OUT!'

Danny slammed to a halt and the sea in his mind sloshed up against the inside of his forehead. He looked up, slowly.

The scene was frozen for a second: the middle-aged woman in the horrible, gaudy jacket; the jigsaw of cracks through her crust of makeup as her face contorted with horror; and the glint of the sun on the sequined leather dog lead, stretched taut between her hand and. . . somewhere in the region of Danny's front axle.

God, what if it was still alive? Should he get out of the car and help? Not looking at the woman, he wouldn't. Her expression was shifting, turning the cracked mask of make-up into war paint. So, just rev up a quick crimson smoothie and put the thing out of its misery?

'Oh, come on!' said the dog owner.

Yeah, too far, I know, Danny thought. Then again, any spray wouldn't show up on that jacket.

'Come ON, Pixie!' the woman repeated, bending and scooping up her poodle, which was rattled but clearly unharmed.

Aww, look! Pwecious is all twembling. Look how those wittle pink-dyed tufty-wufty ears are jiggling around - Mummy make it better!

Danny relaxed back into the seat, ignoring the silly old bint's parting-shot scowl. He'd hate to run over a dog like that accidentally. No, he'd want to do it on his own terms, and savour it, maybe reverse and do a couple of wheel-spins on it, too. Actually, if he hit the revs hard now and let her go, he could get both of them in the same–

White Van Man behind him blew his horn. Danny got rolling, wondering if anyone going to work actually envied Mr W. V. Man as much as he did. Radio on, the open road, even the not-so-open road like they were on now, it had to beat trying to ignore the buzz of the fluorescent lights and Jocelyn all day.

He pulled the car into the delivery yard, parked and went inside.

After casting a quick, suspicious eye over the in-tray, he turned on his computer, opened the *Google* search page and typed in 'fishing' and 'Woolacombe'. Several suggested answers pointed him towards the pages of somewhere called *TheGoldfingerBite.net* so he took the top one of those and got more tips and hints than he could handle, including several technical ones he didn't even understand.

Before he knew it, nine-thirty am had been and gone and Jim was perched on the edge of his desk, rattling his car keys and flicking the laser pointer rifle on the fob to get Danny's attention.

'Nice tie, Jimbo.' It wasn't, nowhere near, but that was the point. 'You decided to come back then. Break time already?'

'Any time's break time, man, and this one's long overdue.' Jim rattled his change again. 'Want anything from the machine?'

Danny screwed up his nose, thought again, shrugged and dug through his pockets. 'How'd it go with Slade? Looked like he was on the warpath.'

Jim frowned a little. 'Dunno. I was just thinking about what a satisfying day it was. See, once I'd heard the phrase, *'Embarrassed us in front of the whole company'*, I knew my work was done. So I threatened to pop down the cop shop and. . . let's say we struck a deal.'

Danny nodded. 'A well-earned holiday, then. Nice one. Good work should be recognised. Bit of a rare thing, him cornering you like that, though, isn't it?'

'What do you mean?' Jim asked.

'Slade. I mean, he hates your guts - he hates everyone's guts - but the rest of us are always getting carpeted, or pinned into a corner somewhere for official slaggings-off. Not you so much, though. Hardly at all. Why is that?'

'You said it,' said Jim. 'He hates my guts.'

'So?'

'So I take defensive measures.'

'Oh yeah? Like what?'

'Serious question for you. Have you ever known me let one go?'

Danny laughed aloud. '*What?*'

'You know, blowing the big brown bugle, shedding sulphur, saluting the sewers, singeing the sofa. . .'

'Ok, ok!' Danny held up his hands. 'I'm with you!'

But Jim continued unabated. 'Cracking the Devil's egg, releasing the hounds, sounding the rectal reveille, giving up the gut ghost, laying down cover for the troops, stoking the Dutch-'

'JIMMY! For fff. . . I get the idea, alright?'

'. . .oven.'

'The Dutch oven?'

Jim shook his head. 'Never mind. But seriously, have you ever seen me blow one backwards?'

Danny rolled his eyes. 'I'd be seriously worried if I could see them, mate. Even a bit scared.'

Jim bowed. 'Touché. Alright, have you ever heard me?'

'How am I supposed to. . .? Mate. . . um, I dunno! No, maybe not, can't say I have, but so what? Who cares? It's like brass band music, really. Some people appreciate the strains of a finely tuned trouser trumpet, others think it's either highly overrated or deeply embarrassing.'

Jim nodded, then yawned and stretched. 'Anyway, re Slade. I save 'em all up for him. Can be all day, sometimes, you know, concentrating it, refining it, letting it age in the cask. Then when Slade wants to get up close and personal about work, I sneak it all out in one venomous hiss and the area's thick with a good dose of Devonshire mace. He never has as much to say as he thought he had, if you get my drift. I told you, it's my guts he hates.'

'Classic,' chuckled Danny, not knowing how seriously to take him. The thing was, with Jim, you could imagine him doing anything. 'So, how come you couldn't evade a kicking for the *Butch e-mail*?'

'Bad timing. Tanks were empty, mate.'

Danny laughed. 'So Jocelyn really did knock the wind out of you!'

'No, not at all. I, um. . . I'd already used it. In a sentence.'

'You *what?*'

'I got tongue-tied. She'd read it, she caught up with me, and she was all in my face, screeching, '*Why do you do these things to me?*' Jim waved his arms about for effect.

'So you told her what you thought of her?'

'Kind of. Let's say I tried to describe her, but I couldn't find the right word. Not up at the mouth end, anyway.' He paused for thought. 'Actually, it was more like a sentence in itself. She must have got seven or eight seconds' worth. You should've seen her face.'

Danny kept his as straight as he could. 'Which is when she. . .'

Jim winced and crossed his legs, carefully. 'Yeah. Worth it, though. Worth every mouthful of Madras the night before, it was.'

'That's dedication, Mr M. The sort of dedication this company needs.' Still seated, he reached up and shook Jim's hand sincerely. 'No regrets, I assume?'

Uncrossing his legs, Jim thought. 'Well, the poppadums were never worth the money.'

He was about to go on but stopped, looking past Danny toward the far end of the office. 'Wait a minute,' he said, eyes widening.

Danny followed his eager gaze and wow! A topless girl, from behind. Well, topless in that no top half could be seen as she bent over getting something from the snack machine, but that was as good as it got on company time; and what a behind!

Jim blew out a breath. 'Now there's a face I don't recognise!'

Already, Danny knew he'd fallen deeply in lust. Jim had, too, without doubt. This meant he'd have to kill Jim, dispose of the body and clean up before she managed to free the drink she'd just bought and turned around.

A face he didn't recognise - the cheek! Danny was entranced by the way that black, pencil skirt was filled out. If that was her face, he'd be stealing the photo from her personnel file. The hope flashed through his mind that, in these times of paranoid security, it might catch on as a method of identification and soon they'd all be wearing clip-on photo Ids of their cheek cleavage. It would bring a whole new, richer meaning to the phrase *'Smile for the camera'*, wouldn't it? He wondered if they would still have to say Cheese.

'Hot chocolate?' It was Jim's voice, urgent and eager. 'I'm supposed to be getting us drinks, Dan, remember?'

'I'll get them.'

'No, no. I'm fine. She'll be Dracula's new PA, I reckon, and what sort of gentleman would I be, not to say hello?'

Danny leapt up and grabbed the back of Jim's collar. 'She's mine,' he growled close to his ear. 'Understand?'

'We'll see.' Jim shrugged free and stared ahead, with a darkly fixed, sarcastic grin. 'I like a challenge.'

Chapter 6

Single white male, 30-something, Barnstaple, no morals, will sell soul to Satan for smoking-hot blonde nymphomaniac with own beachcaster; must be non-talker with allergy to clothes shopping. Allergy to clothes, full stop.
  If unavailable, would settle for tips and advice on local beach marks.

'Hi there, everyone in fishing-land.
  New member here, just posting to say, um. . . hi there, everyone in fishing-land, I suppose.
  Obviously, if there really are any smoking-hot, blonde nymphos here then we can forget all this angling rubbish and get down to business but, while I'm sat here not holding my breath, I thought I'd open with some catch detail of my own. I like the way this site is split into counties. I've learnt a lot just from reading back over all the local catch reports you guys have been posting - I mean, trying to learn how to fish from a book might be a great start, but one thing I've learned already is that up-to-date, local info can't be beat. So anyway, I thought it was about time I signed up and chipped in some info of my own. Plus I have this site to thank for a good night's fishing after a really crap day working, yesterday.
  I went to Instow beach, targeting bass and keeping it simple - selecting lugworm as the bait of choice, on the end of a flowing trace. Got there just as it was getting dark and fished from about two hours after low tide up to when the bait ran out, near the top. Not much action at first but got lots of bites later on. Ended up catching (!) one nice bass of about a pound - a nice fit on the dinner plate and in my freezer now - plus a flatfish that I think was a plaice. Could have been a thick leaf, though, it was that small.

Not a bad night for a newbie. I was pretty chuffed anyway. Except for the damned weather - it rained half the
time!

Anyway, cheers all. Looking forward to pumping you for
information and maybe running into a few of you on the
beach sometime.

Danny Buoy.'

Danny Buoy - the on-line name he'd chosen when he
signed up to the web site - clicked 'post message', sat back
and waited. There: fishing forum joined and entrance
made.

And lies told. *And* twenty minutes fooling anyone looking
into thinking he was hard at work! He grinned and read
through his debut post again, now published on screen for
anyone in the world to see. He thought he had the tone
about right, admitting he was a beginner and eager to learn
but still managing to sound like a competent one, at least.
He liked 'targeting' bass and 'flowing trace' in particular, a
little ring of professionalism casually tossed in.

He refreshed the screen to see if anyone had replied yet.
They hadn't, so he read his lies again and thought through
what a 'Danny with a conscience' would have written:

'I went to Instow beach because my low fuel light lit up on
the way to Westward Ho! I was targeting anything cos I
had never even considered the concept of targeting anything particular and thought you just flung a bait out and
took your chances. I was keeping it simple because I only
had two swivels and no idea how to tie anything more
complex than a flowing trace anyway, which I didn't even
know it was called a flowing trace until I looked it up on
here. The lugworm was by chance, not choice, because a
quarter pound of them, so old they'd have been on their
last legs if they had 'em, was all the tackle shop would sell
that wasn't pre booked by someone called *'reglers'*.

Fished up to when what was left of the bait ran out,
literally, in a slurry of decay and worm innards that I got
on my jeans, can still smell on my fingers, and have a
horrible feeling I may have also wiped in my hair.

The plaice was a fluke - no idea it was on there - and the bass an even bigger bit of wild luck. After spending all night trying to smash Appledore's twinkling streetlights, on the opposite bank, with every cast, I hooked my only other fish when a tired winding arm made me pause with the hook only twenty yards out!'

He could be that sure, that accurate, because the fish had scared the life out of him, splashing in the shallow water like one three times the size as it snatched up his bait, so close that he'd taken two steps back. It still surprised him that the fish came in so close, into such shallow water, and Danny wondered if they'd been mooching around there all night, which he'd spent casting way out beyond them. He remembered just standing there, frozen, holding the rod as the little fish fought for all it was worth. *Amazing, just feeling it. . . that sensation up the line so clear it's like the fish's wild pulse is right there in the palm of your hand. . .*

He'd almost forgotten to wind in. But he had, and had something of the good knocked out if it when he saw blood coming from the twitching fish's gills. He would never have taken it home at all - it was only in the freezer because he hadn't the first idea how to prepare or cook it. It had just seemed the kindest thing to do at the time.

He'd lied about the weather, too, but fishermen were supposed to tell tales, weren't they? Sure, it had rained, just as he'd said, but after the first drops had him pulling his collar up and moaning, he'd quickly grown used to it. It was refreshing, and what's wrong with a little rain on your head, anyway? The ingrained childhood urge to run indoors was easily washed away.

Even though he'd got cold. Only gradually, the heat seeping out of him over several hours of motionlessness, so he'd been as stiff as a freshly-risen zombie when the time had come to pack up. He made a mental note to look up outdoor clothing, oilskins or whatever it was that fishermen wore, then decided to do it straightaway. The message-waves of the Post-it note sea on his desk would never be read, so what chance did a note that didn't exist have?

He opened a new browser, then another: Google in the first; the other, eBay. Now what was he after? It wasn't oilskins, was it. It was that kinda nylonish stuff, proofed against the weather. Lycra? Neoprene? He typed the first of those into Google, including 'fishing' and 'clothing' in the search then turned to eBay.

'Clothing' went into the *Search* box. Also, 'Sports'.

Or was the material more like divers wore. . . wetsuits? That kind of synthetic rubber stuff?

'Mmmmm, rubber-wear. . .!'

He realised what he'd done the moment he clicked the button, so he was expecting the scattering of S&M gear thumbnails that appeared among the choices and clicked one, just for a laugh. He wasn't expecting the soft voice, close to his ear, though.

'Hi there.'

Danny turned his swivel chair around and his jaw fell into his lap.

'I'm Annie,' she said. 'Annie Parkham. New girl, starting today. Mr Slade's PA.'

Danny's mind, heart and hormones freaked out simultaneously. She was stunning, like all the Spice Girls rolled into one, he thought, and not in a multicoloured-haired, twenty-limbed, forty stone harmonizing Hydra of a beast way. She wasn't tall, but still with legs up to the armpits of the girl upstairs, a thought that, in itself, brought a new and wonderful image to mind.

Danny's gaze was so fixed that, in hospital, they'd have turned off his life-support machine.

'You must be Dan.' She offered her right hand but his eyes were on her left. His heart sank at the sight of a single ring, second-left finger. Sank a little, anyway. Rings were just fences, and fences could be climbed. Double-checking for barbed wire, he saw none. Damn it, though. Damn it to Hell.

She looked at him curiously. 'Or Danny, is it?'

That got him back on track.

. . .and the <u>original</u> Spice Girls, too, not the reunion version when they'd all become Scary Spice. And maybe not that one, you know . . .because of that stuff about. . . yeah.

'Yeah,' Danny managed eventually, virtually scraping the word off his sticky-dry tongue. 'Da-Danny's fine.'

She laughed politely and looked down, a little awkwardly, the fluorescent strip-lights reflecting in the shampoo-ad sheen of her tied-back, long, pale hair.

'Y-you must be the new girl, Mr Slade's PA,' he managed, his voice just about dropping into deeper, cooler tones by the end of the sentence. 'I'm Danny.'

He remembered to offer his own hand and she shook it lightly. Hers was cold.

'I know.' She smiled. 'You just told me. And I just told you. Mr Slade told me to wander around the office for a while, get to know the place, you know? See what people are up to.'

Danny recalled his mock personal ad in his Goldfinger Bite post; did she own a beachcaster, too? Wondering when the horned guy with the contract would appear, he glanced around his desk for his signing-pen -- and saw the 'fun costume' he'd called up on eBay, filling the screen in all its high-gloss glory. And it even came with a mask! With a zip!

Danny hit his mouse like a hunting hawk and sat back, desperately hoping he'd closed the picture before she'd seen what he'd appeared to be buying, then feeling his heart sink into his bowels as her giggle told him he'd been just little too slow.

'I'm sorry,' she said. At least she sounded genuinely amused, even if he did seem genuinely idiotic. 'So what *are* you up to?'

'Christmas shopping,' said Danny, thinking fast.

'In April?'

'I was a boy scout: *Be Prepared*.'

She grinned again, the kind of grin you could look at all day, Danny thought. Until it got dark. She nodded toward his computer.

'So who were you shopping for? Nice to see. . . you know . . .you're not looking for the usual bath salts or pair of comedy socks.'

'You saw that?' Danny kept a straight face and beckoned her closer. She chuckled but didn't come. 'You must keep it to yourself, ok? It's for Mr Slade. I'm after a raise and it's top of his wish list.'

'Really?' She had that suffering-bad-humour-politely forced amusement in her voice. It only made her cuter.

'And what do you think of my new boss, then?'

'Really?'

'Really.'

Danny lowered his voice and, frowning, fixed her blue eyes with a glare. 'Get out. Get out now, while you can. If you're still here when the sun goes down, he'll have you, and you'll never leave. Never, I tell you. *Neverrrrrr!*'

A big, real laugh escaped from her but almost at once, Danny's face fell.

'Mr Benton, may I consult with you a minute over the. . . Oh! Who have we here?'

Danny sighed and picked up his phone. 'Annie, this is Jim. Jim, Annie.' He punched out a number. 'And Jim never consults, he conspires, so watch out.'

As Jim said his smarmy hello, Danny turned away, picked up the phone and put on his gravest voice, speaking quietly and fast.

Behind him, he heard Jim say, 'Ain't that right, mate?'

'Absolutely.' Whatever that was. He looked back.

Jim and Annie exchanged furtive glances but Danny didn't mind being the butt of whatever joke he'd been set up for. Suddenly, nothing fun mattered any more. Because Jocelyn was coming.

'Jim, back to your desk, please,' she spat. 'You know how Mr Slade feels about personal calls but this one's urgent, apparently.' She arrived, stopped and stared at Jim like he'd just strangled her cat. 'Go on, then!'

Jim paled and hurried off with a shuffling run. Jocelyn smiled at Annie - 'Hi again!' - glared at Danny, then left.

'You've met *Joestalin*, then?'

'I beg your pardon?'

'You've already met Jocelyn?'

'Yeah,' she said. 'She seems nice.'

Danny nearly choked. 'Sure. She's a sweetie. All that bride-of-Godzilla stuff is just a front.'

'Danny!'

She knew his name!

'Seriously,' Danny said, 'Slade and Morticia there, they're like that.' He held up crossed fingers. 'The Ian and Myra of the fixings and attachments world, they are.'

'Hmmm.' Annie was looking down, fiddling nervously with

her damned engagement ring. 'Did I mention that Mr Slade is my uncle?'

'No!' said Danny. 'Did I mention what a wonderful, caring boss he is, and that I'd willingly work here for nothing, just to spend time in the warmth of his presence?' He stopped. His shoulders slumped. 'I've blown it pretty well, Annie, haven't I?'

'No,' she said, brightly. 'He's not my uncle. I was just checking I hadn't *said* he was, by mistake.'

Danny looked at her open-mouthed, smile spreading. 'Wh. . . why would you have said something like that?'

'Du-uh. Hello? To wind you up? It's what people do in offices, isn't it?'

'It's *why* people work in offices, isn't it? Speaking of which, Jim will be back soon so we'd better make the most of it.'

'Oh yes,' she said, 'I hope it's not bad news.'

'*Only for his chances,*' Danny thought. 'No,' he said. 'It's just some bailiff's gonna take his car over unpaid parking fines in Aberdeen.'

'Aberdeen? Does he go up there a lot?'

'Never,' said Danny, straight-faced. 'I just transferred a recording to his extension. Sounds like you're taking a live call, though. Keeps most people fooled for a while.'

She looked at him sidelong. 'Sounds to me like you wanted him out of the way, for some reason.'

Fighting back the urge to propose marriage to her on the spot, Danny held up his hands. 'You got me,' he said. 'Yeah, cos I hate his guts. And it's best not to stand near him for too long.'

'What?' Annie frowned. 'Why ever not?'

Danny lowered his voice. 'You know. . . diseases and stuff. Catching. Nasty.'

'No!'

'He's gay, too, you know?' Danny added. 'Seriously. Gayer than a range of male grooming products. And he touches people. Elderly nuns, mostly. And small animals.'

'Oh, get out of here,' said Annie, sounding disappointed to have twigged that such juicy gossip was faked.

'So. . . you've worked in an office before!' Danny said. 'That's a turn up for the books. Most people they employ here need training to sit up straight unaided.'

She pulled a face. 'I have, actually. I came down from Taunton branch. Just an order clerk, you know.'

'PA, now, though,' said Danny. 'Going up in the world. At least you know the ins and outs of Barum Fixings.'

'The business, yes,' she said, 'but not this office. I'd never even been to Barnstaple before the interview. I was expecting wicker men on the roadside, on the way here.'

'That's Somerset,' Danny corrected. 'They have a giant one beside the M5, up at Bridgewater. It's very important to the tribes around there, ritual sacrifice.'

She sort-of got it. 'Ha, right. Anyway, what's it like working in here? What's the vibe?'

'The *vibe*?' Danny paused for thought. 'The nearest thing we have is the occasional vibrating snore. Don't get me wrong, we have these little in-house games we play, like avoiding all eye contact or sullen staring, but apart from those it can get a little bit dull.'

'Right. Much like Taunton,' she said. 'Well, I'd better, you know, mingle.'

'Yeah, get in with the in-crowd.' Danny nodded at the others. 'Take it easy, though. Don't let them thrill you to death.'

He got a smile, at least, and she turned to leave.

'Hey, Annie.'

She looked over her shoulder.

'Slade, he's not really your uncle, after all, is he?' He grinned.

She didn't. She looked shocked, 'So, you don't just think the man's some kind of monster, but you also think I could be related to him?' She tossed her hair. 'Huh. I can see I'm gonna have to work on my first impressions!'

She stomped off, trying to convince him she was serious.

Danny raised an eyebrow and watched her go. Intently.

When the door closed behind her he sat back. In his mind's eye, he watched his new business contact approaching, the guy with the black goatee, the pitchfork and the pointy tail. He was angry and waving his contract, demanding a signature for the delivery of one hot blonde. Danny stood and faced him down, eye to eye.

'Get thee behind me, punk,' Danny snarled. 'The order clearly stated a non-talker.'

Chapter 7

'Fishing Report, Friday Night.'

Danny stopped typing, reached behind him to his bedside cabinet and turned up the radio. He was up early for a Saturday, just in time to catch the eleven am news and weather on Radio Devon. Would the rain gods let him get back on the beach again tonight? Much as he liked being out in the rain, there was little point getting soaked and standing there with brass balls shivering loose of the monkey.

He wouldn't be the weather's slave for long, though. He'd bought some clothing on line, which he'd have within a week, fingers crossed; a two piece flotation suit, a warm, water and wind-resistant jacket and trousers, which was pretty much the same as commercial fishermen wore, apparently. Danny wanted his mainly for its warmth and weatherproofing, rather than its seaworthiness, but it was good to know that should he ever get swept away from the shore, the suit could keep him afloat and alive a lot longer than if he were just wearing normal outdoor clothing.

'So,' he'd muttered to himself at the final eBay screen, 'a lonely, lingering death instead of a mercifully quick one.'

Only fifty quid, though! He'd pressed 'BUY IT NOW' and smiled. Spending money had never felt so good.

Danny shook the thought away and returned to his fishing report on TheGoldfingerBite.net. The first thing he did was to retitle it.

THE WONDER-BAIT YOU'VE ALWAYS WANTED!

Is THEGOLDFINGERBITE.NET working TOO well for you?
Are your catch scales overworked, the spring squeaking like a newlywed's mattress as yet another lively, fat bass dangles below?
Are you developing gigantic wanker's wrists, hauling in fish after fish after fish without even a chance to moan once about the bloody easterlies? Who wants a

never-ending procession of duvet sized rays being dragged onto the beach? Fishing should be about RELAXATION, shouldn't it????

Anglers, THE FUTURE IS NOW.

Nobody in their right mind would turn down a bait that gives GUARANTEED RESULTS, and Barnstaple Sandeels® will guarantee you blanks even more surely than a vasectomy from a Rottweiler. Why the constant wind unhook cast, wind unhook cast, when you can have hours of peace, hypnotised by the glow of a motionless tip light?

Scientific tests* have proven that Barnstaple Sandeels® are not ATTRACTIVE TO FISH whatsoever, and are GUARANTEED to remain unbitten 250x longer than conventional sandeels, SAVING YOU MONEY AND TIME on messy and expensive bait changes.

Special offer bargain: One for the price of Two! Order NOW to avoid satisfaction.

* - Tested on Friday night at Instow, behind the sand dunes and down near the rocks. God, those dunes are harder (or softer) to climb over than you think! They were well-frozen, not thawed then re-frozen, which turns them to mush. (You do know we're back to the sandeels now, right?) They looked like quality dead-bait but obviously smelled like the hunger-hormones of live killer shark when in the water, as all fish fled to the horizon faster than the setting sun.

Result: no bites all night and hypothermia, most of it. Looking forward to the arrival of my first floatation suit so I can stay as warm as toast while sod all happens.

'Well, I'll tell you this,' said Jim, appearing from nowhere and staring back into it, lost in a daydream. 'I wouldn't be sending that one home rested and refreshed in the morning.'

Danny followed his gaze across the office: Annie. 'I don't think I'd send her home at all, mate.'

Jim stared at Danny. 'Steady on there, man.'

Mentally, Danny kicked himself. That had come out much too soppy and daydreamy. Just quickly enough, he added, 'Not until she'd made the bed and cooked me breakfast, obviously.'

'Obviously,' Jim affirmed. He actually looked relieved, although his eyes never left the girl. He sighed. 'She does score a lot of Bs, though.'

'Bs? Meaning?'

'Think about it, Dan. So much of what we want from women begins with B.'

Danny did think about it. 'You mean, like, a beautiful. . . busty-but-brainy. . . bubbly Blonde?'

'I was thinking more of a bisexual brewery-billionairess bimbo bondage bitch but I think we're talking the same language.'

'Oh yeah,' said Danny. 'I'm sure we are.'

'Right. So you'll understand me when I say you've got to forget about her. Obviously.'

'You what?'

'She's taken, man,' said Jim, hissing the word *Taken* like he meant Cursed by gypsies. 'Didn't you see the finger-shackle?'

'I saw it.' Danny didn't want to seem to care. 'I'm going through my toolbox when I get home. Gonna find me a tiny little hacksaw.'

'I doubt it, Dan. Seems like a girl who knows her own mind. And if she's got one, she's way out of your league, buddy. Forget her.'

Danny shrugged. 'Maybe I will, maybe I-'

'Can't!'

'Won't.'

Jim shook his head. It would never work anyway. Doomed from the off.'

'Go on. Why?'

'Annie and Danny?' Jim tutted. 'Annie and Danny?! EWWWW!'

He explained further with a series of unspellable retching noises that Danny thought would never end. He drummed his fingers on the desk patiently.

'It'll never work, man,' Jim said, finally, when his air had run out. 'It's like you being called *Gavin and Stacy*, or *George and Mildred*, except it's worse because it rhymes! You'll be wearing matching knitwear in days, my friend, you mark my words. *And* I'll bet you she's a vegetarian.'

'*What?* How can you say that?'

'She'll be an orchid-hugging vegan. . . hunt-sab, I'd bet me left one on it. Chuck her, mate. No, don't just chuck her, Chuck Norris her.'

Danny gasped in mock-shock. 'God! What if she is a veg?'

There were days when Jim was really up, spot on form, and Danny felt like Derek to Jim's Clive but without so much swearing. 'Then again,' Danny continued, 'vegetarians are alright, aren't they? Keeps the queues down at *The Colonel's*, anyway.'

'Not in my book, mate. They're anything but all right. Look, no rump on her, too lean. And that skirt, she doesn't fillet. Doesn't look like she's had her chops around a steak in years. Doubt she's ever had a good bit of beef in her life, mate, actually. Likely to prefer the company of cucumbers, if you get my drift.'

'Being a vegetarian, you mean.'

'Obviously. But you've got to drop her, mate. Drop her like a hot nut cutlet.'

Danny finally took his eyes off Annie. 'So that's your game, Molton! Trying to get rid of the competition?'

'You, competition?' Jim scoffed. 'Naah, you're welcome to her, mate. Let's get this straight. Female veggies are never, ever worth it. No energy when it matters and a bedroom full of methane in the morning. Light a fag afterwards - instant homelessness.'

Danny tried to get a word in. He failed.

'I'm telling you, all veggy girls should be rounded up and put on a well-ventilated island somewhere with lots of live, fluffy baby bunnies to cuddle, and not allowed off until you can't see their ribs through their clothing any more. No food, though - just a few wire snares, a skinning knife and a roasting spit. Sorted.'

Danny sighed patiently. 'Drop it, Jimbo. You wouldn't stand a cat's chance, feller. And even if she is a veg, a good portion of Benton's finest salami will put her right.'

'Danny's dinky chipolata?'

'Oi! You can fff-' Danny spotted movement. 'F-Fine day for fat profit for Barum Fixings,' he continued, loudly, almost without pause. He clapped Jim on the arm. 'Couldn't agree more. I'll have those price revisions with you before you know it.'

Jim, used to this, knew without looking that Slade was coming and fell into the act straightaway. Danny leant into his keyboard, his eager, look-at-me-I'm-working face on and Jim watched intently, pen poised over his notepad like a scientist waiting for important results.

Slade stalked past in silence, with his pet Rottweiler, Jocelyn, padding along obediently in his wake, clipboard in hand and drool slopping from her heavy, black-whiskered jowls that barely covered her three-inch, sabre-like canines. They must have been downwind of her, Danny thought, as she didn't catch the scent of their fear. He grinned as a bright red dot of light appeared on the back of her head as she left, Jim lining up a covert sniper-shot from the key ring at his hip.

The danger passed.

'You're really getting into this fishing malarkey, then,' said Jim, tapping the screen. 'You're sick in the head, aren't you.'

After a quick Slade-check, Danny whirled his chair around. 'Yeah, I am! Hey. . . getting into it, anyway. I'm not sick in the head, though. The voices say I'm in perfect killing condition.'

Jim gripped his friend's shoulder. 'That's good, that's good,' he said softly. 'Remember, the time to make them pay is close. Their screams will be sweet music when the bullets start to fly.'

'Anyway, actually,' Danny continued enthusiastically, barely hearing him, 'I'm, like. . . pretty surprised, myself, at how much! I only found the rods a few weeks ago, only went cos I was bored. It's like crack, mate. No idea why you'd want to try it but do it and you're hooked. Haha, you're hooked. Good one.'

Jim shook his head, grinning. 'No, crap one. Crap hobby, too, if you ask me. Haven't you got anything better to do in the evenings?'

Strangely, it felt like a personal dig and, though he knew it wasn't meant, Danny had to bite back the urge to bark defensively. It wasn't as if Jim had anything better to do, either. Outside of work, Danny barely knew him at all.

But inside of work he was a good lad, so Danny relaxed. 'I know. But what can you do when you're an addict. I'm even thinking about going again tonight, mate, even though the tide's wrong, I've got no bait, no clue which would be the best mark to go for.'

Jim went shrill and camp. 'Ooh, listen to him with his *wrong tides* and his *best marks*. Proper little computer-chair expert, isn't he!'

The word before 'off' was bleeped as the phone started ringing. Danny considered ignoring it completely but gave in, raising his voice a little so the call didn't interrupt talk of fishing.

'Anyway,' he continued. 'Armchair fisherman I ain't, mate. Ha! Sitting in this place, I think I'd be out every single night if I could! It beats drinking yourself into a stupor in the pub.' Jim raised a hand but Danny was already rethinking. 'Ok, that's going too far, but it beats doing it every *single* night.'

Jim was unimpressed. 'Why do you have to do it at night at all, for Christ's sake? How can you enjoy going to the beach in the dark?'

Danny laughed aloud. 'It's not, *going to the beach*, mate! What do you think I do, take a bucket and spade for when they're not biting?'

'Hey,' Jim whined. 'Like *I'm* stupid? Like *I'm* the one standing soaked in freezing rain with my rod in my hand?'

'I'm thinking of getting another rod,' said Danny. 'Maybe another, better beachcaster, get meself some more distance, or maybe something smaller, a spinning rod, for light tackle. Gonna have to have to get myself a decent tripod, too, to hold both at once. Something with extendable legs would be good. Far more adaptable to using on rocks, sloping beaches and the-'

Abruptly, Jim yawned, loud, wide and unshielded, straight in Danny's face.

Danny turned away. 'Jesus, mate! I can see your break-fast!'

'Man, you're boring me so bad I'm surprised it wasn't the seam of my Jockeys.' Jim yawned again, even wider and faker, to drive the point home. Danny leaned forward and peered in.

'No, wait,' he said. 'Breakfast with whiskers?'

'Wha--?'

Danny lunged at Jim with both hands, grabbing his bottom jaw and wrestling his other forearm around his workmate's head. Squawking and coughing, Jim fought to escape but his thrashing toppled him back over the corner of the desk and as he toppled, Danny shifted his grip and thrust his lefthand fingers in, too, under Jim's top teeth.

Jim flopped back across Danny's desk, head and shoulders hanging off as Danny pried his jaws apart and peered deeper. Already helpless twice over - half through laughter, half through rage - all Jim could do was to wail with an open jaw like a sadist-dentist's patient under the drill.

'Oh, of course!' laughed Danny over the noise. 'It's just your hamster coming through! Aww, look, he's smiling. He never thought he'd see daylight again.'

Jim fought less and spluttered more.

'Move toward the light!' Danny continued enthusiastically. 'I command you, leave his body! The power of Christ compels thee! The power of Christ compels thee!'

Jim coughed, gagged once or twice then went limp. Danny released him, sat down and began tapping at his keyboard.

He lasted ten seconds before glancing up over his monitor. There were a few tired glances from the ranks of keyboard slaves, and someone tutted, just the once.

'They're not buying it, mate.'

Jim sat up, brushed himself down and re-coiled the enormous knot in his latest vile tie. Mickey and Minnie must have really hit rock bottom, if writhing poorly drawn and poorly dressed on cheap novelty neckwear was the best gig they could get since Disney hit the deep freeze.

'Gonna have to tidy your act up, too, next Monday,' said Jim. 'Assuming you still want to get all kissy-kissy with the Ice Maiden.'

Danny knew who he meant straightaway. He's been counting the days. He grunted agreement. 'Who starts a new job then goes straight off on holiday, anyway?'

'Anyone who books their holiday before they get the new job, I guess.'

'It's not—'

Fair, Danny wanted to say but stopped himself.

'It's not right,' he improvised. 'Bloody slackers. Shouldn't be allowed.'

Jim stood.

'But why Ice Maiden? She seemed alright to me. Odds on, in fact.'

Jim smiled, one with just a hint of evil satisfaction. 'Don't tell me you haven't seen her ring, Danny-boy?'

'I'm not that fast, mate. I barely know the girl.'

'No! The one she's always fiddling with.' Jim demonstrated, twiddling something invisible on his finger.

'That silver thing?' said Danny, sitting up. 'I've seen it, yeah. What of it?'

'Aha,' said Jim, though he must have strung it for a full five seconds. 'That would be telling. Joe-Stalin was the one doing the telling, though. Maybe you should talk nicely to her.'

'*Jocelyn?* You must be joking!'

But Jim was already gone, leaving nothing but fading, cackling laughter swirling in his wake.

Avoiding work for the next five minutes was easy. Wondering what the Hell Jim was up to, was more than enough reason to stare into space in contemplation, and with Annie involved it justified the full blurred-eyed, slack-jawed coma.

Surely Jim hadn't got in there already, swept the girl off her feet with his mature charm, restraint and subtle wit. No, no, obviously he hadn't. Not Jim.

Eventually, Danny snapped out of it and turned back to his computer. What had he been worrying about? Jim was no real threat at all. He was just too weird to even consider passing on his genes. Wasn't he?

He blew out a big sigh, returning to *TheGoldfingerBite.net* and clicking back to see if anyone had taken any notice of his first post there, in the 'Devon' subsection, the report on his Instow trip.

'Wow!'

Danny leant forward on his elbows. Eleven replies. *Eleven*. Obviously, a lot more people had computers than he'd thought. This Internet thing could catch on.

Six of them were simple 'Welcome to the site' messages, though *Hell* and *the Madhouse* appeared more than once instead of *the site*, making Danny grin. The place had a good atmosphere, always with some kind of banter going on.

He read back over the longer messages, those with more to say than just 'Hi.'

The plaice was a fluke.

Danny's own line caught his eye in one of the replies. It was from some guy with the screen name *Dwarfmeister*, and was almost in English.

you are right wiv the plaice cos of you being wrong. the plaice was a fluke cos it wasn't a plaice it was a fluke.

Danny scratched his head. Reading other replies made things clearer. Another site member, the dubiously named *Bent Rod*, included '*flounder (fluke = local name)*' in his reply and explained that Danny was far more likely to have caught one of those than a plaice, fishing in the estuary as he had been.

Other responses included some valuable Instow info, like lugworm being the best bait over the sand but crab being a great bait upstream, amongst the rocks; and that the fishing dies off a half hour or so after high tide. Also, someone called *Fishslapper* had thought Danny's line, 'look forward to pumping you' (for information) funny enough to re-quote and comment on with just a long line of laughing *smilies*.

Danny was already tapping out a quick note of thanks for the welcome and tips when he noticed the only negative reply of the bunch.

If you have a plate sized bass of 1lb you are break-ing the law. MLS - 'Minimum Landing Sizes' - look them up!!! Newbies like you give us all a bad name. You should stay off the beach until you know what you are doing. Or leave your rod at home and take a frisbee.

The Predator had written that. What a jerk, Danny thought, and almost changed the tone of his thank-you note to something a little more aggressive and sweary. He decided against it, though, not wanting to rock the boat. This *Predator* could be best mates with everyone on there, for one thing. Plus, once his anger had died down, Danny had started wondering what sort of law he was breaking.

You don't need a licence to fish in the sea, he was pretty sure of that. Freshwater fishing, that was different. He'd used to need two for that. No, *The Predator* was probably talking rubbish, one of those stupid gits who get their kicks winding others up on line. Danny chose to ignore it, sent his nice, bland reply and signed out.

He glanced at the papers in his in-tray, then turned his concentration to the wall clock, determined to force it to move faster by the power of his will alone. Come home time, he had fifteen minutes, tops, to reach the tackle shop. And it was going to be tight.

Chapter 8

It was the most exciting place on Earth. It had to be. Winding down the long, tree-lined hill into town, Danny gripped the wheel tightly, trying to crush the tremor of excitement from his hands. There were hours left before darkness and just minutes before he'd be fishing.

It wasn't just that was he was visiting the town that was once home to *Tarka the Otter* author, Henry Williamson; the town where not only the great Peter Sellers first set foot on stage, but also where those giants of cultured entertainment, Joan and Jackie Collins, were educated (though not in cultured entertainment). Oh no, there was even more. Amongst its claims to fame was being at the southern end of the A361. . . only the longest single-lane A-road in the country!

He shouldn't mock neighbouring towns, Danny knew, but being a Barnstaple boy it had kind of soaked into his genes. Or maybe it was just compulsory for Barumites, he wasn't sure. He wound down his window and smelled the sea immediately, although the air was faintly tainted with the scent of urban traffic. Danny breathed it deeply anyway, one small part of his mind already drifting ahead to the shoreline, to the wash of waves, and fish.

Rising anticipation made his right foot heavier and the car picked up speed going into a tight, tree-lined bend.

Bad idea.

Or rather, bad idea to be walking across the road so slowly on a blind bend. Especially if you're a hedgehog.

Damn. Danny wasn't exactly an all-out animal lover but he hated doing that. And wasn't it a bad omen, hitting hedgehogs? Or was that black cats? He'd find out one day, hopefully. A flick of the wipers sent a shower of quills rattling over the roof as he sped on around the next wide bend.

And into a tailback.

The road was up. Smaller, red warning signs blotted out the lower half of the big, white town sign and Danny waited, breath held. Temporary traffic lights showed red, too - just temporarily, he hoped, but already, it already felt like forever. And he wasn't holding his breath through excitement. The car in front had the catalytic converter from Hell, catastrophically converting pure, fresh carbon monoxide into essence of arse-scratcher's fingernail. Danny had wound up the inch of open window and turned off the cold air fan at once; much too late. So much for the environment! What about *his* environment, now that he was sealed inside a steel and glass bubble of the stuff?

Eventually, though, just as Danny began to turn green, the lights did, and as soon as he was out of second gear, Danny rolled down the window, exhaled his whole soul and sucked air in like - because - his life depended on it. The driver in front went up a gear too soon, the engine growled, and the exhaust ripped out a fart that would have shamed Satan on sprouts, straight into the back of Danny's throat.

Too stunned to choke, Danny slumped sideways, praying for death, but turned away from the light when he realised that the last thing he saw before his afterlife comeuppance would be the big white sign: 'Welcome to Ilfracombe'.

The car's sidelights flashed twice as it locked remotely behind him, and Danny strode off, carrying his rod, kit box and the new tripod he had picked up from the tackle shop. He'd needed one anyway but, having decided to try out Capstone Point after reading some good reports on the web site, he needed it straightaway. He'd read that it was a dangerous place in bad weather, and one where care was needed, even in calmer seas, to avoid ending up in or beneath them. Daylight was on his side, though, and for at least another couple of hours, which would let him check out the rounded, lower slopes of the huge rocky promontory and find himself a secure enough spot before nightfall. He'd need proper, secure support for the rod, too, because if a big fish bit, he could lose his whole setup as the rocks sloped straight into deep water. And that deep water and those big fish were, together, the whole attraction of the mark.

Leaving the Landmark Theatre's trademark twin, white volcanoes behind, Danny crossed a typical resort seafront, overlooked by arcades, chip-shops and migrating alcoholics, then took the walled path up and left around the headland. Pausing halfway up he scanned the twilight sea for wildlife. The local paper sometimes carried short column-fillers, reporting sightings of grey seals, harbour porpoises, even the occasional basking shark spotted from the high cliff path. Nothing, though, but hopefully because all the real action was going on under the waves.

There was no real climbing, as such, just a walk down sloping, rolling rock, conveniently coated with barnacles, the fisherman's true sole-mate when it came to the grip of boots on wet boulders. There was no slippery weed, either, so the only real danger to watch for was a freak, high wave. Danny positioned his tripod on a ledge a good six feet above the waterline and quickly assembled his rod.

He was trying a different technique, this evening, due to all the submerged rocks that *The Goldfinger Bite* had forewarned him about. He'd also bought some pulley rigs: simple, pre-tied arrangements of hooks, lines and swivels that helped lift the weight clear of snags when a hooked fish was being reeled in. Otherwise, the weight could easily be dragged along the bottom by a hard-fighting fish until it found itself a little gap and lodged in like a ship's anchor. Loads of good fish were lost that way over rough ground, apparently.

The pulley rigs were simple indeed, thought Danny as he tied one on. He made a note to tie his own in the future, and get a diagram from on-line if he lost the two he'd bought, which he thought pretty likely.

It was a perfectly still Spring evening, with the edges of the high streaks of white cloud just starting to smoulder orange as the sun fell below the horizon. The sea was smooth, almost flat, but undulating gently with about a foot of swell.

Danny reached for his bait, prising a six-inch, three-parts frozen squid away from a boxed block of his former chums, which he'd been frantically defrosting in the passenger's foot-well heater in the car on the way into town. He held it in his hand awhile to soften it up, then peeled away the faintly speckled skin to reveal the solid, white flesh underneath. Memories of calamari tapas lunches on *Eighteen-Thirty* holidays filled him, briefly, with the urge to take a bite, then memories of *Eighteen-Thirty* hangover toiletbowls put him off the idea.

The cast was a pretty good one, for him, Danny thought, as bait and weight splashed down sixty, maybe seventy yards out to sea. He was improving. His early efforts, a few weeks back, would have been good ones for a six, maybe seven year old girl. He kept the line almost taut as the lead pulled everything bottomwards, which seemed to take forever!

This was much, much deeper water than he could reach from any beach. In his mind's eye, he watched the white squid corpse twirling down, fading silently into sunless depths and thought at once of Leonardo DiCaprio sucking in sea in the scene that makes every man punch the air in *Titanic*. Oh come on, you all know you wanted to! God, that had been one hundred and ninety four minutes of lifetime destroyed, and Danny had counted every one in the most ill-judged cinema date he'd ever been on, with a girl called . . .something slightly off-beat and beginning with R. That was all he remembered of her, now, but it had all been a worthy sacrifice, just to watch that piglet drown.

Sunless depths.

He shook away the pleasant vision and stared out into the sea, down to the point where the thought his bait would lie, and tried to conjure up a fish to swallow it. None came, at least, his mind's eye didn't spot any. Not that it would, in sunless depths. Danny wasn't entirely sure what species might turn up but the were certainly tales about big fish taken from the rock in years past, not least the UK's second biggest shore-caught cod, a thirty-five pounder some twenty-odd years ago. There had to be big eels, conger, down there, too. Danny had never caught anything bigger than a twelve-ounce freshwater eel from some pond as a kid, and the thought of a ten or twenty pound monster leaping at him from the deep added a touch of nervousness to his anticipation. They had teeth, those things. Real teeth. He watched his rod tip, quietly pleased, just for the moment, that it wasn't moving.

Twenty, then thirty minutes passed and Danny's pleasure dwindled with the daylight. Nothing was biting. Nothing was even remotely interested. He wound in to put on a fresh-scented squid, remembering to jerk the bait up off the rocky bottom and wind like Hell to avoid the snags.

As he cast again he heard voices, older kids, coming from beyond the curve of the rocks. There were four of them, as far as he could make out. He didn't know if they were fishing but, from the rising laughter and shouting, they were having a good time. At least someone was, thought Danny, eyes still on his motionless rod tip.

More kids voices joined but younger ones, from up behind him on the cliff path. Three kids, one of each, aged about eight or nine, skipped down over the rocks, taking about as much care as they would on a bouncy castle. Didn't they realise how dangerous it was? One slip and they'd be gone, thought Danny, which was at least as dangerous as a bouncy castle session with a gutful of birthday cake, chocolate and cherryade, and probably more.

They had two brightly coloured fishing rods between them, the little ones that come in moulded plastic and cardboard packs, hung with the rubber rings and waterwings in every other seaside trinket shop, and whatever they were using for bait was already attached. They picked a spot annoyingly close to being in Danny's way, but not quite, then two marble-sized leads plopped into the sea, ten feet out at most. Danny grinned, hoping they'd hook a giant conger that would pull them in. Well, *almost* pull them in.

Then at last, some movement from the sea, and Danny jumped to attention, to see if the beer can drifting around the point would brush against his line and break the monotony. It didn't but another, then another bobbed into view, so there was still hope.

Mocking laughter, littered with critical swearing, rose and fell from beyond the rock as though the drunken youths had read his thoughts. Then the younger kids chimed in, whooping and cheering, eventually screaming, as a curly-haired child caught an angry little wrasse. Danny groaned. Not only was that rubbing his nose in his own lack of fish, they would probably want him to unhook it. The hook would be deep in, of course, and even though he'd bought some forceps especially, removing the hook would, no doubt, puree the fish's innards and put the kids off fishing for the rest of their lives.

The little fish had other ideas, though, and when it fell free onto the rock Danny sighed his relief. They were both off the hook. The wrasse posed there long enough for the kids to have a good gawp then flipped and flapped its way seaward and over the edge. The kids watched it go and, thankfully, none of them followed. After all, that might have scared any bigger fish closing in on Danny's bait.

Ten minutes later the kids and the daylight were gone; the children bellowed at and summoned back to safety by rightly worried parents, leaving Danny in relative peace to enjoy the sunset's encore, the vivid salmon-pinks and peach-golds sweeping the vacant, azure horizon. While he could still see, Danny taped a small, pale green plastic tube to the end of his rod. He should have snapped it first, he realised, when he tried to do it through the tape, and had to bring the rod tip down and bite it to crack the thin glass tube it contained.

'Let there be light!' he mumbled as his teeth crunched down. And there was light. Chemiluminescent light, no less. He'd gone for those over the much bulkier, battery operated ones as he could see himself tangling up every cast and probably flicking it into the sea, and at pennies a throw, he could afford to do that with the chemical ones.

The other light, sunset, was failing fast and Danny groaned and tensed inside when he heard footfalls scuffing over the rocks up behind him. They'd been quiet for a while but the stream of beer cans from around the corner was now stretching out of sight in the other direction, and the last thing Danny fancied was a friendly visit from a bunch of vomit-soaked chavs.

It wasn't. It was three more fishermen, the first Danny had come across in real life, on the shore. He was even more pleased that they weren't the sloshed yob brigade because one of them was huge, a good six foot four tall - and wide - and looking like he'd been hewn from solid Capstone rock.

'Evening, mate,' the big bloke growled. 'Anything about?'

Danny nodded hello then shook his head. 'Not a sniff. Should've kept me bait for the barbecue.'

His friends trudged past, grunting greetings then pitching up around twenty yards further along the rock.

'Ah, sure, it'll pick up now it's dark.'

All three were loaded with gear, two rods each, and hulking heavy tackle boxes. 'Looks like you're here for the night,' said Danny.

The man laughed. 'Depends how it goes.'

'Listen, I'm still kind of a beginner at this,' said Danny, squatting to tighten his line with a few turns of the reel. 'I thought dusk was meant to be the best time.'

'Aha! Here after big silver, are you?'

'Big silver?'

'Yeah, what have you got on there? Mackerel?'

'No, squid,' Danny said, 'but what do you mean, big silver?'

'Give you a tip, mate,' said the big bloke, leaning forward. 'Snakes. Whole ones on a big, big pennel. Maybe take the head off. And don't go for anything less than thirty for the hook length.'

Danny watched his rod tip while he considered the advice, then said, 'Eh?'

'Big silver! You must have seen them, giant bass, getting netted close to shore. Everyone with a rod's after them, mate! Where have you been?'

Danny laughed. 'Like I said, I'm a beginner. But, yeah, I read about them on line. Do you really think there's a chance of catching them? Around here?'

'Everyone with a rod seems to think so. I reckon there's half a chance, too, so I'm gonna get going and set up.'

'Yeah, sure,' said Danny, following him along toward the others after a quick glance back at the green rod light. 'But they say they're likely to be open sea fish, don't they? Grown so big because they've never come in near the nets before?'

'Tell you what I think,' said the big bloke. 'I reckon they're open sea, all right, but they're deep water bass, too.'

Danny frowned. 'They're surface fish, aren't they? In shallow, inshore.'

Big bloke shrugged, his chunky weatherproof jacket swooshing as he moved. 'Doesn't matter. They'd have to grow big to survive in deep water.'

Nice to see someone thinking this through scientifically, thought Danny. Then again, what did he know? The big bloke, on the other hand, probably knew a lot, judging from the amount of stuff he was carrying and the battered appearance of his tackle box and clothing. 'Snakes?' he asked. 'What, like, real. . . ?'

'Yeah, real big sand eels. Get 'em frozen, thick as your thumb. You must have seen them.'

Danny hadn't. 'Yeah, course I have,' he said, then turned to watch his own rod, giving the other man a chance to set up. He would never let on, to anyone, that for a moment he had pictured fillets of adder for bait, or possibly pennel-rigged python chunks for the big bass.

'There you go,' the big bloke said eventually. 'Snake launce.'

It was just as he'd said, a giant version of the sand eels he'd used from the beaches; not really eels but long, thin, silver fish with pointy snouts for burrowing into the sand. Great bait, they said. Any fish that eats fish will love sand eels.

'You really think they're out there?' Danny stared down into the dark sea. 'I mean, out there within casting distance?'

The other man clipped down his headless, tailless, oozing length of snake launce onto a black rubber hook above his large lead weight, then threw out a cast of little apparent effort, but that seemed to sail through the new night forever. Danny watched his yellow line stripping off the caged drum of his multiplier reel, until the man judged the weight had landed and stopped the line escaping with his thumb. The line showed up well in the dark, Danny noticed, much better than his own transparent monofilament. Presumably, the fish couldn't see it in the water.

'There's been big fish off here before now,' he said as he set the first rod in the tripod and set about assembling the next. 'Used to be, anyway. I've seen cod of thirty pounds up on these rocks.'

'Wow,' said Danny, wondering how big the chips would be to go with a fish of that size. 'Used to be, though? What happened, did you catch them all?'

The man laughed. 'I wish. No, netted up like everything else of any size. All gone now. A double figure cod is a fine fish these days. Few and far between, an' all.'

By the time his second bait was out, something was tugging at his first.

'Johnno!' he called to the nearest friend. He tapped a finger in the air, lit by his head-lamp. 'Tap-tap-tap.'

Johnno nodded and grunted but seemed unimpressed.

'What do you think it is, mate?' Danny asked, knowing a good eye could often tell a fish by its bite alone.

'That one's a pedigree, chum.'

'A what?'

The big bloke snorted, amused. 'A Pedigree Chum bite. It's a dogfish, mate. Get plagued with them off here sometimes. Pain in the arse, they are.'

'Yeah, I know,' Danny lied. The time didn't feel right to reveal, not only that he'd never caught one, or that he'd love to catch one, but that a whole bubonic epidemic of them would do him just fine! They were fish, to be caught, weren't they? And wasn't that why he had come?

A cheer rose over the rock behind them, followed by a splash louder than a beer can. The big bloke glanced questioningly down at Danny.

'Chavs,' Danny replied. 'Drunk ones. There's been a beer can conga-line going past since I arrived.'

A whole load of voices went, *Whooaaa!* Laughter and a lot of swearing followed. The big bloke shook his head, slowly, and Danny was sure he heard him growl.

'Chavs!' That was definitely a growl. Danny stepped back as the other man stood back from his tripod, cracked his knuckles then strode off over the rock without another word.

Danny glanced toward the other two, who were taking no notice, then watched as the big bloke's big silhouette dropped out of sight over the rock. This could be good, he thought.

The voices fell silent.

A little cheer behind him, from one of big bloke's friends, welcomed a shiny, eight-inch fish onto the rocks but apart from a quick glance over his shoulder, Danny wasn't interested. Just for now, fishing could wait. He was waiting for the first human-sized splash or burst of gunfire.

Tragically, neither came. Big bloke's headlamp rose over the rocky horizon like an announcement of the second coming and behind him, a line of hoodied monks filed quickly but respectfully away.

'What did. . . How did you manage that?' Danny asked as the man plodded back down the rock.

He chuckled. 'Oh, I just- Hang on. Fish on, here.'

He slipped the nodding rod out of the tripod and lowered the tip almost to the horizontal, winding in the slack he made as he went.

The line was taut.

Both pairs of eyes knew only the tip-light.

It tapped twice, then again.

Then *taptaptaptap* and the big bloke struck into it, swiping the rod back upright into a satisfying, bucking arc that showed a fish was on. Danny felt just the same charge as if he'd hooked it himself; he just missed that wild energy, the rod *alive*, tight in his palms, and that feel of direct contact with the quarry.

'Just a doggie,' big bloke groaned. 'Bloody things.'

'You can tell that from the bite, can you?'

'Yeah, they just chow down on the bait, gnaw away at it, you know. And they fight like they died last week.'

He pulled the two foot long fish out of the water without any sense of victory, wetting his hands in a rock pool before clutching it to him with the thickly padded arm of his jacket and efficiently, if a little roughly, removing the hook.

Danny would have been pleased with such a fish. They had to be in the top ten most colourful species, with their bronzy-sandy, black-speckled backs, fading to a pure, white belly. And they were sharks, too, weren't they! True, they looked about as intimidating as an under-stuffed child's soft toy version of a shark, and bore little resemblance to the bite-yer-legs-off, celebrity monsters of stage and screen, but a shark was a shark to anyone who hadn't caught one, and Danny hoped the next one would fall to his squid.

The dogfish flew about five feet, splashed down, righted itself and, with a casual swipe of its tail, faded from the cone of the big bloke's headlamp as though nothing had interrupted its evening.

'So how did you get rid of the chavs?'

The man finished rebaiting before he replied.

'I asked them,' he said, 'if they were there for the GAR-LANDS meet.'

Danny shrugged. 'Garlands?'

'Gay Anglers, Rod Lovers And Naturists of Devon, Sweetie.'

Danny laughed aloud but was left a little nervous by the way it had tripped off his tongue, not to mention the ease with which he'd slipped into a voice that would've made Boy George sound like Barry White.

'Nice one,' Danny added, then moved away one step, just in case. 'It. . . it's not true, is it?'

It was the big bloke's turn to laugh. 'Well, what matters it that they thought it was. When they said no, I told them, ok, enjoy the show, and started unzipping the jacket.' He smiled. 'And they left.'

All conversation stopped by a metallic crash and clatter.

Danny's rod had come to life, leapt out of the tripod, and was jerking its way forward, desperate to escape into the sea.

Chapter 9

'You've never seen anything like it!
Well, you probably have, most of you, but for a beginner like me it was a first, and a pretty scary one, too, if I'm honest!'

I was chatting away to some bloke down there, wondering on our chances of catching one of these monster bass, when all at once my tripod hits the deck and the rod is heading seaward faster than a turd in a sewer pipe!

So I ran towards it - bad mistake, running on rocks - and ended up skidding seawards, too, on one bruised, scraped hip. Luckily, I followed the same path at the fishing gear and, as my feet were kicking out, trying to find an anchor point, my fingers found the but of the rod and stopped it going in. That's when a boot found a toe-hold and, pretty amazingly, I stayed dry.

The bloke fishing next to me came over to see if I was ok but all I was interested in was getting revenge on the swine of a fish that had tried to steal my kit. You can guess, then, can't you, just how disappointing it was to feel less action out there on the sharp end of the line than you get on *Big Brother* at four am.

Never had a slack-line bite before, had I? Never knew what to expect. Always thought hooked fish swam out to sea or dived. I never knew that, sometimes, they head straight for the idiot who just pierced their mouth, and it sure ain't for a sociable chat.

'Wind in! Wind it!' one of the others was shouting. I did.
'Nothing there,' I remember saying. 'It's bitten it off!'
'Keep *winding*!'

I didn't have to. The line tautened and the rod nearly leapt from my hands - I'm not kidding! If I hadn't locked two fingers above the reel seat, the whole lot would have been gone cos, by this time, I was only one good step from a dip, myself!

There was one Hell of a fish on there. One Hell of a fish. I have never, ever felt anything like it in my life. What a rush! It was like trying to reign in a wild horse on a piece of string.

Within seconds, I was hanging on for dear life, trying to back-pedal my way to a safer, flatter bit of rock. The other blokes were getting pretty excited, too. I knew what they were thinking. They were thinking *Silver*.

I don't know if I'll ever find words for that feeling. Excitement doesn't capture it. *Thrill* maybe overdoes it, but don't let that fool you into thinking it's any the less intense.

There's a darkness to that kick, in that taste of being tied into a creature from the black, so big that it could genuinely hurt you. There is fear, but it's a cold, logical fear that doesn't scare you at all. They say fear's supposed to panic us into a *fight or flight* response, but this fear just says hold it, soak it in. It only feels like you're flying.

Then there's nothing but that feeling.

Everything else just fades out.

And then next thing I knew I'd stitched a new, brown seam in the back of my boxers. Suddenly, my big fish was a big, angry fish. Maybe the hook touched a filling, I don't know, but it wasn't just fighting any more, it was head-butting, throat-gripping, groin-kicking battling!

'What the flipping heck is it?'

Looking back to the heat of that moment, those may not be the exact words I used, but excitement does cloud the memory and this is a web site open to minors, after all.

Behind me, nobody replied.

'It's not one of those bass, is it?'

Somehow, three men already not speaking fell even more silent. I could *feel* it, feel them staring at each other, too, chewing lips.

'Might just find out,' the big bloke growled, eventually, 'if you keep that jolly old line tight.' Again, I can't vouch for the wording but, from the vulgarity and sheer physical difficulty of the sexual practice he actually did refer to, I could tell he was hopeful, at least.

The fish, or whale, or Soviet nuclear submarine or whatever it was, hit the brakes on its charge away out to sea and stopped dead in the water, keeping the jolly old line tight without me even trying. A half bend in the rod stayed perfectly still and the line stretched like piano wire, slicing down into the dark water at close to forty five degrees. Nowhere else I've fished has water this deep.

Or fish this big. It just hung there, immune to careful heaving for so long that I thought it may have swapped places with a rock. I didn't know what to do next. Could I really be snagged? Should I yank hard to get the fish going again or would that just snap the line? I glanced back at the other blokes but I may as well have been invisible. They only had eyes for the rod tip and the sea.

The fish made my decision for me, taking off parallel to the shore and heading for the Landmark Theatre. There was me trying to play a fish that was off to see a play and there seemed no way to stop it. A high-pitched revving noise started coming from my reel as the clutch released line just before it reached its breaking strain (thank. . . flip, I remembered setting clutches from childhood piking. I sure didn't remember any pike fight like last night's fish, though!).

'Just hold the rod, let it run,' the big bloke advised. As winding in was not an option, and neither was *not* holding the rod, I complied.

'It'll tire soon,' he added. I hoped he was right. I didn't want that fight to end but I really, desperately, had to see that fish. With the reel whining, my arms aching and nothing on my mind but beating the beast in the water, I took two steps forward. And over the edge.

My boot came down on thin air and I toppled, only to get half-hanged as the big bloke caught my collar and yanked me backwards. Even then, all I could think of was hanging on to the rod, and it's only now that I realise just how close I came to chasing the fish on a more face-to-face basis (*So thanks again, mate, if you're reading this!*). All he said at the time was,

'If you're falling in, always throw your gear back over your head.'

The fish helped pull me to my feet. 'Why?' I asked through gritted teeth, climbing up my own, straining rod.

'Like a grappling hook? Eighteen-pound line ain't gonna hold me, is it?'

He waited while I set my boots into the rock and re-engaged the fish. His headlamp traced the bend from tip-light to reel.

'Nah,' he said. 'Just, it's a half-decent rod. No sense in wasting it, too.'

I began to realise that, if I intended to carry on fishing as a hobby, I was going to have to start going to the gym. Not to work out, though. Just to buy steroids. It's amazing how quickly your arms tire when there's a big fish on there. I think it's because half your energy is spent not heaving back with all your might, and snapping the line, so your muscles are in a constant state of adrenaline-soaked semi-cramp. Not knowing whether they're coming or going really pees them off.

But fish tire, too. It seemed to go lighter on the line and, without me pulling any harder, it wheeled around smoothly like a kite caught in submarine slow-motion. The bend in the rod relaxed.

'Keep the pressure on,' said the big bloke. 'Give him slack and he'll spit the hook.'

Damn. There was more to this catching business than I'd expected, a lot more than just wind and celebrate.

'It's just a dead weight, now,' I said. 'You don't think it is dead, do you?'

'Could be a cod, mate,' one of the others offered. 'Coming in like a sack of spuds like that. They can do.'

'Used to be some massive cod off here,' said the big bloke. 'Thirty pounders. Not in donkey's years, though.'

'Nah, it's no cod.' He looked at my rod, still with a healthy bend but just shaking a little as I wound in, not bucking wildly like when the fish first took the bait. 'No bass, either. It's twisting.'

'It's doing what?' I heaved harder, slowly, and the fish glided easier still through the water. 'Do you know what it is then?'

'Reckon so.'

And then there was a big, white swirl in the sea. A good fifteen yards out and another two under a surface aglitter with reflected, distant streetlights; defining any detail was impossible. Apart from one.

'Christ, that's *long!*'

'Yep, nice fish,' said one of the others. He sounded pleased but not as excited as I'd expected. Or as I was, come to that.

Winding more, I soon had shock-leader - the last length of heavier line tied on to stop snapping on casting and abrasion from undersea rocks - sliding through the rod's eyes, and once it reached the reel I knew the fish was going nowhere. Whatever the Hell it was.

It was in close to the rock now and deeper, and I'd learned my lesson about stepping forward so I waited.

'Bring it up on the swell,' said the big bloke, edging forward at a crouch, ready to grab the fish when it appeared.

I took the strain and almost immediately the sea bulged up as the next breaker-ro-be rolled shoreward bound. It was a big one, too. And so was the fish that came with it.

Gobsmacked. That's a good word for it. I just stood there as this. . . sea monster, uncoiled inside the rising wave and lunged straight out, past the big bloke, and tried to attack me!

Well, kind of. I suppose my falling back in shock and yanking it right out of the sea had something to do with it but, suddenly, I was flat on my arse with a five foot eel in my lap!

And. . . it didn't really attack me, as such. More just sort of laid there, really, at first. Nonetheless, I got the Hell out of there. I'd seen its teeth!

Edging back toward the big fish, half-crouching and with the others' congratulations ringing in my ears, I felt like some kind of caveman, creeping up on a kill to see if it knew it was dead yet. A big, black eye looked back at me. It wasn't anywhere near dead. In fact, it didn't seem to care much that it had been caught.

They're incredible beasts, conger eels. If you're a super-squeamish girly reading this and squealing 'Eew, *wiggly eels!*', I'd like to know what the Hell you think you are doing reading this report, and to request that you return to your domestic duties immediately. However, if you're just a bit squeamish about eels, then you shouldn't be, not about congers. Instead, be scared, be very scared, if only because being squeamish about girls instead makes much more sense.

Anyway, where does an eel's head end and it's body begin? This thing's head was huge, broad, like a marine brontosaurus, but with sharper teeth more suited to snatching live fish than long-extinct Jurassic foliage. Could the Loch Ness Monster be a conger that loves Scottish scenery? It had lips, too, which surprised me, cold, bulging, fleshy things that seemed to sneer at me as it lay there, not caring a damn about the size 4/0 hook poking cleanly and bloodlessly through the membrane under its chin.

'Nice, nice fish,' the big bloke repeated. 'I'll give you twenty on that one.'

'*Twenty*?' I asked. 'Twenty *pounds?*'

'Reckon so. I can weigh it for you if you like.'

'Make it thirty quid and it's yours.'

He smiled. 'Shame it wasn't big silver, though. We thought it might have been, at first. Big eels often bite a bit softer. It's usually the better straps that pull your rod over.'

'Straps?'

Smaller eels, a couple of years old. Some say under ten pounds, some say under twenty. Depends how big they grow wherever you are.'

Watching the fish, I nodded. 'So how big do they go?'

'Not as big in North Devon as they do in the south. They've had them to nearly seventy pounds from the Tamar, the shore record.'

'They go up the river?'

He sniffed. I could tell he knew he was dealing with a rookie. 'Just the estuary, on the whole. But seventy pounds is nothing, mate. Fishing boats have netted them to two-fifty.'

I looked at my eel and suddenly felt inferior. A two hundred and fifty pound eel would be like a tree! Without the leaves and branches, the nesting birds, the romantic summer picnics in its shade and so on, obviously, but you get the general idea. As I had many times before, I dreamt of having one ten times the size of my own. I'd have pictures taken of it and show everyone who was interested, or I could stop in the street. I might even get a shot put on a tee-shirt, with it's big, bulging head reaching right up to my grinning face, and with, 'Look At The Size Of Mine' in big, bright letters.

'Well, what are you going to do with it?' said the big bloke, yanking me out of my daydream. 'Keep it, release it, or should we give you some time alone together?'

'Keep it?' I laughed. 'No, it's going back. I work nine to five and it wouldn't be fair, leaving it shut indoors on its own all day.'

Faint wisps of mist began rolling over us as the breeze rounded a little, coming in from the open sea, and as I dug through my kit for something to remove the hook, a shiver shook my shoulders as an eerie sensation of complete incompetence crept up on me. All I had, with which to pull a large, barbed hook from the snapping jaws of an increasingly angry eel, was a flimsy, six-inch pair of forceps. Oh yes - did I mention? - those jaws were snapping by now, all right, and the great fish was suddenly writhing like a pissed-off python. It dawned on me then, that, as it hadn't swallowed my bait, it was obviously still just as hungry as when it had ripped it to shreds. Someone's headlamp glinted off my shop-new forceps, and the eels teeth, and I knew that it was smiling and would have licked its fleshy, grey lips if it had the tongue.

'Here, try this.' The big bloke held out a larger metal instrument, which looked to me like he'd got it from a very old surgeon or a sadistic and inventive serial killer. I hoped he wasn't one himself. I hate surgeons.

He must have noticed my bemusement.

'A T-bar,' he informed me, stepping forward to do the honours. 'Just fit it on the hook, turn, and the fish's own weight pops it out. Watch.'

'Oh,' I thought, 'I'll watch, alright!'

Looking back, I hate that bloke. Too cool by half. All he did was stand behind the fish, over it, raise it's head by winding my shock-leader around his arm and lifting, then the hook popped out - audibly popped - just as he'd promised.

'There you go,' he said, stepping back. 'You can send him on his way.'

Now, you've probably got it into your head that eels are snotty, slimy things, harder to get hold of than a greased pig, or a copper when there's crime. You'd be right. As no bloke in his right mind would admit on an Internet forum like this, to prancing around the fish like a Jessy, trying to usher it back to the sea without actually touching it, let me tell you, the very first thing that I did was to get it in a judo hold to try to carry it the short distance to the water's edge.

In a very, very short distance, though, the eel had other plans and slipped from my two-arm bear hug like I wasn't even there. Of course, its short fall onto the rock just made it angrier, and I could swear it launched clear off the ground for my throat, but whatever actually happened then, I ended up back on my arse as the fish snaked away into the depths.

It may not be the best word for that feeling but. . . brilliant, just brilliant!

Chapter 10

It was two days before Danny returned to that catch report. He'd spent a sunny weekend wandering the highways and byways of north Devon with only a road-map, the outdoors and a stack of CDs for company, reacquainting himself with childhood favourite seaside spots and searching out new niches and ledges on even more stunning coastal stretches, where sandcastle beaches gave way to towers of rock. He'd returned with a notebook half full of definite spots to fish in the future, and the other half full of spots to check the possibility of fishing in the future. The memory stick of his phone was filled, too, bursting with photographs fit to grace souvenir calendars or chocolate boxes.

All of those marks, though, would need some researching, and not just to up the chance of fish. The thrill of catching a big eel hadn't quite wiped away the memory of that moment's awful, sinking shock, when he'd nearly stepped into the sea from Capstone Point. It was beginning to dawn on him that, if he intended taking his sport a little more seriously, he'd have to start exploring new places in search of new and bigger fish. Getting out and about as far from rescue as possible meant he'd have to take the safety side of things a lot more seriously than when he just pitched up on an open beach on the spur of the moment. And what better place to start working on that, than at The Goldfinger Bite?

And what better time for it than paid time? Danny sighed, leant back in his company chair, laced his fingers behind his head and stared at the clock. Its hands made a lopsided grin, showing ten past nine on a working Monday morning, or suicide *contemplation time*, as it's more commonly known. Danny thought it was BF&A's most productive time of the week. Everyone was sat at their desks, working out any tiny dribbles of enthusiasm for the job that had built up over the weekend, or simply throwing themselves into the task with a sense of desperation and their minds fixed firmly on five on Friday night.

'Well, mate,' he murmured, 'you can slow down time all you like now, at least 'til I've finished reading t'Internet.' He leant forward, staring down the clock with wide-eyed determination. 'Yes, my friend, every last page of it.'

He looked back at the freshly-loaded screen, The Goldfinger Bite forums home page, and breathed deeply. In the weeks since he'd signed on as a member, the whole place had become so familiar that it had become a virtual second home to him. Danny smiled. Even thinking of it as 'the whole place' proved that: it had long since ceased to feel like just a two-dimensional screen-full of bold text headings, thumbnail pictures and never-clicked advertisements. At the bottom of the page, in tiny letters, a list showed the screen names of all members currently on line and, when the list was long, Danny felt like he was entering a busy room, or even the bustling, marbled entrance hall of some grand hotel or university, with each on-screen, clickable link a like a side passage, leading to somewhere very strange.

Devon.

Danny clicked his usual link.

The Devon Area Catch Reports Forum announced itself in big capitals at the top of the page. The place worked like a giant message board, where information was first posted (as a new *thread*) under a title of the angler's choosing, to be commented upon by other members, tacking on their own notes underneath. The effect, on screen, was a long page to be scrolled down through, with each follow-on comment set in its own little box, a slightly corny rip-off of a pale yellow Post-it.

Danny skipped past the list of thread titles, first looking at the bottom of the page to see who was on line in the area. The list of live screen-names was busy tonight. He hadn't actually met any of them but was starting to feel he knew some, just through reading their catch reports, comments, and the odd on-screen discussion. It's surprising how much of a person can leak into their writing, and how much you can glean after reading enough of their posts. His fellow fishermen ranged from teens to pensioners (as Danny found out when he discovered that clicking their name brought up whatever personal info they wanted the world to know); frum da iliterit and/or txt-spk prx, through every conceivable occupation and intellect, right though to the wordy, know-everything angling-professor types. But although all human life was here, Danny thought, it seemed to be getting along pretty well, with everyone surprisingly willing to help and happy to join in the banter and contribute to the community atmosphere.

Well, nearly everyone.

Jim came in, waving a piece of paper. Danny could tell from his enthusiasm that it wasn't work.

'A letter?' Danny asked. A glance confirmed it. 'I'm not so sure. You can't send one from here, anyway. They get franked with our name.'

'No, this is perfect. This one has to be sent from outside. Trust me.'

Danny sighed. 'Give us a look.'

'This is just a rough draft,' said Jim. 'Electronic copy's in your e-mail. You print it off when we're finished.'

Jim thrust the paper at him and he read it. There was no sender's address, just 'Barnstaple Office' and the date.

Dear Mr OOOOO,
I am an employee of The Pasty Boys, Barnstaple branch, and I wish to offer my resignation directly to you because of continued intimidation from my colleagues.

There is an oppressive and hostile atmosphere of hetero-sexism throughout the all-male staff here and, although I am not a practising homosexual, I am a doctorate-level expert on the theory side thanks to many pleasurable, late night hours of study via the company's Internet connection (for which I should thank you - ditto, all the overtime).

However, it is my colleagues' stubbornly negative position on the cross-dressing debate that has driven me to resign. What a man wears to work, however frilly, is his own business in the privacy of his own trousers and should remain that way, as long as his trouser-status does not change. It's in the rules.

And I know what I'm talking about, legally. I have had many letters answered in the problem pages of *Cornwall Fetishist Monthly* and they have a legal advisor answering readers' court queries. His pages take up a surprisingly big chunk of each issue, actually, so he does know his stuff.

That I am forced to 'come out' for the first time in a resignation letter is intolerable, so I insist that you respect my confidentiality: I am not prepared to discuss this matter on the Barnstaple premises and I will go as far as to deny all knowledge of this letter if confronted by anyone. I will be more than happy to work out a period of three months notice in total silence, then simply not turn up again from the first week in August.

I trust you will accept my terms as you continue to hope that I don't bring a discrimination case against you.

Yours etc,

'Yours et cetera, *Dan Benton?*'
'Dan Benton, brackets: Miss,' Jim corrected. 'Anyway, you can delete that, obviously. It was only there to make sure you read it all.'
'Of course I read it all,' Danny muttered, glancing through it again in silence. 'It's a work of genius, mate! No amendments necessary! Only. . . I mean what, exactly?'
Jim let him bluster for a second. 'You mean what, exactly, is their head office going to do about a letter like that, which you're going to sign with a scribble so unreadable they're not even going to be able to work out an initial? Glad to see you're with me there, man.'
'I. . . see where you're going with this. I think.'
Jim stared at him hard and snatched back the letter. 'No you don't, do you?'
Danny bit his lip and shook his head. 'Who's Mr OOOOO, for starters?'
'The Pasty Boys' MD, top man in the company. You're always on line, you can track his real name down, surely.'

'Probably,' said Danny. 'They're a registered company. So, what? We're fooling some old git down in Cornwall? Not exactly a challenge, is it?'

Jim slapped his own forehead. 'You're not even trying, Dan, are you? They'll have to take it seriously. You know what Personnel people are like these days.'

'I think you'll find they're like, *Human Resources People*, these days, mate.'

'There, so you do know. They'll jump onto the words 'discrimination case' like fat chicks on a chocolate orange, but who are they going to call in for sympathetic counselling when they've no idea who their tearful drag-queen is?'

Danny thought, then nodded. 'Ok, I'm. . . partly with you.'

'It's bound to leak out, isn't it. Don't tell me they won't have a cackle at that one over their alcopops in the bar of the *Turnip and Inbreed* on a Friday lunchtime. So. . .'

'Aha!' Danny clapped his hands together and rubbed them. 'So what's the atmosphere going to be like in the Barnstaple branch when it does!'

Jim grinned, triumphant. 'They'll only go into the bog alone, for one thing. They'll all *know* whoever it is will deny it, the letter says so.'

'Enough!' Danny held up a hand. 'I'm with you. Leave me to savour the rest as it develops.'

'Anyway,' Jim said. 'Whatcha doing?'

'Fishing site,' Danny answered. 'Gonna check the report I posted, see if anyone was interested.'

'Fishing?'

'Yeah, man. It's brilliant,' said Danny, leaning into the screen. 'I put a report up a while back, about, you know, that massive eel I had. It's here somewhere. I'll show you . . . 'Jim?'

Danny tore his eyes from the screen just in time to see Jim disappearing through a closing door, heading back to his own desk. He picked up and glanced through Jim's letter again and smirked. He located the e-mailed master copy on his computer, changed his own name to Jim's and printed it off. The phone rang and it was Jim, yawning and snoring down the line. He kept it up for a good twenty seconds, then groaned despairingly, *'Fishing?!'* and hung up.

Danny grinned and returned to the Internet.

He clicked through The Goldfinger Bite's links to the Devon section, then opened the Capstone report thread he had started, 'I got a big long one'.

'Wow.' He sat back.

Thirty replies! *Thirty!* For a beginner's catch report!

He'd noticed before that other threads usually got a good handful of responses, with several numbering double figures.

But *thirty?!*

The first few posts were variations on 'Well done, cracking fish', plus a couple of comments from blokes burning with tongue-in-cheek jealousy. Danny read those, in particular, several times. Someone had picked up on Danny's mention of the giant bass, asking if anyone had heard anything more about them, but from the lack of any answer, it looked like no one had. Danny was getting somewhat bored by the subject, at least when he was on line and away from the water. No more of those gigantic bass had been reported by nets-men, off Cornwall or anywhere else, and no one had heard of them reaching the shore, but all the same the prospect of a freakish record-breaker kept it the hottest topic on Danny's fishing web site, and probably every other in the country. No one seemed prepared to accept it as a one-off freak of nature.

But the main flurry of posts on Danny's thread had nothing to do with *big silver*, and surprisingly little to do with his catch. That *Predator* guy had kicked it off, and he'd clearly decided that friendly congratulations were a little over the top in this instance.

'Reasonable strap. Good luck if you ever hook a real one.'

Well, short and to the point. Nice to see, though, Danny thought, that someone had jumped on him quickly; just ten minutes later, from the time shown by the message.

'I thought you left the site,' said someone going by the name of *Western Anchor*. 'It was good while it lasted. It's a v. good eel for up here and give the bloke a break he's new here.'

Western Anchor and The Predator had history, obviously.

'Only been away cos I go fishing and not sat playing with myself behind a keyboard all night. Been on your deckchair down the Quay again have you?'

Danny noticed The Predator's typing getting worse as his posting times got later into the night, and reckoned he'd been downing a can between each one.

'Anyway,' he continued, 'tell your newby boyfriend that fishing blind don't stop you gettin blind luck. Any idiot can do that. Is the salmon record still held by a woman?'

Danny rolled his eyes, laughed quietly and mouthed a word you wouldn't tell your granny. He rolled the screen down to the bottom, to the space for his own answer, and typed, 'When was the last time you were held by a woman, Predator?'

He moved the cursor to click 'Submit Post' but waited, realising he hadn't read the rest of the reaction. He rubbed his hands and scrolled back up the screen.

One *Leviturdo* had joined the debate, giving both The Predator a lot of constructive advice and the auto-censor programme of the site a thorough workout.

'prediter you are a ******* ****. why dident you **** off and stay ****** off from here. ***** like you only come here to get info but you never post any ******* catch reports of your own. you pleased with yourself with that? ****. ******. **** ******. and lay off the newbie. you should have got the sence not too post rudeness on a open web sight witch children can see. its' waaay not on. and you never know those bass might show up there. like-ly mark for them.'

Danny loved it, feeling a growing, guilty excitement at watching the argument developing. He wanted to post something goading them on, and had to remind himself that all this had taken place the night before, stretching into the early hours of the morning. The Predator's next response had taken him a full half hour of deep thought.

'**** you, Leviturdo. How can it be a good mark for fish that have never been here before? Where are you getting your info? From some jerk who takes illegal fish from Instow?

Danny's smile faded. That jerk was him, he realised.

'If you knew anything more about the area you're fishing than the location of the nearest pub and kebab shop,' The Predator went on, 'you would know that IF those fish are out there they'll be in on the next spring tide.'

Why, he didn't say and no one had dared to ask, but even if The Predator was as big a four-asterisks, six-asterisks as he appeared, something in his tone said he might know his stuff. The spring tide point stuck in Danny's mind as, maybe, worth a try. There's nothing stopping a full-blown ten-asterisker being a good angler as well, just like the teachers he remembered from school, getting plenty of kids to pass their exams, despite being arrogant ****s.

Danny was thinking of letting it pass and not posting the comment he'd typed. Getting further on the wrong side of this Predator would surely ruin his chances of getting more info from him in the future. So Danny scrolled the screen down further and sat back from his office desk to read on, pleased with himself at his scheming self-restraint.

Which was when, right on cue, Western Anchor chipped in again, accusing The Predator of always going for beginners like a playground bully, and starting Danny thinking that they were treating him like a kid. Resting on his elbows, he leant forward.

'They've been out there for weeks,' Western Anchor finished off. 'If you know so much how come you haven't caught one yet? Or maybe you're not as good as you think.'

The Predator had kept them waiting another fourteen minutes, time enough for his cans to really kick in. 'You haven't caught them bass cos you're an average angler. I haven't cos I haven't tried. BIG differnce pal!!! And before you say Yeah Sure I will put my monkey where my mouth is. I'll stake my car on catching one before you Western Anchor. One that beats the old record!'

'Yeah, sure,' Western Anchor replied, all in big, bold capitals. 'Like you would go through with a bet like that. That's a twenty pound plus fish you're talking, dingus. Go and sober up and enjoy regretting being such a tit.'

The Predator had jumped in again in seconds, with a volley of asterisks and accusations of cowardice. He left a big space then, almost as though he'd been taking deep breaths.

'No takers? No one?' he continued. 'What about you, Danny Buoy? You started this. But cos you sound under sixteen you can dig worms for me all the summer. WHEN you lose.'

Danny closed his eyes and sighed. Just when he was learning self-restraint! A thin smile crept across his face, he stretched, cracked his knuckles and stared down at the keyboard.

'Matey. . .' he typed without hesitation, 'you are ON!!!'

Chapter 11

Nothing came of it, of course: no support from the friendlier names on the site, no furiously boastful and mocking acceptance from The Predator. Not the next day, the next week, or by the time that Danny's catch report thread had dropped down the list and into the oblivion of *Page 2*. The thread, not to mention the bet, was soon forgotten.

Not surprising, really, as the thread had been locked by a site administrator, meaning no further posts had been possible, presumable due to its tone and high asterisk content. Nothing had come via the private message system, though, either. As Danny had spent more and more time on The Goldfinger Bite and posted ever more catch reports on his regional forum, he'd become friendlier with quite a number of the other blokes on there, through on-screen exchanges, and had started using this PM system more and more. It was nothing more than in-house e-mail but had proved invaluable in getting to know something of the other beach regulars, and in arranging to meet up with a few, now and then. In the weeks that had passed since the midnight row with The Predator, Danny had been fishing at least half a dozen times with other members of the site. And every one had been an education.

The first one he'd met had been by chance, on a return visit, on a pleasant, early summer evening, to Instow beach.

Danny had spent the day at work working hard, studying the wonderfully detailed satellite photography on Internet sites like *Google Earth* and *Wikimapia*, producing nothing in the way of profit for Barum Fixings and Attachments but plenty of new, coastal spots that looked likely to hold fish. Danny had known about those sites for a long time, with their amazing technology that allowed you to zoom in from space to helicopter close on any spot on the face of the planet, but after a quick visit he had decided they were only really there for sad people who wanted to zoom in to see if their house was visible. After all, that was what he had done. And it was. That opinion had changed quickly, though, once he'd connected outer space with his new hobby. Photographs near clear enough to count the crabs on the rocks let him virtually fly along the coastline, finding sheltered coves and rocky outcrops that he never knew existed, without leaving the discomfort of his office chair. Detail on the estuary was superb, too, with many of the low tide sandbanks visible, and many tiny paths to the banks clear to see; marks that he knew he'd be fishing one day.

And that's how he met Red Rum. On the computer at home, zooming in on Instow beach had led Danny's eye upstream along the river's course. He'd seen more sandy patches in amongst large, spurry outcrops of rock and, from all his online reading, knew that this was prime ground for catching bass. Just ordinary bass, up to a mere ten pounds or so if you got lucky, and not the elusive mega-mutants that were driving some people wild, but certainly fish worth catching. They were sleek, fast-roving open water predators but would move in close, very close, when there was food to be had. That meant, on beaches, they'd be found as near as the second or third breaker, just twenty or thirty yards, hunting sand eels in the swirl. In the estuary, they'd be after stray lugworm from the sand or fat, juicy crabs from the weedy rocks.

Light gear, lug and peeler it would be, then, Danny decided. Pitch up on the sand, against the rocks, and fish the full flood of the tide. It was a bright summer's dusk when the tides next fell right and Danny hit the beach straight from work.

'Do you come here often? Hahahaha.'

Danny groaned inside as he faked a smile. This guy was in his early fifties, with a tackle box the size of a small fridge and a Bobby Charlton Fan Club Member hairstyle. He'd arrived beside Danny just moments before, as Danny was still threading line up his second rod, then, after grunting a greeting, had stood in silence while Danny baited up and cast out. *Red Rum* was his screen name on The

Goldfinger Bite, apparently. Danny had recognised a fellow member from the site-merchandising stickers caking the legs of his tripod, and now wondered if he'd got the horsey name from laughing like a mule.

'No, mate. I'm pretty much new to this fishing malarkey. Haven't got a clue if I'm doing it right, really.'

Danny had discovered this line only recently but was fast discovering how useful it was. Plead total ignorance, even if your ignorance is only in the high ninety per cents, sound willing to learn and most blokes are eager to help. Danny grinned. He was picking up a lot of good tips that way.

Red Rum took a can of beer from his fridge, cracked it, swallowed half, belched like an angry tiger and drained the rest.

'Well,' he said sagely, wiping froth from his lips on the back of his hand, 'it's worth a long chuck now and then but, for your bass, casting far is casting too far. Lazy lob, all you need.'

Danny knew that. Neither of his baits was further than thirty metres from dry land. 'Oh right!' he said. 'I never realised. Cheers.'

'Yeah,' Red Rum grunted. 'That'll catch 'em.'

Danny waited.

'And leave the shell on your peelers if the crabs are stripping your bait. 'Twill last 'ee longer,' he added in a poorly put-on accent.

Danny had read into crabs on line. Peelers were the crabs to have because, when they're ready to shed their shells as they grow, they become one big, juicy seafood bite, then pop out, completely defenceless until they harden off the new shell. Hungry fish are supersensitive to the hormones they release as they change and hunt them down remorselessly, like zombies chasing brains. Marine biologists have devoted many years of research to these powerful attractant properties and have concluded that the hormone must smell, to a bass, like hot, fresh bacon sandwiches with lashings of brown sauce, where the bacon has just singed around the edges to give it real bite but it's lost none of its moisture or texture, and there's just a little mouth-watering, glistening fat dripping from the corner of the fresh-baked crust, the kind of sandwich that would have turned

Linda McCartney carnivorous, and you *know* you're gonna be in real danger of weeing yourself with gastronomic, salivating delight the moment you sink your teeth into it. Or something like that.

Hardbacked crabs are different, he'd learned. There's not much meat in them, no hormones, either, and they're a little on the crunchy side, too. So, with some exceptions, they're not a great bait. Hardbacks were often a problem near rocks because the live ones, free and peckish and frantically feeding as the tide flooded in, have just as much a liking for their dead peeler brothers as the bass do.

'Ever tried mackie down here?' Red Rum enquired.

'Mackerel? No. Never thought to, actually, not in the estuary.' It was a great all-round bait from the shore and rocks but he'd always assumed that an open-sea fish like mackerel would work only in the open sea. 'So. . . should I?'

'God, no.'

A car horn sounded in the distance, somewhere across the gleaming band of dark water, strung with rippling, pearly reflections of Appledore's streetlights. Danny glanced across, wondering what good marks were over that way. Where the river took a rocky bend looked promising.

'Why's that, then? Why no mackerel?'

Red Rum hoisted his mobile tackle warehouse cum booze-chiller onto his shoulder.

'Crabs again, innit,' he said, as though it should have been obvious. 'Strip it down to the bones like piranhas.' He paused, grunted and added, 'Be a fine thing if we had piranhas in here, wouldn't it! Hahahahahaha.'

He even ended it with a huge snort. Danny winced and prayed to the fish gods that he'd move on. Maybe the mule of a laugh had got him the name, but at least it didn't sound like he was talking through his ass about fishing. It often payed to be nice and let people chat awhile, even when, occasionally, Danny's first instinct was to fake something like Polish nationality, madness or rabies, or to whine, *'Sorry I am deaf,'* but saying only the vowels, inventing sign language and pointing to his ears. And he wasn't chancing that one again, not after last week, and the old guy with the two hearing aids that just didn't show up too well after dark. Deaf people ought to be forced to display large, flashing warning lights during the hours of darkness, Danny had resolved at the time as his blushes were diminishing, green on the port aid and red on the starboard. Or was it the other way around? Just in case, they should be banned from boat ownership, too.

Danny wasn't always so antisocial. Most nights, he didn't mind company at all and often relished it, but sometimes, particularly after a hard day's work-avoidance or, worse, having actually worked, Danny wanted just the stillness, the quiet and the dark.

Red Rum waddled off to wherever his own mark was, slowly fading, with the light, into the silhouette of the first Yelland pier, upstream. A gunshot belch echoed back from the gloom as it swallowed him.

Teat, Danny thought. Job done, though. Potential rearache repelled, but sent on his way feeling good, and Danny a little bit wiser. He smiled. The night-world was his, now; just him, the *shush* of low waves on the sand and the silences in between. He wound in, replaced the gnawed peeler's remains with a fat one, leaving the shell intact.

He went on to blank spectacularly, that time.

However much you think you know, you'll never know why some nights just ain't got fish.

Other nights were different, though. Other nights had fish aplenty.

Like the next time out, when he did investigate the Appledore side and ended up fishing sat on the wooden crosspiece of a tarnished ornamental anchor, the town lights behind him. The breakwater was covered in distinctive, grey blocks, double-drilled, and Danny was surrounded by a honeycomb of holes, each a little flowerpot for weeds.

The faintest haze clung around the stars, just enough to blur detail in the high dome of night. Below, the air was next to asleep, barely stirring the water as it calmed at the top of the tide. Nothing had bitten in over an hour and a half, although Danny had just missed his first rattle when they arrived.

They were fairly young, early twenties, maybe and seemed a little hesitant at first, hanging back and muttering quietly; considerate, at least, Danny thought. Eventually, ushered forward by his colleagues, one approached and courteously introduced himself.

'EeeeAaaayAllHicAlrightMaaaate?' he slurred at the top of his voice, swaying in a gale that wasn't blowing. *'Owwwwzitgoingthen?'*

His three chums followed, bunched close together and staggering in step, propped in a kind of loose, mobile human tripod that just about kept them on their feet. Not from the web site, these guys; they were straight from the pub, via the chip shop. They muttered a few monosyllables of greeting. Danny nodded. One nodded back, which seemed to throw his balance somewhat and his knees bent, then he flopped down on his backside with a thump.

'Pull up a chair!' Danny said it smiling but he was eyeing them all up and down from the corner of his eye, assessing them. Drunk like this, did they pose any kind of threat?

But who was he kidding? They were so completely drunk that he could have flattened them all with one strong blow - the kind strong enough to blow most of the head off a pint.

'Haaay I know one I can errrr. . . like give you a fish. . . I mean a tip on fishing, how to. . . catch em! I used to fish . . . here and all over North Devon. All of it. And south Smerzet. . . Smummer. . . Smu. . . Smu. . . Dorset.'

He sounded really pleased with himself and after all, Danny thought, he had done so well with that long near-sentence. He hoped his sigh wasn't too obvious. 'Go on, then.'

The young bloke swayed back a little, looking pale as death but happy as Larry as a street lamp lit his face. He swallowed hard, twice, and emitted, 'Garp!'

Danny stared at him. 'Ok.'

'Carp. No. Wait a minute. What looks like a carp?'

Danny stroked his chin. 'Another carp?'

The young bloke laughed. 'Ahhh, you winding me up you are! Mullet. No. Oh, I dunno what the scientists call 'em. The brownish ones.'

A breeze must have stirred, Danny thought, because suddenly he could smell the chip shop.

The drunk beckoned him closer, like he didn't even want his semi-comatose mates to hear,

' 'fYouu wanna cash. . . brown fish. . . ma man,' he said, clapping Danny on the shoulder, as much in need of support as being friendly, 'youuu gotta. . . you gotta use. . .'

He was swaying badly now but Danny was desperate to hear his tip, just in case it was a true diamond in the rough, the one, single gem of truly useful knowledge that this clown had ever acquired in his whole, intoxicated life. But he'd suddenly fallen silent, putting all his concentration into keeping his eyes pointing parallel.

'Come on then, mate, what would that be?' It felt like being by a pirate with a cutlass in his guts, trying to get him to spit out the treasure's location before he walked the biggest plank of all. Danny wanted to shake the bloke. 'What have you got to use?'

'I. . . I. . . Oh crap.'

Danny never got his answer but his hope for a night of fish aplenty was fulfilled; by the chalk-written blackboard menu-full. Cod, or possibly *haddock, semi-digested and served on a bed of chip-puree, in a Stella and pork scratching coulis*, cascaded down the side of the breakwater, pooling in the honeycomb of holes and filling several.

'Ground-bait, then,' grunted Danny, stepping aside and immediately starting to pack up. 'That's the word you were struggling for, was it?'

He left soon after they did, deep in thought, wondering, confused.

If they'd been to the pub and the chippy, where on Earth did he get the diced carrots?

Chapter 12

Then there was the night he found himself fishing beside another fellow Golfingerbiter, *Bent Rod*, whose name he remembered from more than one thread, partly because he wondered if he was.

He was - called Rod - but he wasn't. The proof was that he had with him one of those rare, wondrous creatures - beings that, to this day, many men believe to exist only in the realms of fairytale fantasy - and one that was certainly a first to Danny's eyes. His wife, stood there in waders, a weatherproof jacket and with her own headlamp on, bold as brass, threading big, fat, lively lugworm up a bright, 4/0 Aberdeen! A woman! Fishing!

'No wonder you married her,' Danny said when they'd been chatting for a while. 'Most blokes would sell both lungs just for a woman who lets them go out. Rare as hen's teeth, her kind, ain't they?'

'They sure are,' said Rod. 'And just as henpecky.'

His wife, Lorna, made a loud, dismissive *Pfff* noise and trudged down the sand to cast.

It was Croyde sand, part of a beach often washed by the best surfing waves in north Devon and known to throw up all sorts of good fish through the summer. The offshore reefs that help stir up good riding-waves are alive with large species, he'd learnt at work between tea breaks, like big conger eels, bull huss and large smooth hounds. The latter, a shark of rough ground that could commonly reach twenty pounds or more, was a highly valued fish among the membership of The Goldfinger Bite. They were fish that hit crab baits like missiles and battled like lip-hooked cage fighters. Danny would, most certainly, be targeting those babies one night soon. Lots of nights, soon, come to that, but not this one. Tonight he was still after bass, although the conditions for them were less than perfect, with the surf that drew them inshore to feed a pitiful foot high, at best.

He had a fair selection of bait, though, and was banking most on his latest investment of sand eels, blast-frozen at sea. Allegedly, this preserved the fast-deteriorating flesh and scent of these six-inch, pencil-thin fish. Danny had another theory. The look of horror at the sight of the blast-freezer, permanently permafrosted onto their silvery little faces, was probably exactly the same expression they wore in the wild, whenever they looked over their shoulder to see a hungry bass a hundred times their size bearing down on them.

'So how often do you have to beat her?' Danny said, chuckling. 'Or any woman, generally, to get her to come fishing?'

Danny stared off to the horizon, wondering if Annie would like fishing. He didn't wonder for long. Knowing her, she would be some kind of militant anti-animal-abuse-activist something or other, and probably shunned quality male company because she spent all her spare time harassing scientists and firebombing furriers. Yes, she had to be. *Suddenly*, it was all coming together. . .

So he could never let her near his car. Her kind was sure to smell death on it, and not just that tiny squid tentacle, stuck fermenting somewhere but impossible to track down. No, Annie would probably read all the dents on the front, know every animal he'd hit and hold him to account for each and every one.

It wasn't as though he was *trying* to hit the poor creatures - anything but! Devon simply had too much wildlife, that was all, and therefore it wasn't all his fault. That didn't lessen the impact of tonight's victim, though. That impact was going to cost hard cash to get beaten out, not to mention the extra damage Danny had added, using his tripod to crowbar out bits of badger from the front grille and wheel arch. God, it had been horrible. It looked like he'd ram-raided a convent.

Bent Rod coughed and scratched his chin. 'Hey, day-dreamer! I said, I don't beat her at all. Not for that reason, anyway.' He added a wink. 'No, she'd be out anyway. I actually met her out fishing, out Crow Point way, up through Braunton Burrows. Lorna Dunes, I calls her.'

Conversation died as Danny's tip light leapt into life, the green glow diving erratically in the darkness like a firefly being yanked back to Earth by an ant with a lasso, a cowboy's aim and great night-vision.

'Bite, mister!' Bent Rod advised but Danny was already on it, snatching up the rod but resisting the urge to strike straightaway, knowing bass sometimes hit the bait first before wheeling around to swallow it, so he dropped his rod tip, tightened the line. . . and there it was! Rattle-rattle BANG and the tip light dived again, veering left as dawned on the fish that diving deep in just three feet of water wasn't going to get it very far.

Danny struck, felt the hook lodge in something heavier than expected, and braced himself for a run that would bend his rod along half it's length.

It never came. The fish gave a lurch, then another, the line went tight as Danny would in and everything. . . just stopped.

Danny swore. His rod was bent along half its length but not from a mighty bass run.

'Snagged, mate?'

'Don't think so,' said Danny. The rod tip confirmed it, tugging down twice, just an inch or two but firmly, then relaxed, halving the bend and allowing Danny to regain a few feet of his line. Then everything went taut again, including Danny's muscles.

'Raymond,' said Bent Rod.

'Good to meet you,' said Danny, through gritted teeth. 'I thought your name was Rod.'

Rod laughed. 'Raymond. A ray. That's what you've got there, mate. I'd bet sick squid on it.'

Danny gently applied more pressure. His rod bent more; it got him nowhere.

'It. . . must be massive!' He'd hesitated, saying it, but it felt like he'd hooked a ditched getaway car. He wasn't snagged, though. The fish would move occasionally - just a little, wherever it wanted - always reminding him it was more than a rusting chassis.

'Oh, I'd give you about five pounds on that one,' said Bent Rod. He knew from the web site that Danny was a relative beginner. 'Strong flatfish like that, they clamp onto the bottom, see? They'll part-bury in the sand, too, if you let 'em. Imagine trying to pull a dustbin lid out from six inches of sand under the ten feet of sea, from an angle, with fifteen pound breaking strain line. Ain't easy.'

Lorna trudged over to watch, all swishing-nylon noises in her oversized weatherproofs.

'Now you tell me,' Danny said, hauling steadily. He reckoned he'd used about a bargain bucket in calories to gain himself four yards of line. 'How am I supposed to get it up?'

Mrs Rod laughed, a quiet shriek. 'Well, he's tried *Viagra* but, you know, we still live in hope.'

Under constant pressure, the fish shifted and glided in, quite easy at first but he could feel there was definite weight to it. It livened a little as it guessed it was in trouble, pulling the tip light down through a glowing arc with slow, steady yanks on the line. A flat, brown shape slid into the shallows, flashing crescents of white as its edges curled and flapped against the tiny surf. Catching the beam of Danny's headlamp, red eyes glowed back; eyes set a healthy, satisfying distance apart.

'Raymondo!' squealed Lorna and Rod was on it like a rat-dog. It looked a good size as he hauled it up but when he turned around, Danny was amazed to see that the fish could have wrapped its wings right around Rod's chest and, extended, they were broader than his shoulders.

Rod laid the fish down on the sand a few feet above the waterline, wet his hand and smoothed away a few smears of sand across its back. 'There you go, Sir!'

Danny crouched close beside it. Well, fairly close. Even though he felt he was fast gaining experience, he was a little hesitant about such a big, weird beast. He'd had a flat fish before - a flounder on his first trip out - but this was a ray and way, way different. It looked prehistoric, like geologists could have named *The Devonian Period* after things just like this, cruising Croyde beach four hundred million years ago. Although, probably, their word for it would have been different.

Looking on, Lorna let out a gaspy, happy sigh, whirled on her heel and trotted away.

'I'll get the camera!' she called back.

The fish was sandy brown, a big square with a tail at one corner. The tail caught his eye first, the two triangular spikes near the tip looking dangerous at first, until he saw they were soft and fleshy. No Steve Irwin heartache from this one.

'That is a nice fish, Danny,' Bent Rod said. 'Very nice.'

Laura was almost hopping from the ground with excitement. 'Get the scales! Get the scales!'

He turned and trotted back to his kit, calling, 'Slip the hook out first. You might well have a double there, mate!'

'Slip the hook out, right.'

Danny was still debating whether to touch it. He wasn't one hundred per cent sure what species it was, either, but preferred to keep his ignorance between himself and the fish.

He knew it wasn't a thornback ray, the clue being in the absence of thorns on its back. Small eyes suggested a small-eyed ray but how big were big eyes by comparison? He was pretty sure it was, though. He'd seen enough pictures on line. A blond ray, the other option, wasn't as prettily patterned, lacking the white flecks and vague, iridescent, blueish-white lines that traced over the faintly striped wings.

'Small eyed, is it?' Danny asked as Rod returned.

'Well, yeah,' he said in a way that meant *Obviously*. 'All you'll get around here at the moment.'

'Course. You get blonds around here sometimes, though, right?'

Rod squatted and did Danny's unhooking for him. 'Not seen one in a few years, myself. Well, only bottle blondes, chasing the surf gypsies.'

Danny watched him spread a canvas weighing sling on the sand and flip the fish over onto it. Its underside gleamed brilliant white, spot-lit by all three headlamps. Rod turned on his electronic balance with a beep, hoisted the sling into the air and squinted at the readout.

'I make that. . . hang on, let it settle.'

Danny chewed his lip.

'I make that. . . Hey, nice one, mister. Twelve - two! That's a bleedin' good fish for around here. They'd be pleased with that out on a charter boat!'

Danny took the scales, not doubting the weight, just wanting to feel it. Inside the sling, the ray had its wings curled over its back, with just its pointy, translucent nose and long tail hanging free. It sure felt heavy! And he didn't need to force a smile when Lorna's camera started flashing.

Rod showed him how to return the fish, by holding it by the soft depressions behind and out sideways from the eyes, where the ray can be, within reason, be gripped as tightly as necessary without hurting it. Danny took it to the waterside, lay it flat on the surface and stepped back to avoid the lashing tail.

Which didn't lash at all. The fish dropped to the bottom like a plate in the kitchen sink and didn't move.

'It's ok, isn't it?'

'Yeah, they're never in a hurry. One of them told me they don't even mind being caught.'

Confirming this, the ray rippled its wings and glided forward a couple of yards, right to the edge of the reach of Danny's headlamp. In its own good time it rippled again and was gone. Danny watched the black water for a good half minute. It was a great feeling, just sometimes, to see a big fish get away.

Fish came fast, after that.

Danny had the next one, too, a school bass of around ten inches and soon he and Laura were matching each other with fish to a couple of pounds, pulling them in for a pastime. Rod must have smelt of bones because all he could find was dogfish, an entire pack apparently marking their territory all around where he was casting. An hour later, Lorna caught their next night's nosh, with a much finer bass, four glistening, silver pounds of chilli and ginger fillets to be.

Rod cleaned the fish there on the beach. 'Always best,' he advised. 'And a must-do for some. Cod family, that's everything right down to yer wee rockling, pouting and the like, they carry worms in their guts. As soon as they know their host's heading for the table, they chow down on that fresh flesh, same as you would, and before you know it, they be out of that batter and across the plate after your chips.'

'Right,' said Danny, not that he had any plans to take more fish himself. He checked his watch. Late. 'Anyhow, you're making me hungry, I'm knackered and almost out of bait. Time to hit the road for me.'

Once his gear was packed and his rods strapped to his folded tripod, Danny went to say his goodbyes.

'Hey, Saturday week,' Rod said. 'Whatcha doin'?'

Danny shrugged. 'No plans. So fishing, most likely.'

'You've done alright tonight, mate. How do you fancy fishing in the Devon-V-Cornwall Open?'

With an eerie sense of chapter-ending *deja vu*, Danny heard himself saying, 'You are ON!!!'

Chapter 13

The nine on the digital display turned to zero and a torrent of cricketing punditry and analysis burst through Danny's bedroom. Coming awake, he groaned. Why the Hell hadn't he retuned it to a music station? Then a spark of panic had him tossing aside the quilt, leaping out of bed and standing in the middle of the room, slapping his face hard with both hands before the cricket seeped in and sent him comatose 'til Christmas.

He rubbed the last sleep from his eyes, snapped the radio over to the cd player, yawned, stretched, scratched and sat at his computer, all to the strains of a little light waking-up music.

'Finished with my woman,' the Brummie sang, *'cos she couldn't help me with my mind'.*

'People think I'm insane because—'

'I go fishing all the time.' Danny quickly decided to let Ozzy take it alone from that point but did provide backing headbanging for the next few moments while the web pages reloaded. He felt pretty good. Life in a box flat did have its advantages. For one, he hadn't had to wait for the computer to start up; read all the fish-porn you want until you fall off your chair into bed, and there, it's all wait for you as soon as you need it in the morning - sweet!

There was a PM waiting for him. Danny grinned. If he hadn't already met the bloke, a 'private message' from 'Bent Rod' would have got him worried. He might not even have opened it, in case it had an incurable virus.

It was short and to the point.

Nice one last night Buddy. Good fish. Pic's with the report HERE. Let me know for sure about the match and I'll put your name down.

He checked his diary pointlessly. Any clash, this was gonna win, no question. Rod's word 'HERE' was a link that took Danny to a report almost as curt as the message.

Took She-Who-Must-Be-Outfished down Croyde last night, squid and sand eel baits on long & low rigs. Quiet start but Lorna got a couple of these on small baits. Not exactly Big Silver but. . .

Two bluish, slightly blurred phone-camera photographs came next. One was a woman's hand, flat, holding a bass that didn't overhang it anywhere and the second showed the same hand holding up a two-hook rig hung with a pair of even smaller bass, with only just enough focus to prove they weren't actually Toby lures.

Bent Rod continued.

. . . caught dogs meself but we all know what they look like. He'd added a little smiley icon there, a round, yellow face, gnashing its teeth in frustration.

Then good to meet another site member, Danny Buoy, who turned up and showed us how it was done with this nice small-eyed.

The pictures from Lorna's camera were far better. The colours were right and the focus was spot on, so the first one caught the stupid expression of wide-eyed, childish glee on Danny's face with perfect, embarrassing clarity. Thankfully, there were three more, two of the ray on the ground with Danny's rod alongside for scale, and the last a proper magazine-pose: a dignified half-smile and a whacking great fish blocking out his whole torso. Numbers two, three and four, Danny saved to his own machine immediately. Especially four. The big, flat fish looked like a dustbin lid in that one.

The responses were already coming in. Comments from a Cornish bloke called Bobso Green came next as he scrolled down the screen.

Wow. Cool, cool fish man. Love catching them. They look like things from prehistoric seas. Well done.

Danny thought they looked more like plasticine cod that had fallen from great height onto concrete but, yeah, the guy had a point. They looked like prehistoric cod that got trod on in the shallows by a dinosaur.

One *Sprattacus* spent six lines moaning about how he had never caught one before slipping his congratulations into the last one and ending with some clapping smileys. A Viking-sounding chap, *Unglaka Norse*, praised *Bent Rod* for posting the info and Danny for both the catch and releasing it alive. Good to see *Western Anchor* back again, Danny thought, especially as he described him as 'on fire' for his recent catches, while someone just called *Strangulated* just said 'Magic' with roughly twenty exclamation marks.

'On Fire'. Danny liked that and, as he read on through a few more messages of praise, he could feel the warmth spreading already, like a gulp of Christmas sherry in his gut.

And then there was *The Predator* again.

Boring fish. All the fight of dragging in a puppy in a sack. The only point in catching them is eating them.
But all that effort and you put it back. Gaylord.

Danny felt like he'd been e-punched in the gut. The piece of filth! Jealous, obviously, he reasoned, and after the third or fourth read through he hit the keys.

Thanks for the positive input, Mr Gaylord. No need for the hissy fit, though. If you want to catch a decent fish yourself, drop me a line and I might give you some tips.

That would sort him.

It didn't. It took only five minutes for The Predator to respond, this time with himself with an even bigger ray. '13.9lb small-eyed, Putsborough,' it was labelled, and dated just three weeks before. Annoyingly for Danny, The Predator's face was obscured by a full-face balaclava and the glare of an over-bright headlamp.

'Pratt,' he said, and refreshed the screen.

'Don't worry about that walking butt extension,' said a new name, *Dr Clapp*. 'He's notorious around these parts - as popular as glass in a crab trap. Needs taking down a peg if you ask me but best just ignore him, the. . .'

He finished with a brief nudge to the asterisk machine. Danny wondered if Dr Clapp might actually be a clap doctor, or maybe just Chinese and rubbish at medicine.

Leviturdo must have been waiting for someone to warm up the swearing filter as he had waded in soon after with a similar message, but one far more colourfully put. One whole line of text looked like a sweep of automatic bullet holes, with tiny stars replacing every word except '*your mother*' near the end.

That Predator again, always goading, always on about his bleeding bass. . . Danny was glad of Dr Clapp's diagnosis, which felt kind of weird in itself, as he'd always managed to dodge his clinics in the past. Taking The Predator down a peg or two sounded about right, though taking him down to low water and pegging him out might just top it. He was lost in the screen, grinding his teeth, when, suddenly, fear gripped him as he realised he'd gone stone deaf.

No he hadn't - panic over - but the cd had finished with him barely having noticed anything past track three, and it meant he was going to be pushed to get into work on time. He got up reluctantly, hoping no one would notice he'd skipped the shower and wondering where he'd left his keys, razor, phone, the new hooks he'd bought, his wallet and a whole shoal of other things. Those new hooks would do the job on any bass, any size, should he ever be lucky enough to get his bait in their big, hungry gobs! That would show The Predator, hauling in the first Big Silver and claiming all the glory. That might even beat the incoming tide torture-murder idea, although it might not prove so popular. Bloody Predator. Danny tried to think of something else, a complete change of subject.

The Devon-V-Cornwall match, that should be great fun. As long as The Predator didn't show up.

'Ha!' A right turn-up it would be, if The Predator turned up in the Cornish team! And it could happen. True, his on-line profile said he was in Devon but he was probably an incomer, who'd see the richer shade of the grass on the good side of the River Tamar. To Danny, at least, he *sounded* Cornish enough.

'Ha!' he said. 'Again!' In a truly ironic world, The Predator would turn out to be the boss of Pasty-Boy in Chief. Danny looked across at their offices and—

Across at their offices? What was the unofficial Cornish Embassy doing in his bedroom? And with that, it all came crashing in, like the sea on a rusty submarine. The real world, the whole clock-staring, soul-freezing office of it, and the last twenty minutes felt like a fading nostalgic dream, from which he'd snapped awake aged ninety five and bedridden, waiting for a god none too keen to show up. He'd been so lost in his developing feud that he'd driven in to work like a mindless robot!

Worse, he'd left everything but his car keys where they lay. So, not even lunchtime to look forward to, now, with no money to help keep the fast food industry afloat and a boring round trip back to grab a sandwich. His mobile? Still in his fishing coat. His razor? Still dry and sharp. Frank Thuck, at least, he'd managed to get himself dressed!

Bloody Cornish. All their fault.

Danny took his time over the first big sigh of the day, tipped forward from the waist until his forehead hit the desk and decided to stay there, motionless, until the day ended or someone called an ambulance.

It was his second big sigh that moved him, snapping him back to attention as his sinuses and lungs filled with a gag-inducing cloud of pickled onion. He glared over the top of his monitor.

Dressed in loose, shabby clothing and shambling along with glazed eyes fixed on some dark horizon only she could see, Joan Lobb had recently fed.

It was always sandwiches with Joan, four of them, oblong, with the side crusts cut off, and always in the same flat, plastic sandwich box with the slightly transparent lid. She had no set time to eat them, either, unless she didn't fully understand the clock and thought she was already on lunch break.

Carrying papers from the cluster of printers at the far end of the room She trudged past with a parting cough of vinegar fumes, just to prove she was actually alive. Ugh. Danny rocked back in his chair and groaned. Cheese and pickle today. Or cheese, pickle and sneaky slug of gin, by the smell of it. But things weren't all so deathly boring. Danny returned to his duties, and the incoming mail.

Jim hadn't shown up for work. Again. Danny had feared the worst when he'd noticed Jim's battered old company car still hadn't reached its usual parking space, gone nine, but Jim liked playing fast and loose with the time-sheets and often took his own sweet time getting in. Danny still wished he knew how Jim had got a car out of Barum Fixings, when only management and above usually did. With the amount of time Jim took 'off sick', he'd have been better off with a company ambulance!

It was a summer cold, this time, allegedly. Very fluey, apparently, according to Janice Bodley, who took the message. Danny wondered what Jim really got up to in his spare time. What was certain, though, was that Jim was more likely to be genetically engineering a new disease than genuinely suffering from a real one.

This was worse news than normal, as there had been a little gem in Danny's in-tray. The Pasty Boys had hit back, and in style.

And what totally pathetic style it was! He turned their answer to the closet cross-dresser resignation letter over in his fingers. It was a truly pitiful offering, a ransom-style note, made of letters and words cut from newspapers. Nice touch, but all it contained was simple abuse. Had they posted that on The Goldfinger Bite, Danny thought, the bad language filter would have spat asterisks like a Gatling gun. Newspapers didn't print asterisks too often, it seemed, so the words were there, letter by letter, in full. Danny regarded it as a small victory, if all they could muster in reply to their little masterpiece was cut and paste cursing. If that was all they had left to offer, the battle was close to an end.

Jim would have loved it, of course, particularly the section about 'Barum Fixers cottaging in every bog in Barnstaple', especially as they'd spelt bog with two Gs. Stupid Cornish.

Damn it, why wasn't Jimmy here?

Their own last letter had definitely hit home. To know the full effect they would have needed an inside man at The Pasty Boys, of course, but from the complete lack of their usual provocation - usually various hand and finger gestures but sometimes the full split moon - Danny and Jim had known they had to be smarting. Three days after the letter was posted, the blinds came down and stayed down the rest of the week! So what if it was summer? It had been summer the week before the letter, too!

He glanced down at The Pasty Boys' ransom-note rantings again. A poor, poor effort; not that his own latest was coming along too well, either. It started had out fine, nice and nasty, but, in the edit, it had veered away from the vindictive and just gone, well, a bit silly. Silly with a capital S. Danny smiled and saved the file on his computer. Jim had got his way after all, getting Danny to do the dirty work. All the same, Danny decided to wait for him to recover from his cold before printing it off for inspection. After all, office summers were always slow and hot, so what was the rush?

'In a rush, Daniel, are we?'

Even though he'd been staring at the clock for a hundred and ninety three counted, motionless seconds, Danny froze.

It was. . . It was HER!

Panic-sweat prickled his scalp and he fumbled blindly for the crucifix that suddenly he wished he owned.

No, not Her. . . HER!!

'Jocelyn.' The poison name stuck on Danny's dry tongue, hissing.

'How. . .' He paused to swallow, put his voice back in its box. 'How wonderful of you to drop by.'

Danny had long since learned the value of leaving genuine Barum Fixings paperwork scattered, not too untidily, over his desk. His decoys, he called them, and he dragged a few sheets casually toward him, covering the Pasty-thieves' note. Even Jocelyn would have spotted that as definitely not an official BF&A document.

'You'll have to work twice as hard without your boyfriend here,' she said, all fake-friendly and deliberately ignoring the fact that Jim's work had nothing to do with Danny's. 'Swine fever, is it? Filthy swine fever, if you ask me.'

Danny looked up. 'Are you medically qualified, Jocelyn?'

'No, but. . .'

'Then that's probably why nobody asked you.'

She scowled and folded her arms. 'So where is he?'

'Haven't you heard?' Danny tapped his nose. 'A heavy cold.'

'Oh sure, yeah, right.' Sarcasm hung about her words like halitosis.

Danny shook his head, disgusted. 'You're so cynical. He could be seriously ill, you know. But you just assume it's all *atishoo* of lies.' He added, 'Duck!' as he watched that one sail over her head.

'What?'

'Nothing. I was just swearing.'

Jocelyn ignored him but stayed, shifting from foot to foot. 'So. . . ?'

She left it hanging like punch line too obvious to deliver but Danny knew from experience that she'd just run out of thoughts. She perched one bony buttock on the corner of his desk and he wondered if she'd scratch the veneer. She was in a good mood because Jim was out of the way, that was clear. First thing that morning she had positively beamed when pointing out to anyone still awake at five past nine that Jim's absence was becoming a regular thing.

Good-mood Jocelyn was still as annoying as a pebble in a pair of waders, though, especially when her amateur attempts at being friendly were usually mindless comments about mindless tv shows or ended up having a dig at Jim. Today was no exception.

'He's probably off having electric shock therapy,' she said, clearly expecting gales of laughter in return.

Danny stared ahead.

'On his brain.'

Oops! Danny had left his Pasty hate mail up on screen. Two discrete mouse clicks swapped it for a decoy order sheet, nearly complete.

'Cos that's what they do, put shocks in their brains. Mental people.'

Danny closed his eyes and breathed deeply, then turned around, all smiles.

'Well, that's one thing I've learnt today, Jocelyn. Thanks for that. It makes coming in so much more worthwhile.'

She looked at him blankly for so long that Danny became convinced she was channelling instructions from Satan. Such an ability would explain an awful lot about Jocelyn. She'd have to be destroyed, of course, staked and beheaded and buried on consecrated. . .

But it was just another case of *Does Not Compute* as, eventually, she drawled out, 'Whaaat? Whatcha mean?'

'Well,' said Danny, 'if it had been me up there in the padded cell, treating him - cos you're quite right, that's exactly where poor James is today - I'd have pressed the electrodes onto his elbows. Or possibly his nipples, just for fun. Actually, it's one of the main reasons I'm sat here and not a practising consultant psychiatrist.'

Evens the sneer, sniff and wander; two-to-one the foul-mouthed slapper response; five-to-one, threats of violence; tens, violence. When Jocelyn got it, sarcasm always got to her and Danny was striving to perfect the art. He waited.

He should have gone for longer odds. The witch raised one eyebrow, enjoying Danny's growing confusion, and her lips parted a little. Danny was surprised that her teeth weren't as jagged or pointy as he had expected, and lacking the shreds of torn employee-flesh that—

OH SWEET GODS OF THE SEA she was actually smiling!

A chill ran through Danny as if someone, probably an obese elephant, had walked over his grave. As he watched the smile spread and the sparkle in her eye, he began wishing he was already in it. Jocelyn was. . . she was. . . *She Who Must Be Destroyed* was flirting with him!

Now Danny knew how it felt.

Now he knew how it felt to find 'N. Bates' has checked you into your motel, or 'H. Shipman' signing your hospital notes. Panicky eyes flicked about, seeking his best escape and settling on the fire exit, which led to the stairs down from the roof. Jumping would be a messy end but quick, efficient and with nice, brief views of the estuary. Anything was better than this. With luck, he might even splat Jocelyn's car.

'So you'd better get busy,' she purred, pointing at the papers in his In-tray then tapping them with her index talon, 'or I'll have to. . . *supervise* you.'

Images flashed through Danny's mind, the like of which no sane man should ever suffer.

'Maybe we,' she began.

Danny panicked. '*We?*' he thought. '*As in me and. . . that?*'

'. . .should go out sometime, just for, like, a work drink, you know. What do you think?'

'I think—'

'And definitely not with Lithium Jim, neither.'

Danny took a while, then, considering his answer, but in the end he couldn't hold it in.

'I think I'm going to vomit, Jocelyn.' He smiled a thin, almost sympathetic smile. 'All over you.'

There, that felt better already.

'Yes, that would be nice. A real ankle-splatterer, diced carrots an' all. And then I think I will smash my head against Mr Slade's door until brain damage has permanently erased all memory of ever hearing you say such a wicked, filthy thing.'

That took well under four seconds to get through. Jocelyn's face went through the whole range of colours from puce to infra-red until Danny thought her head might explode, *Scanners* style. He held up a ring binder to shelter his face from the blast but couldn't help peering over the top, just in case. He'd never stop regretting missing a sight like that. Somehow, though, she managed to bite her lip and swallow her rage, just hissing two words - one of them 'off' - before storming away, no doubt to find a cat to kick, or a baby cat. Come to that, knowing Jocelyn, any kind of baby would do.

'You're as bad as he is,' she called, far louder than necessary. 'And just as mental!'

Danny tried to ignore it. He failed. 'Face it, Jocelyn,' he called out, loud enough to fill the room, 'No man's going to want you, not unless he has diseases to spread. And only if he's in a big, big hurry.'

Jocelyn stopped in her tracks, giving Danny time to enjoy the cartoon steam that only he could see, jetting from her ears. When she turned, though, she was surprisingly calm; clearly seething, but well in control.

'Ha! Look who's talking.'

'What's that supposed to mean?'

She sneered. 'At least men don't live a lie to avoid me.'

'What's that supposed to mean?'

That felt stupid, repeating himself, and he felt himself redden with rage as she came back over. She gripped the edge of his desk and leant across, wearing a face straight out of *The Exorcist*. He wanted to strangle it out of her but he couldn't, not in front of witnesses. She'd tell him, obviously. She was bursting to.

'Well,' she said when she had calmed, stretching out the word a full four or five seconds for maximum annoyance. 'What about your darling little Annie?'

'She's not my Annie! We haven't even-'

'But you'd like to, wouldn't you, Daniel? I bet you'd *love* to just-'

That was enough for Danny and he yawned and returned to his screen. 'Haven't you got work to do, Jocelyn? Babies to eat? Corpses to defile?'

He'd said it with a smile but she responded with a stream of words that would have melted The Goldfinger Bite's profanity filter. Danny was immediately impressed. He didn't think Jocelyn knew so many words in total, never mind such a long selection of rude ones. On and on it went, too, as she searched ever darker and more lurid corners of her bedsit mind for every single reference to improper or inadequate sex or excretion she'd ever encountered, then coughed and spat them up like a gull regurgitating lunch for the little ones.

And Danny was lapping it up, now settled back in his seat with his arms lightly folded to enjoy the experience to the full. Like being caught in farmyard traffic in a leafy lane, he thought, unable to take your eyes off the leak from the septic tank truck in front but fully confident in your windscreen and safe from getting splashed. True, she slowed and lost her rhythm toward the end but it was a grand performance that only stopped completely when Danny couldn't contain himself a moment longer and burst into spontaneous applause.

He even let her compose herself afterwards, before going in for the kill with his own super-putdown, which she'd given him so long to prepare and refine; after all, she had a lot of blue air to suck back in. She looked totally lost, then, for words or thought, so it was time to go in for the kill.

But she wasn't. From somewhere, she came up with one more shot of nastiness, blind-siding him with a wild sucker punch out of nowhere.

'That ring of Annie's? It was all a lie. From the bubblegum machine outside the newsagent, it was. It had a sparkly plastic butterfly on it but she broke it off. Just to get rid of you, Daniel. Just to make a fool of you.'

Danny was dumbstruck.

'Done a good job, too,' Jocelyn added, casually victorious and turning to go, *'din' 'er, muy luvver?'*

Chapter 14

Danny sat with his head in his hands, though he'd have preferred to be holding Jocelyn's, neatly severed.

'There, everyone's happy,' she'd told him. 'You're not being laughed at behind your back any more and we're free to laugh in your face!'

That Jocelyn had known all along made it much, much worse. How. . . why would Annie confide in someone like *her*, of all psychopaths? Annie being in any way close to Jocelyn was like discovering the old Queen Mum had been an insatiable, Satanic serial killer. Danny tried to resign himself to another crap week in the office, just, this time, all crammed into one day. Annie's blatant snub was just par for the course and he consoled himself in the sure and certain knowledge that, outside of work, he could sweep her, or any woman he chose, off her feet at the drop of a hat.

And there she was, again, Annie, bold as brass across the room, trying to look busy with the photocopier. She might be avoiding his eye and keeping her head down but she was there to gloat, really, after a girly gossip 'n' giggle update from Godzilla, no doubt. She'd probably been waiting outside the door or had been watching all along. Danny glared, daring her to look his way but she didn't, granting him only a toss of blonde hair as she turned her back on him, then bent across the copier, pressing buttons.

He rotated his chair for a better look but however far she bent, however tight her skirt was, Danny didn't want her pressing his buttons, not if she was infected with Jocelyn's evil. He glared harder, wondering if he could burn it out of her, or burn her as a sorceress on the spot before the evil overwhelmed her, which was surely the kindest thing to do and something the police would be sure to understand when he introduced them to Jocelyn. And then they could help burn her, too.

'Witch!' Danny hissed under his breath, and thirty feet across the room, Annie whirled around and stared him straight in the eye. And, god damn it - and give the girl her due - she held his stare. But then, she would, wouldn't she. . .

Danny shivered, then flushed as Annie's eyes burnt right back along his own stare, piercing his sockets and searing into his brain as she used her newfound powers from Hell to spellbind and corrupt his deepest, darkest—

He yawned.

No, perhaps not. She'd just glanced and smiled casually, like she always did, like nothing had happened. He watched her dip down, retrieve her copies and breeze for the door to Slade's office.

Danny slumped back into leatherette-upholstered boredom and swivelled back to face his computer screen, and the single page website for *Basham's Bodywork Repairs*. He was going to have to start doing overtime, if he wanted to keep himself in both hooks and wheels. Overtime, yes. Voluntarily helping out the company, too. That would be nice, and in the unlikely event that he did get bored, he could always stare out of the window and soak up the view of Hell freezing over.

Then to add to his troubles, Annie was back in the room again. No casual glance or furtive peek from behind a stack of copier paper, this time, but right out in the open, brazen and unflinching. One eye was partly closed, defiant, like she was Mickey Rourke calling out another hairy, Lycra-ed wrestler. He'd have to remember to tell her that she looked like Mickey Rourke. But something in her eye, a raised eyebrow, a subtle change in posture, made her suddenly seem less hostile.

What was he supposed to do now? It was like a Mexican standoff, except neither was from Mexico, and Annie was the only one standing. But the air was so thick with tension that, when Danny threw down his pen in angry frustration, it took three times as long to hit the desk.

He took a chance. Hand trembling, he drew a two-finger pistol from his hip holster, aimed from behind the cover of his monitor and squeezed off one high-calibre round at her, savouring the weapon's satisfying kick. Annie stayed standing, though, just watching him, half smiling.

How had he missed? He was out of practice. Duelling wasn't commonplace in modern, bustling Barnstaple. He blew cordite smoke from his fingertips and, when he lowered the weapon, noticed Chappell the accountant standing there, just watching him, half scowling. He sniffed, rolled his eyes, and continued on his important job of carrying paperwork across the room, shaking his shiny head just noticeably. Danny split his pistol into a V and flicked it, rapid-fire, at the baldy's back. If Chappell was so high and mighty, why did he stop to dodge the bullet?

As his target disappeared, slumping back in his chair for the return sink into boredom came as a reflex to Danny, but Annie was still there and he snapped back upright, staring at her from beneath a suspicious frown. She was smiling, though, behind her hand; the end of a laugh at V-signs, perhaps? Not if she were one of Jocelyn's minions, and by the way she was giving him the finger now, it looked like she had been recruited.

A closer glare, though, showed him it was not *The* finger but the *ring* finger, the one now free from the stupid piece of costume jewellery she'd had no right wearing in the first place!

'*Aww, poor baby!*' her expression seemed to say, then she laughed again and suddenly didn't seem quite so deeply evil, after all.

But she could still be a witch, just one in disguise, like all female traffic wardens without exception. Danny needed a test, and fast, before it was too late. A swivel-chair ducking stool would be easy enough to set up but where to duck it? The river through town was a fair way to drag them both, especially if Annie wouldn't come quietly. Jim - who else but Jim? - had once told him that they used to test for witches by the flammability of their intestinal gas. Blow out the match and it was, '*Have a fine day, my goode Ladye,*' but scorch the Puritan's eyebrows with a jet of fire and brimstone and it was barbecue time, with stake instead of steak. Jim said he had read it on the Internet, so it had to be true and would work, but following her around the office all day, holding a naked flame to her backside was likely to arouse suspicion. Then Slade called her, she rolled her eyes and ducked into his office and the moment was broken.

Only momentarily, though. He'd just wanted the papers she'd been copying and then she was back, stood watching him again and, this time, with no excuse. She looked faintly amused but with a slight, lopsided frown of curiosity. Was it his move, or something? What did she expect him to do?

Danny scratched his head. No, he doubted it was that. She sighed, visibly. Was she challenging him?

Well, if it was a challenge she wanted. . .

One brow raised, he locked eyes with her, jerking his head back once to beckon her over.

'Me?' she mouthed, pointing to her breastbone and feigning surprise.

Danny tore his eyes away and looked down, opening his word processor to bring up the file marked 'ISD', his Pasty boys vendetta letter. He'd make it look like a printed-off e-mail, he decided, adding fake *To* and *From* lines and that day's date. Jim's e-mail address went in as the sender. Danny chuckled to himself. If the lazy sod couldn't even come in to work to join the fun, he could take a little credit in his absence. He clicked Start and, behind Annie, a small printer jolted and rattled into life. Raising one eyebrow and nodding, Danny motioned her across to collect it.

INTERNATIONAL SILLY DAY FAQ

'WHAT IS INTERNATIONAL SILLY DAY?'

International Silly Day is a day of silliness that is international.

'ARE YOU SERIOUS?'

Absolutely. And absolutely not. It's like Comic Relief, except it costs you nothing and it's funny.

'WHEN IS INTERNATIONAL SILLY DAY?'

International Silly Day is now, today. Time is short.

'SO WHY HAVEN'T I HEARD ABOUT INTERNATIONAL SILLY DAY? BEING INTERNATIONAL, SURELY IT'S A BIG ORGANISATION?

No, that would be silly. Organisation means sensible method, rationality and planning; unpleasant behaviours from which International Silly Day wishes to formally distance itself.

International Silly Day was created on the spur of the moment, appearing in a flash out of nothing but infinite boredom. You, too, can recreate that divine instant simply by forwarding this e-mail to everyone in the whole universe, instantly, or simply to everyone in your address book, when you have a spare minute.

'I HAVE A FRIEND WHO THINKS YOU ARE JUST BEING STUPID. WHAT WOULD YOU SAY TO THEM?'

Potato, Triceratops and, quite probably, Ukelele. All in a soothing, high-pitched yodel, naturally.

'NATURALLY. BUT WHAT IF MY FRIEND STILL REFUSES TO JOIN IN?'

Tell them to stop being so silly.

'I LOVE IT! WHAT CAN I DO TO HELP?'

International Silly Day means that you MUST do the silliest thing you can think of, IMMEDIATELY. . . or don't you care at all about hot, starving children with only flies for sunglasses?

'OF COURSE I DO, THEY'RE GREAT, BUT WILL PARTICIPATION IN INTERNATIONAL SILLY DAY INCREASE MY ATTRACTIVENESS TO THE OPPOSITE SEX?'

Without any doubt whatsoever. And not only the opposite sex, but all sexes, and with immediate effect.

ACT NOW - PROVE YOU'RE ALIVE!

D O   S O M E T H I N G   S I L L Y

Then loosen your clothing, take a deep breath and brace yourself.

Annie picked up the printed page by one corner, letting it hang from finger and thumb like it was another, quilted-softer sort of paper, badly soiled. It flapped audibly as she approached. She didn't read it.

Which was fine by Danny. He gave her the shortest, tart smile of thanks, took the letter and folded it into an envelope. He wrote Joan on the front and passed it back to her.

Still without a word, she took it, again, pinching just the corner and letting it swing. She grinned, the faintest gleam of evil on her teeth, and waved the letter threateningly toward Slade's office. And what if I take it in there instead?

Danny hoped he hadn't paled too visibly. Obviously, she knew it wasn't work-related but she delivered it anyway, to

Joan's empty in-tray, as requested, and not into Slade's lap. He drew a deep breath as she released it. She was clean, uninfected by Jocelynism. He wouldn't have to kill her, after all.

With Annie stood beside his chair, not too close but close enough, they watched Joan oblivious to the letter on the desk beside her, She stared into her screen, mesmerised, rocking gently back and forth to some unheard, monotonous beat.

'She only does that so we don't call the undertakers,' Danny was about to say but he didn't want to break their long silence. Neither did Annie, apparently. Having lost interest in Joan's meditation, she was looking at his screen, curious, intrigued, but she didn't say a word either. Danny watched her, waiting for the look to change to boredom, mockery or outright disgust when she twigged it was a fishing site.

They were so intent on the screen that neither noticed Joan stop rocking, nor her hand inching flat across the desk toward her in-tray.

Amazingly, Annie was actually reading the site, and looked almost. . . interested? In what was technically, occasionally, a blood sport? And this was the girl who Jim had bet his left one was an orchid-hugging vegan? Ha! Guess again, sucker, thought Danny. He should offer Jim double or quits.

But, first Bent Rod's wife, now Annie? Another woman fisherman? What was the world coming to? Coming to being entirely taken over by women, at this rate, and then where would we be? No football, No wars, No Page Three, and 24/7 nagging channels replacing anything daring enough to show Top Gear or Deadliest Catch.

It was Danny's duty to break the silence then but Joan Lobb beat him to it, standing bolt upright and knocking her chair over backwards with a crash. Danny jumped and his eyes widened as he tried to see what was wrong with Joan but he couldn't get past Annie's grin. She was staring at Danny again, not caring what the mad woman was doing a few feet behind her, and holding his eye with another, brighter sparkle of that same evil in her own. The good kind of evil. Danny's head spun. Wasn't it a law of nature that women were never, ever, ever fun or naughty at work? God, she was stunning. He wondered what other kinds of naughty she knew.

Obviously, she knew that Joan had read the note she'd delivered, and she must have heard the sound of Joan's clothing shredding behind her, but all she did was look Danny straight in the eye. She wanted something. Was it . . . was it him?

Distant strains of the most dreamy, romantic music he knew caught his ear, too, though when he finally recognised Lemmy on lyrics he realised that it was just his mobile ringing. He groped for it in his pocket then threw it over his shoulder.

'She's lost it! Get her off me!'

'Danny,' said Annie, her voice soft and hoarse. 'Danny, take me.'

'What?' he said, with both of them oblivious to the whirlpool of chaos all around. Colleagues' gasps grew to howls of alarm, then disgust, and someone was crying, 'For pity's sake call an ambulance!'

Someone else - and it sounded like a man - was just crying.

But what did Danny care? He was so pumped he thought his heart was about to reenact John Hurt's death scene in Alien. Was he dreaming? 'Pinch me,' he wanted to say, but that was always dangerous as you never knew who might overhear and take you up on it. Of course, though, being a bloke, all he did was scratch under his chin and mull it over, making her wait for a just-slightly-grudging, 'Ok then.'

Never would there be a working day more perfect.

'Take me,' she repeated, grinning, but spoilt it all by looking at his damned computer screen. 'Take me fishing.'

Chapter 15

'I can't believe you brought me here! It's dangerous!'
'Dangerous? It's supposed to be. This is where I was gonna come and drown myself.'
'Drown yourself?'
'If that ring of yours had been real. I had it all planned out.'
'Oh, come on, I've said sorry for that.' Annie looked down embarrassed. 'Not that I had any reason to apologise! That was on the day I walked in the door, so it wasn't aimed at you. Just. . .'
'Just all men, everywhere?'
'Well, I suppose so.'
Danny nodded. 'Lez! Thought so.'
'What?'
'Oh, my mate Les Jones thought so. You know, you might be doing it just cos you needed some space. Like you said. Maybe after a. . . a recently terminated relationship. And . . . that's what Les thought. When I told him all about it. Which I did. In. . . the. . . pub?'
She stared him out. 'You aren't friends with any Les-es, are you, Danny?'
'No.' Danny looked down, then brightened. 'But if I was, d'you think they'd let me watch?'
He dodged a half-hearted slap, then raised his cola can to his lips, sipped and swallowed. 'Anyway, girl. Dangerous? Are you mad? Saturday teatime in Instow is about as dangerous as yer granny asleep!'
Sunblock scents mingled with the sluggish breeze. Gulls and children screamed their delight as ice-cream chimes tinkled on the edge of earshot and, washday white in the brightness, two mute swans drifted past, saying nothing. Danger wasn't a feeling that sprang readily to mind. Even so, they were cowered down against the low stone wall like

they were sheltering from a raging blizzard, Annie having dived there for protection and Danny because it got him closer to Annie than he had ever been.

She peered down at the birds and shuddered. 'Granny doesn't keep swans, though, does she.'

'Swans?'

'Swans can fly, you know!'

Danny looked long at her, rubbing his chin. 'University girl, then, are you?'

Already, he'd had enough of birds today. The feathered kind, anyway. When they'd parked on the seafront behind the low stone wall overlooking the beach, how he'd managed to steer Annie clear of the thick, bloody streak of *pâté de pheasant gras* sprayed out from under the nearside wheel arch was anybody's guess! He was warming to this bird, though, and her apparent swanophobia. Not-being-afraid-of-stuff in front of girls had been a winner since his playground days, and hadn't many a fair maiden been won by a bloke unfazed by spiders in the bath? He sipped his drink again, extra nonchalant.

Annie huffed and rolled her eyes. 'But they might fly up *here*, Danny! They could be up here in a second, if things turn nasty.'

He spluttered, just stopping cola hosing from his nose. 'If things *turn nasty*? They're swans, not alligators!'

Annie looked at him aghast, like he'd casually tossed piranhas into a playground paddling pool.

'A swan can break a grown man's arm with it's wing,' she snapped, noting him grinning at her terror. 'And that would knock the smile off your face.'

'That's complete crap,' said Danny. 'They're all feathery, for one thing. How's that gonna break even an un-grown man's arm?'

'It's true!' Annie insisted. 'Everyone knows it.'

Danny sighed. 'Look, I'll show you.'

He stood and leaned over the wall of the stone quay and looked down at the pair of swans drifting by. It looked a great fishing spot, the short stone jetty protruding from the middle of town, from where the ferry ran across the mouth of the Torridge to Appledore. Silt flats made up the upstream shore, with sunbather-strewn sands sweeping away to the right. Danny had fished there twice before and had a couple of cracking bites, but hadn't yet landed a fish. 'Give me some bread.'

'Some bread?'

'One of our sandwiches. I'll sacrifice a bit of crust. . . if it'll save us from those big, nasty, arm-breaking birds down there.'

'Oh, shut up.'

Danny didn't look back but held out a hand behind him and waited until she filled it with parallel corners of butter-stuck bread.

'My god! About time!' he exclaimed, rubbing a stiff shoulder and forearm. 'Me hand was killing me.'

The sun had dropped a little. 'Yeah, I know,' Annie sighed apologetically. 'I never brought our packed lunches. I left them in the fridge. Sorry. Almost no cash, either, so had to bus into Bideford and get some on plastic.'

Danny grunted. 'Anyway, never mind that, swans are cute and friendly and wouldn't dream of stooping to violence in the first place. Breaking arms is just a total myth.'

'But I'm sure I've heard,' she began.

'Yeah, everyone's *heard* it, darlin', sure. But, ask yourself, how many actual recovering swan-victims do you know of? How often does it get in the local paper, '*Swan Named as Only Suspect in Recent Spate of Male Arm Fractures*'?'

Annie stood up and laughed nervously. 'I, uh. . . think I get the message.'

She watched over his shoulder as he dropped the bread in front of the birds, who sniffed it, then shot both of them a look of hatred and disgust before turning to set sail across the estuary to Appledore. Annie moved forward to the wall, beside him. Close beside him.

'It's like drunken red-necks in America,' Danny rattled on, oblivious, 'making up stories of alien abduction to cover those *missing hours* sleeping off moonshine in a ditch. But in this country, we get too drunk to stand, fall on our arms, break them, then struggle to come up with an excuse that beats, *I was too drunk to stand, your Honour*. Obviously, you need something better.'

'Obviously,' said Annie. It was all she could manage.

'And, obviously, being attacked by one of the biggest bits of British fauna sounds a lot better. You can say you put up a great fight and only got drunk afterwards to numb your shock and anyway, surely you deserved a drink, fighting off rampaging, feathery wildlife like that and protecting the general public, free of charge. Also, you can claim it's swan poo, not your own.'

Annie laughed but he stopped her. 'It's heroic, not funny.'

'Heroic?'

'You'd probably get a medal. I did. And I wear it with pride. It warns other swans that I'm not to be messed with.'

Annie watched him, her head shaking slightly but holding his eye all the time. 'You're nervous around women, Danny, aren't you? Babbling on like that.'

That did make Danny hesitate, but only briefly. 'I'm nervous around women who think the swans are planning to attack.'

'So that's why you didn't bring me a rod of my own, is it? You wouldn't trust me with one.'

It was true, he hadn't brought a rod for her, but not just because she was a girl and he didn't trust her with. . . Ok, obviously he wasn't going to trust her with a hundred and fifty pounds' worth of quality carbon fibre rod above a drop into ten feet of water but it was because she was a beginner, not because she was a she. At least, not very much.

'But. . . bright orange string on a lump of plastic from a seaside tat-shop? What next? A bucket and spade and ice cream later? You really know how to show a girl a good time, Danny Benton.'

'Let me tell you something,' he cut in. 'Not long ago, there was a crabbing competition, right here, which a little girl won - with a crab line - and do you know what the winning catch was?'

'I'd go for. . .' She scratched her head. 'Lots of crabs. Or a really big one.'

Danny shook his head. 'A gurt great bass. Snapped up a big lump of bacon and headed for the Atlantic. Nearly pulled her in, by all accounts. . . would have paid to see the look on her face, cos you just know there was a moment when she thought she had the mother of all crabs on there!'

She looked at him long and hard. He liked it at first, but when the hint of a wicked smile started spreading it unnerved him, made him feel like she had, somehow, sussed him.

Perhaps she had.

'So,' she began, 'what you're saying is. . . that bass are not hard to catch. That even a soppy girly can do it, even without a fishing rod. It's that simple.'

'No! Obviously not!'

She smiled. One of those forced ones, impossibly pretty but so annoying Danny wished he was carrying a baseball bat. OK, maybe not a real one, just something flexible, some kind of soft rubber device that he could use on her to. . .

'How would I explain that to the other guys?'

'Explain what?' Annie asked. 'And what other guys?'

'Nothing, nothing.' Quickly, he leant over and checked his line tension, cranking the reel a couple of turns to stay in taut contact with the bait. 'Well, OK, yes, that's exactly what I'm saying. Bass are dead easy to catch but I'll never admit it in public.'

'Interesting,' said Annie, nodding at Danny's rod tip, which wasn't nodding. 'Where's your bass, then? Or perhaps you need the help of a soppy girly.'

A small boat ploughed past a few hundred yards out, the cabin windowcatching sunlight and flaring like a floating, daytime star. Danny shielded his eyes.

'It'll come,' he said. 'Might take a while, but it'll come.' The little boat turned, the light died and it headed for the white band of surf coming over the bar at the estuary mouth. Three small figures were visible, all anglers from the number of rods in holders on each side. 'Doesn't really matter how long it takes.'

Annie nodded. 'Patience?'

'This is no time for card games. But it might help pass the time.'

She prodded him. 'But, you just need patience. It's that simple?'

'Once you've got the basics right, yeah.' He glanced at her, smiled, but quickly drifted back to the rod tip. 'Bass are easy to catch, when they're there and when they're hungry. They're strong, fast fish, roaming feeders, with the biggest mouths in their bit of sea and they don't take no for an answer. They'll hit a crab as big as their own heads, BANG!' - he mimed it, fist in hand - 'CRUNCH! And swallow the bugger whole. If you're there when they're hungry, you ain't gonna go far wrong.'

He fell silent, feeling her watching him too intently, sure she was trying not to laugh. She didn't try hard.

'You love your bass, don't you!' she said, chuckling. 'I don't think I've ever seen you enthusiastic over anything, Danny. I wish you were as keen at work!'

He stared back. 'Really? What would I be like then? You'd rather have me in a pinstripe suit, yeah? A centre-parted, head-down drone?'

Annie sniffed. 'Boring folk do boring sports.'

Danny was shocked. 'This isn't boring!'

Annie thought about it. 'No, actually, you're right,' she conceded, nodding at his motionless rod. 'It's a real white-knuckle ride. Thill a minute stuff.'

'Ah, you just wait and see,' said Danny. 'Did you know the name Bass comes from the ancient Anglo-Saxon word for Bus? It's true. You wait for one for ages, then three come along at once.'

'Hmmm.' Annie pulled up her crab line, sighed and lowered the untouched bait back into the depths. 'Well they must be running a Sunday service today.'

'But this is just the calm before the storm,' Danny said. 'You're probably just thinking of coarse fishing, all big umbrellas and folding chairs and fish you could fit in a lunch box.'

'Possibly, a bit. But-'

'But the sea's a world apart from the freshwater lark,' Danny cut in, 'rivers, reservoirs and lakes and so on. Take carp fishing. *Serious business*, carp fishing. And officially the most boring sport on Earth because the equipment catalogues sell beds! *Beds!* But out on the coast, even when it is boring, you're always in with a chance of being swept to your death, which tends to stop you nodding off, if you know what I mean. And you just can't get that kind of excitement down the local pond.'

The sun blazed on and nothing was moving, but for a lone fulmar, gliding high overhead. 'You're not *seriously* telling me you're in it for the adrenaline, though?'

Danny frowned. 'Are you mocking me, woman?'

She grinned. 'Just interested to know why you do it, that's all.'

'I dunno. Been doing it since I was a kid, I suppose.' Danny really wasn't sure why. Already, fishing was simply something he did, not something he did for a reason.

'Or, what I mean is, I did it a lot as a kid. With my Dad. It kind of faded out in my teens but, like, old habits die hard or something, I dunno. Tell you what, though. I've read exactly the same story with most of the other guys on the site.'

'That's actually quite worrying,' Annie said.

'Worrying?'

'That there are more men like you out there with access to computers.'

Danny pulled a face. 'Oh, yeah. Me and some school-mates used to go teasing trout, too.'

'Don't you mean tickling trout?'

'No. A whole gang of us used to go down the river after the football, line up on the bridge and chant, *'You're JUST pa-THET-ic SALMON!'* He repeated it, adding taunting pointing gestures for effect. 'And they weren't at all tickled by that, I can tell you.'

Annie checked her crab line again. The bait had been stolen but the thief was long gone, too. 'Are you ever serious, Danny Benton?'

'Christ, no!' said Danny. 'That way lies madness. Alright then, here's serious. Seeing what so few other people ever get to see. That's a motivation.'

'Like what?'

Danny's mind drifted to some of the marks he'd fished in the last months, from rocks to beaches in all weathers. And always at night. Freestyle mountaineering by torchlight. Huge waves welling up out of blackness and stars, or stiller seas, pulsating with the phosphor glows of jellyfish or clouds of neon shrimp. Even seaweeds in the rock pools glowed. It was magical.

'Like. . .' he said at last, a dreamy, lost look in his eyes. 'Like once I saw this bloke swallow a live king ragworm, whole. Drunk as a lord, obviously, but like a bleedin' sword swallower, he was.'

'Danny!'

'Ah, but how many people you know have seen that?'

'How many would want to, Danny?' She shuddered, the question 'Is he serious?' clearly playing on her mind. She showed him her bare hook and an upset face.

'It's not happening, is it?' Danny stated. If there's not even crabs, well, it's obviously some kind of fishy day of fasting out there.'

'Shall we go?' Annie asked. 'I mean, it's lovely here but . . .' She smiled. 'There are other places.'

Danny checked his watch. 'There sure are.'

Annie wound her glowing string around the spool while Danny cleared up his bits and pieces and checked about for litter before winding in. When he did retrieve his rig, his hook was equally naked.

'Damn,' he said. 'Lost it.'

'A fish? You're kidding.'

'Yeah, just then, on the way in. I think it was hit by a ray. Bang: gone.'

'A ray? One of those big flat ones?' Annie looked back along the still-busy beach as Danny broke down his rod, scooped up everything and began to amble back along the quay. 'Don't the kids paddling. . . don't they tread on them? It wasn't a stingray, was it?'

Danny laughed aloud. 'No, no. None of those in here. My fish must have been hit by an invisibility ray. At least, I never saw it.'

It the top of the short gravel track back from the water they had to pause before joining the pavement, for a gap in the current of holiday-makers departing the beach.

'You really go climbing over rocks at night?' Annie asked him. 'Isn't that a bit. . . slippery?'

'Naah. Rocks, beaches, anywhere. Can't beat the night, baby!'

'But you go out at night alone? In the middle of nowhere? That's got to be dangerous! You could get, I don't know . . . raped!'

Danny nodded thoughtfully. 'Yes, there's always that hope. Fishing's just filling the time, you know, until my prince comes.'

'You're impossible,' she said, then noticed they'd stopped walking.

'Nah, I'm lovely really.' Danny said. He checked his watch. 'And, well, it's been a lovely day and all that. . .'

'Oh. That's it then?' Annie frowned. 'Danny, this is a bus stop, not the car park.'

Danny dug into his back pocket and pulled out a fiver. 'I'm going to need the car. Sorry. But here you go, get yourself a nice seat upstairs. Amazing views over the estuary as you go back towards Yelland.'

'You. . . what? You're not coming?' Annie paled and held her forehead. 'You're. . . you're just dumping me on a bus?'

Danny clapped her on the shoulder, just as he might have to a bloke. 'Yeah, sorry again and all that, but I've got to get over there pretty quick.' He nodded across the water to Appledore. 'It's a fishing site thing. Got a match against Cornwall in ten minutes.'

CHAPTER 16

Some men were gathering, dubious characters, lurking around the public toilets at the back of Appledore's large car and coach park like fans arriving early for a George Michael performance.

The town hosts many other types of water-sports, though, and fishing rods soon appeared, tips rising vertically like a tribe raising camp in a clearing.

Danny trotted across the tarmac, weaving through parked cars and slowing to a walk halfway across. Friends or foes? Several flags settled that one at once, the green, white and black adorning tackle boxes, teeshirts, even the full rear window of one competitor's car.

Kit boxes and rucksacks were being dumped on the ground as he arrived, and five tripods were propped against the whitewashed toilet wall.

He cleared his throat. 'Alright, Gents?'

A familiar face emerged from the yawning back end of a green estate car.

'Danny! How's it going, boy?'

'Alright, Ladies?' Danny continued, with a quick nod to the other toilet door, then went over and shook Bent Rod's offered hand.

'Have you met the other guys?' Rod asked.

'Probably,' said Danny, unsure. 'Only on line, though.'

'Oh, yeah,' said one of the others, 'you go to those disgusting web sites, too, do ya?'

Danny laughed, turned, and shook another hand; a tall, thin man, well into his forties, with a small but disturbing Elvis quiff.

'Unless you mean The Goldfinger Bite, of course. Hi, there. Awesome Wellies.'

Danny stopped cold, glanced from side to side, then down at the other man's boots. 'Cheers. They're. . . they're just wellies, though.'

'No, no, buddy. That's my screen name. I thought it was funny, the night I joined. But, to be honest, it had lost much of its gloss even before the hangover set in.

'Anyway, we're one man down, so good you came,' Wellies went on. 'And them, they're late.'

'Who's missing?'

'*The Chiropodist*, we call him,' Wellies said. 'Doesn't post on line much, just lurks about reading the reports. Always turns out for the meets, though, does the weights and measures, tallies the scores, writes the report and stuff.' He paused to scan the roads. 'Trouble is, he's also the only one with Cornwall's contact number.'

'Right,' said Danny. 'So why do you call him The Chiropodist?'

Wellies gave him a look that suggested one of them must have a screw loose.

'Because he's. . . a chiropodist.'

'Understood,' said Danny, nodding slowly. 'So, Rod there tells me there have been a few of these competitions, home and away, right?'

Wellies nodded. 'And I've fished all of them.'

'An expert, then. So, you the team captain?'

Another hand tapped Danny's shoulder; another one to shake.

'We ain't got no captain, mate.' This guy's growl was difficult to place, more Pre-Cambrian than Devonian. 'Just a bloke in charge of clearing up the bodies.'

'The bodies?' Danny asked. 'I thought we'd be throwing them all back today. Nothing too big going to come out of this stretch, is it?'

The other guy stared back at him like he's said something deeply stupid. 'I meant,' he growled, 'the bloody Cornish.'

Now, there was a man after Danny's own heart! Barum Fixings ought to employ him, and the war against The Pasty Boys would be won in one fell swoop.

'They probably won't even turn up,' Danny said, trying to lighten the mood. 'East of the Tamar? They'll be like, *That be trespassin', that be, in the forbidden lands of magic. Tiz yon they make them new suns every mornin'!*'

The other guy still didn't smile. 'You think I'm kidding? Ernie, where's the corpse-hook?'

Danny spotted a gaff among the tripods, a six-foot aluminium handle topped with a hook big enough to hang a dolphin on. As far as he knew, he was at a school-bass and flounder mark, while gaffs like that he'd only seen in photographs, on boats, bringing conger eel or sharks on board. Perhaps he was serious.

'He's not serious,' an older guy said, around the side of the stub of a roll-up. 'Good to see some new blood in the side. I'm *Strangulated*, mate.'

'I'm sorry to hear that.' Danny grinned. 'It's not a corpsehook, then.'

'Naah. Not even mine. Anyway, we just kick the corpses over the side and let the current do the work.'

'Mine, actually.' Bent Rod was back, clapping him on the shoulder. 'My lucky gaff. I get no luck if I leave it at home and, luckily, I've never had to use it.'

One of the others grunted. 'Yeah, well I'm not superstitious, touch wood. I'll use it. I'll use it on them as soon as they set foot on the tarmac.'

Danny lowered his voice. 'A bit touchy, isn't he?'

'Horace?' Wellies put in, not copying the quietness. 'Irritable to the core, Dan. Ain't you, Horace?'

'Even got irritable bowel,' he snarled back.

'And I bet he don't hesitate to use it.' Danny said, trying not to smile.

He failed, but Horace just looked at him, expressionless, then went back to knotting a heavily-sequinned flounder rig onto the end of his line.

Rod clapped his hands for attention. 'OK, this is Danny, everyone, though you might know him better as Danny Buoy. Or maybe as that jammy sod with the conger off Capstone.'

'And as you know,' he said, turning to Danny and steering him left, 'this is *Horaceorifice*. He's not a Horace, really. Nobody knows his real name cos nobody dares ask. Or cares. We just call him that cos he's such an-'

'Shut yer hole, Wellies. At least I remember to bring my *rods* every time I fish an important match.'

The grin straight dropped off Wellies' face. 'Oh, yeah. 'Nuff said. Maybe you've got a point there, Horace. And he does catch a few good fish, now and then, has to be said.'

Wellies patted Horace's shoulder and turned back to Danny. 'Is that everyone? You've met Strangulated, yeah?'

Strangulated, a Scottish-sounding but Transylvanian-looking, mid-grey, mid-fifties bloke now puffing a longer roll-up, got to his feet like it took every ounce of strength.

'Kind of,' said Danny, shaking his hand. 'So why do they call you Strangulated, then?'

'Real name's Ernie Hay,' he sighed, as though he'd answered that a thousand times before, or was close to exhausted just by standing.

'Well up for this one then, are you?' Danny asked.

'Straining at the leash, mate,' Ernie said, rubbing the back of his neck like he'd just been released from a tight one. 'Strainin' at the bleedin' leash.'

Further pleasantries were interrupted by Rod, calling them around for a team talk.

'Alright then, lads. I think we know what we're here for: to catch lots of small fish and kick some Cornish arses.'

Danny glanced around. There were a few dry sniggers but no cheers.

'IF they come,' someone grunted.

'They'll be here. But seriously, we're here for the smaller stuff. This time of day, this tide, it's not gonna show off its best fishing to our visitors, is it? While the tide's flooding, I'm going to be fishing lug on 1/0 half-circle hooks, close in, and hopefully bag up on the better school bass without deep-hooking them. Always the chance of a flounder, of course.'

'Any mullet about?' Rod asked. 'Good spot for them over there,' he added, nodding downstream.

'Good point,' said Wellies. 'We heard the Cornish boys were thinking of targeting them, so hopefully not.'

'They haven't had the chance to get down here and bait it up, though, have they?'

Danny knew what Rod meant. Mullet are the supreme cowards of the sea, so skittish that they'll skit themselves at the slightest sound or movement from the shore. The fish themselves would probably try and justify this by blaming their childhoods, grazing the treacherous shallows of heron-ridden estuaries, but Danny knew that was just an excuse for the backbone of a jellyfish. There were millions upon millions of mullet fry out there but how many herons do you see? A few a year, and most of those are probably the same one, somewhere else. Also, mullet, with their super-sensitive mouths, used to browsing soft, slimy silt for even softer, slimier algae, mean that only the lightest, finest tackle can be used and, even then, you're still highly unlikely to catch one unless you've lulled them into a sense of vague security by ground-baiting their feeding area every day for a week before you even fit your rod together.

If only they didn't fight like Joe Calzaghe, they could be scared out to sea and forgotten about.

'We, of course, have had the chance to get down here regularly,' Wellies continued, rubbing his hands with enthusiasm, 'and, knowing the Cornish fancied some mulletting, I've had my two lads down here, same time of tide for the last five days, with orders to lob in as much of the shoreline as possible. And you know what kids are like for chucking stones.' He tutted, grinning and shaking his head. 'There ain't a mullet left this side of Lundy Island, mate.'

And that, with a few hoarse laughs, was that: team talk over, down to business. Breath bated and match tactics whirling in his mind, Danny awaited instruction.

None came. Rod was rocking back and forth slightly, like he'd been standing waiting for a bus for an hour, Awesome Wellies was motionless, staring expressionlessly in the direction of the water. Only Horace was noticeably conscious, already well into his packed lunch, orange, scotch egg chest-dandruff sprinkling the front of his khaki coat.

'So, what now?'

Rod blew out his cheeks. 'Pub, Dan, if they don't show up.'

'Yellow scroats,' Wellies spat, then returned to his standing coma.

Rod chuckled. 'Most likely scared off by our walking dose of beginner's luck, here. Young Daniel.'

Danny looked at Rod sidelong, not sure how to take the comment, but Rod was thumbing text into his phone and giving no clues. Danny sniffed. Perhaps he should take it as a compliment as, after all, he had caught some good fish. Some blokes fished for years and never managed a fish bigger than their worms. He hoped there was no jealousy or resentment from his teammates.

He went for a simple, two-snood rig with size one hooks, which he'd load with a choice of lug or rag. There was a small bag of leftover crab legs thawing in his bait bag, too, which he'd use if he needed to raise his luck. Danny would be fishing today, even if the Cornish didn't come. He hoped that the others would, too.

Tiny, away across the water, a big bus edged along Instow seafront and he wondered if Annie was on it. It hadn't been the best way to end a first date but she would understand. It was a solid, fishing-related reason, a proper, organised competition, and fishing is what she'd come out for in the first place, right? She would understand, wouldn't she? 'I knew they wouldn't show,' Wellies sighed. 'No balls, see? Not enough for a game of snooker in the whole county. Hey, Rod, didn't I bet you fifty quid they wouldn't *dare*. . . oh, here they are.'

Danny sniggered and followed the others' eyes toward the road, just as a bulky, black van, complete with A-Team style trim, slewed a hard right into the car park. All four of the van's tyres stayed on the tarmac, though, and there was little - in fact - no harmless machine gun fire, and Danny's heart was already beginning to sink by the time they got close enough to see that, even through the tinted windows, the driver looked nothing whatsoever like Mr T.

He should have known better. A big white cross on top turned the whole roof into a giant Cornish flag, which wasn't something likely to be sported by a crack commando unit sent to prison by a military court for a crime they didn't commit before promptly escaping from a maximum security stockade to the Los Angeles underground.

And those bursting from the rear doors were certainly no soldiers of fortune.

Danny could only stand and stare.

A car-park's width away, six genuine, smock wearing, floppy-hatted, straw-chewing Yokels spilled out. Shrouded in a visible cloud of cider fumes, staggering, falling and chanting rubbish without end, Cornwall's finest assembled for duty.

Danny was ready to burst into mocking laughter when the smile dropped from his face.

One of them had the Devon flag, and another was flicking a cigarette lighter!

Chapter 17

'RESULTS - D v C match, Appledore.

'So The Chiropodist had hopped it (off on his toes for some corny reason, if that's not being too callus) and for some reason (threats of violence) yours truly, Danny Buoy, volunteered as temporary war correspondent. The pen is mightier than the sword, after all, and less illegal than the flick-knife.

And there we were, face to face with a bunch of the ugliest, inbredest, drinkinest yokel savages you ever did see, and it looked like they were spoiling for a fight. Like a cast reunion for *The Hills Have Chainsaw Massacres III,* it was, or the staff Christmas do at Banjos R Us.

One of them approached cautiously, probably the alpha male, I thought. . . relatively speaking. Hesitantly, he extended a gnarled, hairy hand toward Awesome Wellies, and his turnip-stained lips began to part.

'Mr Boots! Long time no see, old chap!' He had a toff-school accent with just a trace of the countryside burr. 'How are you doing? Wife and kiddy well?'

Wellies shook hands vigorously, and I was shocked that he didn't wipe his palm or count his fingers afterwards. Rod told him it was kiddies, plural, now, and that Marie had plopped another one out in February!

At this point, I want to stress that this was my first D v C match and the first time I'd met Mr Wellies, so I have no idea who Marie actually is. I just hope his Mrs isn't reading this!

Well, it was obvious that these men were old friends, despite one of them being from Cornwall, and I have to admit that, over the next few hours, I've had to reassess the Cornish as a species.

They didn't burn the flag, of course, and most of the bumpkin smocks were soon replaced with light, weatherproof jackets and waders. The guy with it was smoking a short cigar, still flicking at his lighter but nowhere near the sacred cloth. Turns out they were bringing it back, and with apologies! At the last meet, I'm told, one of their guys caught a five foot conger and Ernie lent it to him to catch hold of the thing securely. Do that in America and they'd probably reopen Guantanamo Bay just for you, but when you've tried controlling one of those greasy beasts to get the hook out, you don't want it finding any opening in your flotation suit, I can tell ya!

All machine-washed and pressed it was, too - the flag, not the eel - so it's nice to know that electricity's finally reached our country cousins down there on the edge of the world!

Anyway, we were there to fish, not talk laundry, and once the introductions had been made we all set off together to pick our marks. The Cornish lads suggested it would be friendlier to alternate team members along the shore line, but I was pretty sure that they knew they'd need a witness on either side of every Devon angler, just to believe the size and number of fish they'd be watching us catch.

It, er. . . didn't really turn out that way but, early on, it looked like it the fishing might exceed our wildest dreams! I didn't see the bite myself but I think the whole of Appledore heard Awesome Wellies' ratchet going! What he was doing even setting the ratchet at Appledore, I don't know, but it was a good job you did, mate!

The fish took a half-launce bait on a single 2/0, apparently. I say 'fish' but whatever he had on seemed more likely to be a stray torpedo, or even the submarine that fired it. The first I knew was hearing Wellies screeching like he was on a ride at Alton towers. Or maybe drugs. But the next second, Corn-Will, next to me, was winding in fast to get out of his way as he ran (or was dragged) toward us behind a beachcaster bent to ninety degrees! Seriously, it looked too big to even be a fish, not unless the tope were in after the flounder. Not as stupid as it sounded, he knew, as flounder is a bait of choice for tope. . . just, big, ocean-going sharks aren't too common in the estuary!

We didn't see the fish, of course. If Wellies had landed it, I reckon it would have been splashed all over the newspapers, never mind this web site. I don't think the fish knew we were there, either, because it didn't batter away like a bass, or show any sign it even knew it was hooked, come to that. It just cruised off seaward in a straight line, like it wanted to tow Mr Wellies right over to Wales!

No surprise - the line snapped, taking Wellies' entire rig with it, so we couldn't even get a clue to what it was from teeth marks on the bait. Corn-Will thought it might not have been a fish at all, and that a boat steaming past might have caught the line. Not likely, as there were just a few canoeists drifting about. Unfortunately, it's still a mystery.

But how do you follow that? We couldn't, not even with a good. . . ok, a *fairly* good haul of other fish between us. After an intense period of nothing happening, Cornwall stormed into a commanding lead with a flounder the size of a Pringle. Next to me, rubbing our noses in it, Will hauled in what we think was a dab but, as nobody had thought to bring a microscope, we'll never be sure.

Yours truly led the fight-back with a shore crab the size of my hook but then it quietened off again until an hour before the high when the bass finally showed up. Just tiddlers, schoolies, for the most part, and most of them were primary-schoolies at that. At least it got some points on both sides of the board, though. Lugworm just kills with these little ones, and they went from being a welcome sight to a bit of a bleedin' plague! When I'd reached ten, none of them over a pound and a half, I switched from a size one hook to a 4/0, and from worm to crab, hoping to weed out mummy or daddy from among the kids. I did get, maybe, an older cousin, a solid three pounder that actually seemed to object to being caught and put up a bit of a fight, but just as I was returning it and patting myself on the back (no small feat, simultaneously!), I saw Figgy Obbin Robin, further downstream to my left, hauling in one half as big again. That tested my newfound liking for the Cornish, I must admit, but beer and exaggeration flowed free and friendly in the pub for hours afterwards, and I knocked Robin around the pool table like he was the cue-ball, so honour was satisfied.

We waved the lads off home at about ten pm and Devon retired to the curry house. I went for a bring-it-on lamb Jalfrezi, with its complex blend of the finest exotic spices, hints of fruit combined with mellow sourness, and a truly sadistic afterburn from which I suffer to this very day. Then again, a curry's not a curry unless it leaves you psychologically scarred.

And as to the final result of the match. . .

Oh, god. . . so many chillies!
Gotta run!

CHAPTER 18

Half and hour after the prison gates had slammed, the office was still quiet, short on staff, with those that were present typing diligently or yawning and sighing discretely. Joan's desk was still empty and Chappell was off at a wedding. His own parents, most likely. Slade and Jocelyn were somewhere about, but tucked away in an 'very important meeting' with some drone from head office, probably discussing how many staples the branch used or the correct, environmentally-friendly disposal of pencil-sharpenings.

There had been no sign of Annie yet, either, but that could be a blessing in disguise. Danny had forgotten the tin hat and body armour, and was sure he had a whole lot of explaining to do leaving her in the lurch at the bus stop.

Danny stared at the screen and frowned hard, confused. There was something wrong with that match report, there had to be. They were his own words, sure, but they didn't sound like him. He must have been possessed by an evil force, or remotely controlled when he wrote them.

Had he really said he liked the Cornish? Could it be that the ascent of man had finally crossed the Tamar, and turned the natives beyond into decent, friendly, upright-walking human beings? Surely not, or there'd have been at least a David Attenborough programme on it, wouldn't there?

Just in case, Danny moved the computer mouse to close down the Internet browser and its *'Homemade nuclear warheads for dummies'* instructions. 'For the moment,' he thought, and saved the link to his Favourites file before clicking X.

Or maybe he'd just misjudged them. They'd won the match, after all, even if it was on a technicality. He drummed his fingers on the desk. OK, they had won by technically catching a hundred and twenty five percent more small fish than Devon had, but that didn't matter at all, looking back. Gallons of post-match Guinness had sluiced all that nonsense away, not that it had ever been there in the first place.

But how could he have been so. . . *countyist*? How could he have tarred a whole people, based on the actions of just a few knobs? And those damned stones, of course. Resting his head on one hand he yawned and looked out of the window.

Oh, that was how.

Not all the Cornish had evolved. Some had crept over the border and set up stolen-from-Devonshire pasty shops. They were the last problem he wanted on his mind at the moment, though. With mixed feelings, he wondered how long it would be before Annie arrived. Time always ran slowest when he knew he was in the wrong, so he didn't need to see the clock to know it would be ticking through treacle.

Where was she? He had to face her eventually, and had long since given up trying to word an excuse for why he had dumped her for a fishing contest.

'*Bloody Cornish,*' he mouthed, then corrected it aloud. 'Bloody Pasty Boys.'

It was all their fault. He wasn't sure how, true, but somebody had to be blamed.

A can of Coke hissed '*Pepsi*' as it popped, jolting Danny awake.

'My god! The dead walk!'

'Daniel, my boy. Nice to see you working hard, as always.'

Danny flipped the screen around toward him, showing him the fishing site by way of excuse. 'You should have seen it! There was some *huge* fish there, just cruising right through where we were fishing!'

Jim rolled his eyes and faked a yawn. 'So what do you mean, the dead walk?'

'Hardly anyone in today,' said Danny. 'Off sick, all sorts. So what's been your excuse?'

Jim glanced toward Slade's room.

'Just been into town,' he said distractedly. 'See a man about a dog, you know.'

From the bulging paper bag he was carrying, it looked more like he'd seen a sweetshop owner about a week's wages worth of jelly snakes. Danny laughed. 'Did you *know* he'd be in late?'

'Did I care? That's the question, mate.' Jim pulled out a licorice Catherine wheel and began unwinding it with his teeth. 'Kiddies' Pick 'n' Mix,' he explained. 'Best breakfast in town. How's it going, anyway?'

'Crap,' Danny said. 'Same as always, only worse.'

'Then it can only get better.'

'Never does, though, does it?'

'Aha!' said Jim, a glint in his eye that always meant trouble for someone, and usually amusement for Danny. 'Could be a big day, today, if you get your cards right.'

'*Play* your cards right,' Danny corrected.

Jim grinned. 'Depends what hand life deals you.' Then something caught his eye, over Danny's shoulder. 'Look out, she's here.'

Annie? he mouthed, then turned and gasped in shock. '*Eeugh!* God, you made me jump! I thought you were a woman there for a moment.'

He glanced back but Jim had vanished as if Scotty had beamed him up. Jocelyn stared at him through slitted eyes, then brightened. 'Well, if you mean your darling Annie, you're out of luck. She phoned. She's off.'

'She's what? Off sick?'

'Dunno,' Jocelyn said casually. 'Worried she caught something off you, is it?'

Worried that Annie was sick of him, maybe.

'She couldn't even catch crabs,' Danny sighed. 'Maybe I should've sent her around your place.'

She ignored him, and snapped, 'Where's Lithium?'

Danny didn't answer. Something wasn't right. Her refusal to bite when he rattled her cage? The look in her eye, the evil keenness to find Jim? Something was missing. Jocelyn just wasn't as chokingly vile as usual.

Danny had to warn Jim. He scanned the room and spotted him first, leant in the corner staring out of the window and draining the contents of a yellow sherbet fountain down his gullet like it was his last meal before dieting.

Danny would have phoned him if Jim had had the sense to carry one, but then Jocelyn sighted him, too, and called out as she crossed the room, so keen she almost broke into a trot.

'Uh. . . Jim? Mr Slade would like to see you in his office. In a minute. Whenever you're ready.'

Danny was amazed. He'd never heard her sound anything but hostile, but suddenly she was politeness itself! He might have had Jocelyn wrong, all along. In reality, she could be a robot, malfunctioning, programmed for evil but suddenly developing conscious thought. He took a step back, in case her brain went into meltdown and blew up. Just a very small step, obviously. But then a gaping wound opened in Jocelyn's face, an awful, dry splitting of the flesh that—

Oh.

She was just smiling. B-b-but. . . Jocelyn, smiling? She *never* smiled - just that one *awful* time that Danny was trying to blot from his memory. He pulled his eyes away from the nauseating sight and watched Jim, watching her intently. Danny sucked up the last of the fountain's sherbet and chewed the straw up into his mouth.

At last, Jim said, 'Cool.'

That was all. Danny had expected a comeback, a snipe at the boss or Jocelyn herself, but nothing came. Even giving the *Obergruppensupervisor* a heel-clicking, straight-armed salute, behind her back as she marched back into Slade's room, got little response from his workmate.

'What do you reckon that's all about?' Danny asked. Jim was distant, and Danny suspected he might already have some idea.

But Jim shrugged. 'A bollocking for something,' he said, draining cola through a spreading grin. He tossed the can, spinning, over his shoulder toward Joan's empty wastepaper bin. It missed by a mile. 'Let's see if we can guess what that something is!'

He nodded Danny toward the open door to Slade's office. It was dark inside, the blinds drawn, and twin, red computer LEDs glowed out like demon's eyes. Danny shuddered.

But Jim didn't feel it. 'Come on,' he said, holding back a snigger, 'we'll say I've requested your presence as the new union rep.'

Danny hesitated, but laughed as he stood up. 'A *union!* He'll die in his damned chair!'

Of course, Slade would groan like an over-stressed care worker, grunt about not being stupid and ask Danny to leave before any of the real fun started but what else was he supposed to do while Jim was in there? Work?

Jim turned, executing a perfect turn straight from the manual of the *Ministry of Silly Walks* and Danny fell in behind him at once, copying his stupid, loping strides and getting right up behind him, like a two-man remake of a *Madness* video. Slade looked up and didn't even see Danny. Danny saw Slade, though, and the fury in the scowl he was directing at Jim, and was glad of the human shield. His eyes must have widened because as soon as he was near enough for Slade to see their whites, the boss bellowed, in one syllable, 'GETOUT!'

Danny whirled on his heel. This was serious. Slade was a miserable sod but he never got hot under the collar. Sarcasm was his forte, not rage. If he was going to avoid the heat, Danny knew he had to be seen to be working, so dived straight to the Xerox machines and began photocopying his hand.

It was almost the ideal viewpoint. Through the half-open door he could see Jim, slouching, and the front edge of Slade's desk, but most importantly he could hear everything.

Jim nodded to one side, at someone else Danny couldn't see. 'Alright, gorgeous?' Jim asked. There was no reply.

'Right, we won't beat about the bush,' the boss began. '*And get your hands out of your pockets!*'

Where did Slade think he was, the Army? Danny was pleased to see that Jim didn't comply. Instead, there was the pop-hiss of a drink can being opened. Danny watched Jim raise it to his lips and sip it slowly; like a non-smoker's last cigarette before the blindfold was tied.

'First, we've had protests from The Pasty Boys offices, opposite.'

Jim rubbed his hands. 'Excellent! I was hoping they would-'

'*Shut up!* Protests from The Pasty Boys include harassment by telephone and e-mail, indecent exposure-'

'*Indecent exposure?!*'

Slade just waited while Jim repeated the question at an even higher pitch, then cleared his throat. 'Indecent exposure, namely. . .'

There was a pause, and Danny, outside, heard papers shuffled and straightened. He wondered, *letters of complaint?*

'Namely,' Slade droned on, 'the pressing of buttocks against the office windows.'

Slade had pronounced the word so formally - '*But, Ox*' - that Danny couldn't stop the snigger. Jim heard him, taking half a step back and glancing his way. There was, maybe, a half-smile, and otherwise a look of boredom. He swallowed a large draft from his can of Coke and turned back to face the charges.

'That wasn't us, me,' he said. 'The arse thing, it was just for the *craic* anyway, but-'

'Shut up,' said Slade. 'And gross sexual harassment in the form of printed letter. A signed letter, Mr Molton.'

'Well, that wasn't even signed by me.'

'Really?' asked Slade, and Danny heard the sound of paper being slid from a stiff envelops. 'But you do know what I'm talking about, then.'

'I know I've been set up,' said Jim, 'That letter shouldn't have been signed at all. It was supposed to be anonymous.'

It didn't sound like an accidental admission, but more like Jim just didn't care any more. Outside, Danny clenched both fists, knowing it had to be the homophobia-resignation letter they'd come up with the week before. Damn. The letter Jim had originally signed, '*Danny Benton,* brackets *Miss*', which Danny had changed back to *J. Molton.*

'Pathetic!' said Slade. 'You sent it in a Barum Fixings envelope, you fool, franked with a big fat Barum Fixings logo. It couldn't have been much less anonymous, signed or not!'

But the boss made no more of it. Danny knew this meant there was more, and worse, to come.

'Then there is your grossly unacceptable behaviour towards another member of staff, Mrs Lobb. 'It may interest you to know that she's quit, for health reasons, citing mental persecution.'

Jim swallowed more fizz. 'Her health's very sad, but it ain't my concern.'

'Mine neither,' said Slade. 'Head office will be handling her constructive dismissal case. I doubt we'll even hear the result, nor do I care.'

'Well, you can't hold that against me.'

'No need, Mr Molton, no need.' Danny heard a popping sound that could have been Slade cracking his knuckles. 'We have a copy of your stupid note to her. . .'

'*My* stupid note?' Jim cut in. 'I wasn't even in the day Joanie freaked out!'

'Indeed,' said Slade. 'But alibis are cheap as chips. What was yours for that day? Delayed winter vomiting virus? A touch of leprosy? Ectopic pregnancy? Who do you think you're kidding now, Mr Molton?'

He didn't give him a chance to answer and went on. 'We know it was printed from your machine. You see, it's always handy to have another computer expert on the job, a legitimate one. Isn't that right, Mr Stibb?'

There was the sound of more evidence being slid from the stiff envelope, then Joe Stibb piped up. 'That's right, Sir.'

'Sir!' Danny nearly puked on the spot. He ground his teeth. He should have known Stibby wouldn't miss a chance to stick the knife in. The bloke was a bigger backstabber than a Stoke Mandeville surgeon.

'It's easy to see what anyone, or any computer station,' Stibb continued, 'is up to at any time, and the information's all stored on the system so it never forgets.'

'There's a full record here, of everything you've mentioned, plus. . .'

'Who asked you, Stibb?' Jim said.

'I did,' said Slade, gruffly. 'It's his job, remember?'

'Game over, Jimbo,' said Stibb.

Silence. Danny waited, sure that Jim would lay into Stibb and praying that it would be physical. But the assault never came, just the bizarre sound of someone's stomach growling violently. Usually, Danny would have laughed but, for once, he felt sorry for Jim, realising what his insides must be going through beneath the couldn't-care-less manner he was fighting to maintain.

'And then there was the padded envelope you took over there,' Slade said, gesturing behind him in the vague direction of The Pasty Boys' building, 'the one that started this whole, pathetic feud nonsense off in the first place. I needn't go on and I won't. It's sickening. You're sickening.'

'I've had enough of this,' said Jim.

'Oh, so have we, Mr. Molton,' said Slade. 'And the images on your computer are more then we could ever want.'

Jim laughed harshly. 'Want for what?

There was a long pause then, broken only by the sporadic rattle of background keyboards. Danny heard Jim swallow loudly again, although he hadn't seen him lift his can to his lips.

'What images?' Jim's voice was quiet, measured, not quite shaky. He raised it. 'Don't you grin at me like that, Stibb. What images?'

A chair scraped quietly on the carpet tiles.

'Images,' said Stibb. '*Images*.' sadistically, the machine that Danny was leaning against clicked and whirred to a pneumatic stop. He picked up the pile of copies, ninety nine shots of his hand that made a good flip-book animation of a black and white fist being clenched.

'Mr Slade,' said Stibb, all formal. 'These. . . these *disgusting* images, were stored on the C drive of his computer. Here, in the same folder as the originals, and the crudely altered, photographs from last year's staff Christmas party, which have been causing so much trouble within the company. Look.'

The dark inside of Slade's lair glowed dimly as a computer screen was turned around. Danny leant around the gap in the door as far as he dared and saw Jim take a step and lean forward. He heard him too: a weak laugh, then a coughing gasp, before exclaiming:

'But. . . But they're all *Oompa Loompas!*'

Eyes wide in shocked imagining, Danny clamped a hand over his mouth and nose to trap the laugh.

'Wow. Ooh! Eeew!' Jim's voice was low; intrigued, amused and horrified in one. Then,

'Nooo!' he squealed, delighted. 'Right in Charlie's choco-late factory!'

But, just as Danny's laugh began to hiss around his fin-gers, Jim twigged. 'You what? On *MY* computer? Hey, I'll hold my hands up for the Christmas shots but not-'

He was sure he heard a snigger from Stibb. The short silence was heavy - was Jim going to thump him? If he'd been in there himself, Danny would've knocked the face right off Stibb's smile, boss or no boss, job or no job.

But no, the silence was just Jim finishing his drink and was broken by his last, loud gulps and crushing of the can.

'Nothing to say?' Slade asked eventually.

Apparently, for once, Jim hadn't.

'Well, as I said, we won't beat about the bush. You're out.'

More silence, still nothing from Jim.

'That's right, you're sacked, fired. Get out.'

Danny heard just one little noise from Jim, a half-laugh, a derisive snort.

Slade exploded. 'Go on, piss off, right now. And count yourself lucky we don't make you shine the arse-prints off their windows, boy!'

'*Boy?*'

Jim had already turned to leave and walked back into Danny's view, but that stopped him cold, whirled on his heel and looked ready to launch himself straight at the boss!

But it wasn't himself that he launched. He released every-thing he had been bottling up - that was, the full gaseous product of an entire can of cola mixed with sherbert, liqorice and Space Dust - in an awesome, ear-splitting, cup-rattling eruption of gastric vapours that just never seemed ready to end. Danny's jaw fell open. It was a belch like King Kong choking on Godzilla, a harmony of roars and guttural regurgitations like a chord from the massed voices of Hell's own choir.

Finally, mercifully, it ended, in a carpet-soiling splat and a cough, spit and laugh from a breathless Jim.

'ENOUGH!' Slade leapt from his chair and slammed his desk with both fists.

'But I haven't finished.'

'You *filthy*. . . GET OUT!'

Jim bowed deeply, turned to leave, and bowed even deeper to whoever was by the door. He stopped, though, staying bowed, a hand braced behind his hip and a growing look of pain across his face. It looked like he'd put his back out, but Danny had seen that look before. As Jim bent further and all eyes zoomed in on his arse as one, Danny moaned, 'God preserve us. . .'

Jim had meant it. Jim certainly hadn't finished. Lithium Jim had barely begun.

So far, he'd only fired a warning shot. Now, he unleashed a full arsenal.

Whatever roared out of Jim Molton's body was not of this Earth. Danny could have sworn the room shook as it erupted, an ear-splitting blend of heavy-duty canvas being torn and whale song played through a whale-sized kazoo. How long he had actually been holding the killer blow in reserve was anybody's guess, but it sounded and smelt like he'd ripped open a velcro-sealed plague pit. The stench tumbled out of the room before its victims. Crouching by the door, a hand clamped over his mouth and nose, Danny shot a sniper's glance inside.

Slade was all shades of purple, a mix of rage-red and hypoxia-blue, and chain-retching unstoppably, stuck between swift suffocation or the horrors of the poisoned air. Jocelyn tottered nearby, hands on her ears and horror in her stare, and Stibb, wide eyed and fighting to keep his cornflakes inside, feared failure and bolted, choking, for the door. Danny tried to trip him as he passed but didn't get good enough contact. Maybe he was suffering enough.

Danny withdrew, keeping his head low to the ground to fill his lungs with fresher air and thought they should have had floor-level lighting installed, like in planes, to guide any survivors to the exits.

Out of Slade's office, out of the fog of death, strode Jim, head held high and the subtlest grin of triumph on his face. Jocelyn stepped in front of him, clearly about to launch the mother of all slapper-attacks, but Jim must have been driving a bow-wave of stench ahead of him because she gagged, coughed and stopped in her tracks, and stepped back.

Jim paused at the door, tossed his company car keys over his shoulder, hard, then turned a half-circle, arms high, waving slow victory Vs at the rest of the office.

Danny watched open-mouthed as Jim was leaving, like James Bond strolling from a burning, baddy-littered set. Slade's suffocations dragged his eye back to the office door just in time to see him crawling out, looking like he'd been nerve-gassed and gasping at ground-level oxygen in the desperate hope that hot air really rose. Danny was too awestruck to laugh like the kid in him was desperate to. This was. . . this was brilliance! But. . .

Jim was leaving.

As he began the applause - and someone had to do it - Danny felt a lump in his throat. There'd be no way back for Jim, not this time, and the coma of the working day at Barum Fixings would get a whole lot deeper without him.

Danny shook his head slowly. Just look at him, imagining the cheering crowds! When the bottom should have been falling out of his world, the human skunk was prouder of what had fallen out of his bottom. But at least he was going out with style, and deserved the ovation. Danny was about to break into a cheer when Jim turned and glared daggers at him. Pure hatred.

Danny's clap-rate slowed quickly to nought.

What the Hell was that for?

Or, not hatred. . . maybe? Blame. Definitely blame.

Jim held him on a skewer stare, then whirled and left the office for the last time, slamming the door behind him.

Chapter 19

'WwwwA-A-A-AH!'
Danny turned it up until the pile of loose CDs on top of his computer began to vibrate. If *Disturbed* were *Down With the Sickness* again then tonight was pub night, definitely. No: pubs, plural, night. Or, if not, then a blow-out at the offy and a night of drunkenness, munchies and rerun DVDs.

'Damn it!' His foot caught in a Playstation-controller snare and as he kicked it free he pulled the console off the tv stand with an unhealthy thump. One day, he'd get this pigsty tidy. One day, when he'd trained the flying pigs to airlift out the ton of crap.

Perhaps he'd meet Jim, out drowning his sorrows or, more likely, celebrating like he'd won the Lotto. No, of course he wouldn't run into him by chance. He never had. Danny had no idea where Jim would be. There was no telling what some folk did with their time alone. He thought about Annie, too, wondering what she'd done with hers while she'd been off sick. . . allegedly.

Huh. *'Alleged Sickness'* could be a disease name in itself, and an infection that Annie had caught from Jim. God, he'd really blown it with both of them! He thumped the table and the silver CDs clattered down over his keyboard, stopping the screen-saver slide-show of fish photos and returning him to the last web page he'd been viewing, *The Goldfinger Bite's* home page. He refreshed the screen and watched the number of logged-in members more than halve. All gone out fishing, if they've got any sense.

Well, it would make more sense than going boozing. Cheaper, less hangover. Fewer women, though.

Cheaper won out, especially with the amount of bait he had in the freezer. He'd smiled but had mixed feelings the other day, when he'd noticed there was more bait than human food in there, by a factor of three drawers to one. That was counting those boxes of frozen, foreign squid as bait, of course, even though they looked like they'd fry up a treat. He hadn't had the nerve to try, yet, but tonight was not the night for food. Danny just wanted to get outside.

He sat down at the computer, opened pages showing weather and tides, then watched himself zoom down from moon-high to his own flat's roof as he clicked on *Google Earth*. He pulled the image back until the aerial view became a khaki mosaic of village-strewn fields, then dragged it down and right until he found the coast. A quick scan of forecast winds and waves ruled out the beaches. A chance of good bass in the choppy surf, true, but summer squalls far out to sea had made it much too rough for rays or much else, close inshore. The breeze would be strong, west-north-westerly, too, and a few degrees colder than was seasonal.

'Do-able,' Danny muttered to himself, but he didn't fancy the effort involved. He'd rather sit down and chill out than get wind-chilled and chased up the beach by the tide, so he overflew the sands of Croyde, Putsborough and Woolacombe and headed for the top coast.

Ilfracombe. . . the pier? Not likely. It would sound like Santa's sleigh-yard up there tonight, packed with sunburnt holiday anglers foul-hooking mullet and insisting on casting and winding with their stupid little tinkly bells still attached. No, he wouldn't get a quiet night's fishing there, not until they made machine guns legal.

Lee. Just left of Ilfracombe. Yeah, he'd read the odd report from Lee Bay but never fished it himself. Never even been there, come to that. He zoomed in, a long channel of sand between submerged rocks catching his eye straight-away. It looked like a riverbed, driving out to sea, although there wasn't even a stream visible from overhead. But sand on the top coast was rare enough, plus the rocks looked fairly smooth, easily scrambleable, (so he could stand on the bank and follow the waterline. Had to be worth a shot. If only he had some worms.

Come to think of it, hadn't he spotted worms in the fridge when he came in? Not loose and grazing a strange, foreign buffet, but the plastic butter container he'd recycled into a worm pot. He couldn't remember the last time he'd used lug, though, and shuddered, wondering just how long they had been festering in there.

In the kitchen, Danny opened the fridge first, then the window before leaning out and daring to lift the lid, crudely altered with a permanent marker to read, '*I Can't Believe It's Not Lugworm!*'

But lugworm it was. Or it had been.

Mercifully, the estuary breeze carried off the cloud of stench before it reached Danny's nose and he let the pot air for a few moments, hanging his head in mourning for the lives that would be ruined downwind. Then he drained off the red juice into the garden below and, as next door's cat raced, yowling and stinking, into the nearest hedge, he snapped the lid back in place and packed the pot into his fishing bag.

'Waste not, want not,' he said aloud, then swore under his breath. God, sometimes his fridge was worse than Jeffrey Dahmer's.

'Clear summer skies the whole day,' the weathermen had said, but - damn the Met Office! - the sun was nowhere to be seen. Then again, it was getting on for midnight, so Danny would let them off with that one.

Rucksack on and rods in hand, he stood beside his locked car, readjusting his ears to the silence as echoes of soft, whispering strains from a Sepultura cd, still threatening to shake apart the bones of his skull, slowly began to fade.

He'd found his way to Lee Bay via Ilfracombe, shunning the other route he'd picked out because he'd never have remembered his way through a new maze of country lanes at night, not in the state of distraction he was. He'd driven through the village almost without noticing, the white-streaked black of the gleaming night sea drawing his eye far more than the quaint, stone-built houses on the front. The windy, walled road swept uphill steeply as he left town and he must have driven a quarter mile before he found a place wide enough to turn the car. He stopped on the edge of the village, just above where he wanted to fish, and left the car tucked in to a hedge as tight as possible, with the car at the steepest angle he'd ever parked it.

But it still seemed impossible to concentrate on anything.

The reasons were obvious, of course. They were, oh. . . something or other, but how the Hell was he supposed to find a route through *those* rocks?

But he did, first getting a good low-tide look at the distribution of rocks, cleanish mixed ground and bare sand of the main bay. The path through the fractured headland to the little bay beyond was easier to find than it first looked. The stony track between high, sheer walls led to centuries-old steps cut into the rock itself, and, with only darkness overhead, Danny felt like he was in a huge cave with no roof. As the seaward wall fell away, he found himself winding through a narrow landscape of deep and shallow rock pools, full of the glittering eyes of shrimp and prawns, gazing up bemused at the new light-on-legs in their shiny, rippled sky.

The steeper sloping beach beyond was a mix of sand and shingle, and offered a shot at deeper water, which held species as varied as fine, daylight wrasse to good sized conger over slack, dark water. Danny recalled that the web site had said to expect a seaside aquarium's-worth of variety to choose from, from rockling and flounder, pout, pollack and dogs, to red mullet in summer and cold season cod. The cod is a fish with a curious beard. A barbule, it's called, and at first it looks weird. True, it hangs from its chin but it helps to find food, so to call it a beard is a little bit crude. It has one single tuft, rather like Gary Glitter,

Glam rock's fallen star who took kids up the—

Danny slapped the side of his head, hard. He hated lapsing into Dr Seuss. Parents should never read books to kids, he realised. It can scar them for life.

So, with all those fish to choose from, how come he hadn't had a single bite yet? He could have done with a bite to eat, that was for sure. Why hadn't he fed himself before leaving? He was soon wishing he'd brought his squid bait grilled instead of raw, or maybe had the sense to pack a gas barbecue. He knew his route through the cliff would flood at mid-tide, and that he faced a fair climb out up steep steps and muddy slopes. He hadn't located the steps out yet but, hey, why would you need first-hand local knowledge when you have the Internet?

'LOL,' Danny muttered. 'PMSL. ROTFFLMFAFO.'

He really wasn't in the mood, for the climb on an empty stomach, or the fishing, come to that. He was on his second cast with both rods and already aching for the settee and a DVD. He knew should have changed baits a lot more often than every forty minutes - especially with the warm sea and run of the near-spring tide washing the scent out of them faster than *Shake n' Vac* -ing the dog - but his heart wasn't really in the fishing. He was just grateful to be out, and alone. He checked his phone for the time, watched the day become yesterday, and looked up just in time to see the first sign of fish.

It wasn't a hard bite. The blue tip light bounced like the rod was being lightly shaken. It stopped, did it again but putting a little more bend in the rod, then fell still. Danny stuck his hands in his pockets and blew a sigh. He'd put a thumb-sized piece of mackerel out on that one, 3/0 Aberdeen, so it was pretty much bound to be a dogfish. Whoopee.

It was, as he found out when the rod twitched once more a minute later and he wound in without striking. A goodish fish, if there are such things as goodish dogfish, definitely over two pounds. Danny angled his headlight to unhook it, and the barb, part-crushed earlier, slid back through the flesh of the animal's cheek with little effort. With its leopard-hide sandpaper skin glittering, and graceful, tapering body, Danny wondered if doggies got a bad deal, the way so many other anglers hated them with a passion. Reading online, he knew they were like plagues in many parts of the country, mobbing baits before they hit the bottom then putting up all the fight of a centenarian pacifist. Maybe north Devon was lucky. Not too often more than a couple a night, and all of them pretty good sized. Then the dogfish coiled its tail in a half knot around his wrist and flexed, and Danny joined the haters in a blink.

Dogfish are cat-sharks, with skin more like a leopard's claws than fur. And not only that, they wee through it. Industrial strength abrasive bit into his skin and removed it, and he swore he saw the dogfish grinning as he wrenched it off and heaved it seaward, hard.

Washing his wrist at the water's edge revealed the kind of skin-deep wound he hadn't had since falling off skateboards in his teens. It bled well, too, for just a graze. Probably the ammonia, he thought. He remembered learning from the site, about how dogfish excrete urine through their skins and washed again, a little harder, cursing. What would it be like to sweat wee? He'd have to ask Jocelyn when he got back to work, though it was more likely bile or venom seeping through the pores in her thick hide.

Then the green-glowing inch on the other rod was bouncing in the darkness. A more positive bite this time, several good hard tugs, then more. Danny crunched back to his tripod, lifted the rod and, when the fish pulled again, struck lightly. It fought well for a small fish but Danny wasn't in the mood to appreciate it and wound straight in.

A pollack, about a pound and a quarter, clean hooked through the bloodless membrane under its tongue. Danny wet his hand and picked it up, tracing its steeply humped lateral line - yep, definitely a pollack. He found that the easiest way to tell them apart from the odd coalfish that showed up. Theirs were straight and nearly white. Then again, they only came in during winter. . .

He was staring into space, night-daydreaming. The fish in his palm gasped a quick reminder, staring up at him with its oversize black and gold eye. He dropped to one knee at the water's edge, slipped it in and sent it on its way.

He groaned. Now he had no rods out. The dogfish had chaffed his hook-length, which needed replacing, so first he'd take care of the smaller hook on the rod he'd just brought in. And that was no barrel of laughs, either. The rancid lug was so soft and slimy that it seemed to have come back from the dead, the way it slipped and slid its way out of every attempt to keep it hooked up, and the thick stench made his head reel and his empty stomach knot and cramp like he'd been offered vegetarian food. Fresh bait was always best but lug would catch fish as long as it was solid enough to cast.

Which it was, just. And it did catch a fish, within moments. As he was replacing the hook-length on the other rod, the rattle of the rod distracted Danny from the knot he was trying to tie in the light from a failing head lamp. He lost the end of the line and stabbed his finger with the hook as he grabbed for it.

'Bloody fish,' he muttered, then shouted, 'Can't you wait?' into the night as the rod bounced on, obstinately. All he wanted to do was sit, mope and watch nothing happening, but the damned fish just wouldn't leave him alone.

He reeled in, unthrilled by the lightweight battering on the end of the line and only vaguely interested by the first rockling he'd ever caught. A pretty, whiskery fish, bright orange with brown blotches all down its back, it was shaped like a salami with fins, or something rude in an adult catalogue. Danny unhooked the end where the batteries would go and slipped it back into the water, unphotographed.

Six more fish came out as the tide rose, all either dogfish-dull or too small to bother identifying. Danny's only excitement of the night came from inland: sirens, engines, gunshots and screams, on top of the cliff behind him.

Chapter 20

Danny sat at his desk in the empty office, staring blankly through his computer screen, the only one still flickering. Even the cleaners had gone home.

Where else would he be? Fishing? Not tonight, Josephine. Not for many nights to come either, after the last one's nightmarish events. Elbows on desk and face propped on heels of hands, he stared through his computer screen and blew out a long, noisy sigh. At least the origami was coming along well. He'd just turned *Basham's Bodywork Repairs* business card into yet another fetching ashtray, boat, bathtub, athletic support or whatever the Hell it was this time. The card was wearing thin now. He'd been turning it in his fingers all day, unable to bring himself to make the call. True, they were already on first name terms with him at the workshop, those that weren't calling him *The By-Pass Butcher* or *Kid Road-Kill*, but they were never going to believe this one. If, or rather, *when* they did, though, they should give him shares in the company.

He flicked his folded model away across his desk and it came to rest in the Post-its Sea. There: it was a boat. He sighed again.

'Keep this sigh-rate up,' he thought, 'and you're hyperventilating.'

So he called it a yawn and had another one. He wasn't going to post catch a report at *The Goldfinger Bite*, not a chance. Enough of the nightmare was already plastered across the Internet and the last thing he wanted was to have his name linked to it in any way.

One silver lining to the clouds had been Slade's insistence on Danny doing overtime. If Danny had still had transport, he would have sworn that Slade wanted him to miss the tide, out of spite. Of course, Danny would rather marry Jocelyn than face Slade's ridicule over the car thing, and it was none of his business, anyway. No, he'd kept him there to catch up on Jim's work, specifically, for a reason. It was the closest company policy let him get to showing Danny Jim's severed head on a spike, a warning that the same fate awaited him if he stepped out of line.

Overtime, of course, and a good rate, too. Maybe Slade had needed Jim more than he'd known. Maybe they all had . . . but double time for a couple of week-night hours extra? Danny'd had to wring time and a half from them last year, and that was coming in on a Saturday for the restock! He wondered if Slade had put his hand in his own pocket to pay him, and snorted. He wouldn't have done that, of course. Rumour had it that you'd only see Slade with his hand in his own pocket, reading the top row magazine covers in filling stations. And he never carried cash.

But Danny was left with the problem of actually doing something, work-wise, because without Jim, or anyone else in the building, Danny had no one else to blame for distracting him. Staring at the fishing web site all night wouldn't help, and certainly wouldn't make him feel any better, so he closed it down and immediately wished he hadn't. Behind it was the BBC local news page he'd read as soon as the office had emptied, and the story, complete with photographs, of the carnage he'd returned to when he'd climbed out of Lee Bay the night before.

Fame at last.

Danny's head fell into his hands. If he was ever to go fishing again, he needed a miracle.

'Oh, hey,' it said.

Startled, Danny peered over the top of his monitor.

'Are you ill or something?' Annie breezed over toward Slade's office door, barely looking at him.

'No,' said Danny.

She stopped in the doorway. 'Then are you insane?'

'Why, what have I done?'

'Stayed at work after hours. But. . .' She turned and stared at him sternly. 'But you're thinking, what else have you done? I can tell.'

'Ah. That.' Danny went to stand but felt awkward and just straightened in his chair, not knowing what to do with his hands. 'That was pretty bad of me, I suppose. I mean, I admit.'

Annie folded her arms. 'Exactly what was so bad of you, Danny Benton, and exactly how bad was it?'

'You're going to make me suffer, aren't you?'

She nodded, slowly. 'I'm a woman.'

'Ok,' Danny said and drew a deep breath. 'I was a bad boy, dumping you to go fishing without a word of warning. I'm sorry. I am.'

She looked at him like he was dirt. 'How bad? And how sorry?'

'Very bad. I should have told you about that competition. It was booked weeks ago but. . . I mean, we had a shot at the afternoon and I didn't want to waste that. God, you really are twisting the knife, Annie, aren't you.'

It wasn't a question. He got no answer anyway.

Danny held up his hands. 'And I'm very sorry. Very, very sorry. Very, very, veryveryveryvery-'

'Enough!'

Annie held the face of doom expression for a few seconds more then burst out laughing, all big, bright smiles and, for a moment, Danny thought she'd lost it.

'You fool, Danny Benton! You must have such a guilty mind.'

'I did pay your bus fare,' he said meekly.

'Danny, you did tell me about the competition! All the way there in the car, you were going on about it. You are just . . . I don't know, fishing-obsessed! I couldn't get a word in edgewise!'

Danny frowned and stared ahead. 'Yeah, I suppose. . . perhaps I did mention it but. . .' He stared up at her. 'But weren't you upset?'

'Of course I was bloody upset! But not about the match. I just thought, we'd had a really good afternoon and, you know, you might have wanted to give it a miss.'

Danny's jaw fell. She didn't need to be smiling. The one raised, shaped eyebrow was enough, more than enough, to tell him what he'd missed out in, just to stand in the mud and lose to Cornwall. His devastation must have showed.

'Aww!' said Annie and bent forward, resting her elbows on the far side of the desk, resting her chin on interlaced fingers and staring deeply into his eyes. 'Don't worry, baby!

You're forgiven. You're obsessed, remember? You can't control yourself.'

He wouldn't have been able to control himself if he'd know what was on offer, that was for sure! Danny couldn't believe he'd been so blind! Was he turning gay or something? Annie stood and he studied her picking off the dozens of Post-it notes now stuck to the elbows of her tight fitting sweater. Breathing hoarsely Danny crossed his legs, relieved. No, he definitely wasn't turning gay.

He had to swallow a few times before he could speak. 'So where have you been, since then? I did, like, miss seeing you. Um, you know.'

She smiled demurely. 'Then you don't know me as well as you think, yet.'

He liked the 'yet'. 'Meaning?'

'Meaning, blokes aren't the only ones who throw sickies. I hate working for that pig as much as you do, and I've only been here a few weeks! I just took a few days off, that's all. No harm in using up your sickness allowance, is there? Maybe pushing the boundaries a little, here and there?'

Danny, he thought, this is your kinda gal! 'Well I never! And I thought you were as honest as a nun.'

Something in that made her smile turn just a little dirty but, disappointingly for Danny, she changed tack entirely and brought his mood crashing straight back to Earth like a monkey-nation moonshot.

'Why so blue, anyway?' she said. That was all it took, but she rubbed it in more with, 'What are you doing here, anyway?'

'Huh. Not fishing, that's what.'

'You see? Obsessed.'

'Not any more,' Danny said. 'For the foreseeable future, I have given it up.'

'You're joking! You are now, Danny. I know you are!'

He looked her in the eye, held it, then turned his computer screen around to face her.

'I went fishing last night.'

Annie gasped. 'Well, there's a surprise!'

Danny grunted, retrieving the business card boat and fiddling with it. 'Not as big a surprise as I got.'

'Oh.' She noticed the car repairs card. 'You haven't hit another poor animal, have you?'

Obviously, she hadn't read the screen yet. She seemed genuinely upset, almost angry, and, considering what had actually happened, Danny couldn't help but laugh.

Wrong response.

'You do think it's funny, don't you? I knew it!'

'No, no,' he cut in. 'Not this time, anyway. This time, the animals got their revenge.'

She gave him a questioning look and he nodded at the local news page.

IF YOU GO DOWN TO THE WOODS TODAY. . .

In your local pub tonight, you might hear some colourful local character relating tales of huge, hairy ape-like creatures creeping around the leafy lanes of North Devon. But scrumpy meltdown may not, for once, be to blame. There may actually be some truth to his bizarre, slurring story.

This lumbering, grunting monster is not just some charming local myth, no Yelland Yeti or Saunton Sasquatch. Explanations as diverse as 'nothing unusual' to tourists from Somerset have also been ruled out. Because, last night, just outside the small village of Lee, near Ilfracombe, an adult male gorilla escaped from a transport vehicle and ran amok, causing local damage before fleeing into the woods.

The animal, thought to be from a regional zoo and on the way to a specialist veterinary hospital to have a banana removed, saw its chance for freedom as the vehicle was negotiating the steep and narrow roads near Lee Bay, when it stopped to manoeuvre around a parked car, partly obstructing the road.

'Danny, that wasn't. . . was it?'

He nodded grimly. 'You can skip down to the picture.'

Annie, though, read on.

How the beast broke free from its heavy restraints is unknown but it punched through the roof of its truck and leapt onto the parked car, which it entered, also by punching through the roof. Early reports that the gorilla drove the car away are considered unlikely - more probably, it simply released the handbrake and happened to indicate correctly only by chance - but the car did start to accelerate down the steep, winding hill toward the village. Much damage was done to both roadside walls and the car itself, which eventually came to rest in the Old Bandstand viewpoint.

Local resident Mrs Sandra Courtney, who heard the crash and whose pet cat, Fluffywuffs, was later scraped from the front bumper of the gorilla's getaway car, described the scene as chaotic.

'We watched Crimewatch before bedtime, so we was expecting nightmares, but we heard this crash, then the deafening explosion. At first we thought it was just a seagull being stupid again. But when I went out and saw that thing running off, I just thought, well, the Cornish are back on the campsites. But you would, wouldn't you? The last thing you expect to interrupt your bedtime cocoa is an eight foot mutant monkey-man on the rampage. This is Lee Bay, after all, not Torrington.

'Your car was wrecked by a *gorilla*?'

Danny couldn't speak.

Give Annie her due, she held onto that laugh until she'd turned the last few colours of the rainbow, but when it came, it came in huge, lung-emptying gales that sent the Post-it Sea into a frenzy like a sudden summer storm.

It took an age for her to recover, both her breath and from the pains in her ribs.

'Oh god, oh god!' she hissed breathlessly; a sound Danny immediately etched into his memory.

Slowly, she recovered. 'Oh, I thought I'd heard everything. I hadn't, not 'til now!'

'Wrecked is one way of putting it,' Danny said coldly. 'Total insurance write-off is one other. Plus, what policy covers joyriding circus livestock? A classic Act of God, isn't it? And what kind of god plays Grand Theft Auto with gorillas? What kind of god?!'

'Oh, come on. You're having me on, aren't you?'

Danny closed his eyes and drew a slow breath.

'Yes, of course I am. I made the whole thing up, even hacked into the BBC web site and faked the page just so I could be stuck here in the office after hours, when I could be winning a big, fat bet and catching the fish of a lifetime. No! My car's just outside, getting a full valet and polish from Mr Slade himself!'

She stared at him. 'Yeah, but there's so little left that it could be anybody's-'

She glanced down at the photograph. 'Oh. That's your numberplate there, isn't it? Or, most of it.'

Danny nodded grimly. 'I'm telling you, it's Karma, for everything I've hit in the past.'

Annie had an idea. 'Don't you mean. . . Carma?'

'That's what I said.'

'Hang on.' She'd noticed something on-screen. 'Scroll down.'

What else had she found, more humiliation for him? A shot of the gorilla making sweet love to his exhaust?

'It all fits. Even the place name. Damage Cliffs, it's called. Can you believe that?'

'Huh, right,' said Annie, motioning him to the bottom of the screen.

'Look,' he said, pulling up a picture on his phone. 'The sign on the gate says, 'The National Trust - Damage Cliffs.' Shouldn't they be stopped? I mean, you'd think they'd know better.'

'Scroll down, Danny!'

He did, and leant closer. 'That wasn't there before.'

BREAKING NEWS:

Following a number of alleged sightings today, at 5pm today police issued a statement, warning of a highly dangerous six hundred pound silver-back gorilla on the loose in Braunton. The army has been called in and people are being urged to lock themselves in, keeping all windows and curtains closed. A high number of casualties were already being reported before all communication with the town was lost.

However, rumours that the transport vehicle was not from a zoo, but from a government veterinary facility, and that the gorilla was infected with some kind of genetically engineered 'rage virus', are described by the authorities as unworthy of comment.

Frowning, worried, Annie stared long and hard at the screen, then at Danny, then back at the screen. She tried to speak but had to swallow and wet her lips first, to make the words come out.

'That's awful,' she said, 'about your bet. What was it?'

Now Danny stared. 'Eh?'

'What was the bet you could be winning?'

'Oh, that. You know, I nearly forgot, what with King Kong tearing up the town and everything.'

'Never mind that,' she said. 'What about that fish of a life-time you mentioned? And what can you win? What can you lose?'

Danny closed the news screen and set the computer shutting down. 'Everything,' he sighed. 'Almost everything. I've already lost my stake.'

He filled her in on the details, the row and the bet made with The Predator.

'Gambling debts aren't covered by the law, you know? He can't report you or sue you or anything.'

'That's hardly the point.'

Annie gasped, exasperated. 'Don't tell me, it's the princi-ple.'

'Sure it's the principle,' Danny said. 'It's the principle of rubbing the arrogant bastard's nose in the dirt.'

They looked at each other, no smiles.

'Well, at least you can't lose your car twice.'

Danny just shrugged.

'You're really upset, aren't you?'

He didn't look up. 'Does it show?'

She didn't answer. Danny heard her digging in her bag, the rustle of papers, the jingle of keys and coins. . . and the keys just kept on jingling.

'Would a ride help?'

He looked up then. Beyond the outstretched key-fob, she was smiling at him.

'Ride with me?'

Chapter 21

'So, you're stalking me, right?'
 'What? Why?'
 'You never said how come you came back in, madam.'
 'Don't flatter yourself, Danny.'
 'Huh. You must love Barum Fixings, then. Nothing better to do on a Friday night?'
 'That's for me to know and you to find out. Actually, I left my phone behind. Couldn't have it going off in front of *him*, could I? Took it out to mute it and. . . *bleh*! In here. Come on.'
 'I can't go in there, girl! There might be. . . ugh! Who knoooows what horrors dwell in such dark hollows?'
 'It's only Slade's office, for heaven's sake. Now do you want me to take you fishing or not?'
 'Ok, ok. You take point and I'll cover you from the rear. Not cover in the racehorse sense, I mean. Or maybe if-'
 'Danny!'

'Eew. What's this supposed to be?'
 'How should I know?'
 'Because you're his PA. You're in here all the time.'
 'Yes, but taking the dictator's dictation, not studying his novelty pencil sharpeners. Put it down. Just help me find the mobile, will you? It's not here. Someone must have moved it.'
 'Forget that, then. If anyone working here moved it, it'll be on eBay by now.'
 'Don't be stupid, Danny. Hurry up.'
 'You're nervous, aren't you? Is it being alone in a darkening room with a man who doesn't know when to stop and laughs in the face of Viagra?'
 'It certainly is not! It's just, what if Slade decides to drop back in, too? It. . . you know. It wouldn't look right, us poking around in here.'

'We're not poking! But I mean, if you've got five minutes to spare we could always-'

'Look, open your eyes, will you? It's right there next to you on his desk.'

'Sorry. I'll bet he's run up a massive bill for you. Here y'are.'

'Ta. Lost without my moby, I am. There's my *enormous* list of friends numbers, obviously, but I wouldn't know what time to get out of bed without the organiser on there and then there's the. . . What's the matter? What are you looking at?'

'I'm not sure. Here, on his screen. Come and see.'

'So? It's just a fish. A big fish, true. Whoopee. Now let's go and you can catch one just like it for me.'

'Believe it, Annie, nothing would give me greater pleasure. Well, almost nothing. But that's not the point. This is *The Goldfinger Bite.*'

'Oh, your fishing site. So what?'

'So why's it on Slade's computer?'

'If I'd got a parking ticket, you would have been paying it. How long does it take to grab one fishing rod?'

'Sorry. Couldn't find it at first.'

'I thought you said it was huge. How untidy can your flat be?'

'Play your cards right and you might find out. And I wasn't talking about my fishing rod, either.'

'Very funny. Now will you hurry up?'

'I had to get my bait, too.'

'But you were gone nearly fifteen minutes!'

'And my kit bag. And some kit to go in it. And I remembered your crab line, the Instow Special. Spare light, too. Boots. Reel, of course. And the new hooks I bought. Look. You could hang a cow carcass off that.'

'I'm not interested, Danny. Well I am, but can we just go? Get in. And put your seatbelt on. I don't want you getting me a ticket for that, either, thank you.'

'Oh no. You're not one of those tetchy women drivers, are you? White-knuckled wheel grippers, bitchin' at everyone else but scared to make the slightest manoeuvre.'

'

You're a brave man, Mr Benton. It's a long, lonely walk to the coast.'

'Ah. Withdrawn, ma'am. A very scenic walk, though. Patchwork fields, wooded valleys. Herds of wildebeest, sweeping majestically-'

'It's nearly dark, Basil.'

'Good point. There's still moths, though.'

'Quiet a minute now, would you? Let me pull out, if someone will just. . . Bloody traffic!'

'It's still bugging me, you know.'

'Shhh.'

'*The Goldfinger Bite*, being on Slade's computer. Being left on there, too. On purpose. Why do you reckon that is?'

'Danny, Shhh! Look, you've made me miss a space now!'

'Perhaps if you used your indicator, they'd know you wanted to get out.'

'You haven't even told me which way to go yet.'

'Forwards would be nice. Just follow the main road.'

'*Grrr.* Come on, come on.'

'Careful. You're turning into blonde van man.'

'Danny, just. . . Just put some music on or something and let me concentrate. There's a stack of CDs in the glove box.'

'Nice one! Now let's seeee. . . Oh yeah, I was saying about Slade's computer? You know why he left that on screen?'

'Go on then. Why?'

'Hang on. Damn it. How am I supposed to keep this shut?'

'The catch is faulty. You've got to close it, then push it. That'll hold it. Oh. No music, then?'

'No way! I mean, I. . . think I might be getting a headache.'

'I thought that was supposed to be my line.'

'He did it out of spite. I'm telling you.'

'Who? Who did what?'

'Slade, keeping me behind after work like a naughty schoolboy. Bloody cheek.'

'If he was *all* bad, he wouldn't have offered you overtime.'

'Oh he's paying me overtime, you better believe it. But there wasn't much of an offer involved. He made it pretty plain that I was staying.'

'You know your problem, Danny? You're too cynical. You are! He probably knows about your car and felt sorry for you. Hmmm. . . Maybe, anyway.'

'He certainly does not know about my car! You're the only soul I've told.'

'Aw, I'm touched.'

'Yeah. But what, give Slade the satisfaction? See old miseryguts laugh for the first time ever? He'd never let it go. I'd never get a moment's sleep at work.'

'Then why? What's fishing got to do with him?'

'Nothing, obviously. That's my point about the overtime, too. He's letting me know he's on my case. He's got me doing Jim's work. He fired Jim on the basis of what Stibb found on his computer, partly anyway, and now he's had Stibb go into my machine. He knows where I'm spending my cyber-time all day and he's making sure I know he knows it, too. *Get on with your work, Boy!*'

'My god, you sound just like him. I thought he was in the car with us, there.'

'Really?'

'No. Danny, I'm trying to drive! Just let me concentrate.'

'Yeah, I'm sure you're trying very hard. But some things just really aren't for girls, are they?'

'I'll kick you out, you know. I will! If I thought you were genuinely this sexist, Danny Benton. . .'

'You'd what?'

'I'd. . . oh, I'd probably bat my lashes at some big, bronzed Croyde surfer and get him to bash your lights out.'

'You've gone very quiet.'

'Thinking, sorry. About where to fish tonight.'

'What? We're on the way there and you don't even know where there is?'

'Just keep going out of town for now. We're spoilt for choice. Make sure you go north not south, though.'

'Why's that?'

'No sea, south, is there.'

'I thought you were admiring The Stones.'

'I. . . wouldn't go that far. Touchy subject with me, The Cornish Stones.'

'I think they're a disgrace.'

'Ha! That's my girl!'

'What's painted on them, I mean. And the people who keep doing it. And that one, wow. That's just so *rude!*'

'It's high art, that's what that is. Clever, too, getting your message to fit perfectly, one letter per rock.'

'But all that security. . .'

'Just adds to the challenge, I expect. And the fun.'

'Danny, cameras I can understand. But Rottweilers? And isn't that razor wire?'

'Electrified. If you ask me, all that power should be used to grind them into a new beach somewhere. Somewhere else.'

'Oh, come on! Are they *that* bad?'

'Well, now you make me think about it. . . Yes. Definitely yes. They're supposed to be Devon but they're just the bits of Cornwall even the Cornish didn't want, and the taxpayers' money spent on buying them meant fourteen hospitals never got built. Fourteen!'

'Danny, that is just not true!'

'It is! Children's hospitals, they would have been. Great big ones. Huge, with cleaners and everything. And only for the most angelic kids, and only treating the nicer diseases, the ones that don't smell or leak.'

'You're a sick individual yourself. You know that?'

'Oho! But you try getting Jimbo on the subject of the stones! Jim'll tell you! He'll just. . . I mean, you should have. . . done that.'

'It is a shame about Jim, though, isn't it? Do you miss him?'

'Miss him? I used to work with the guy, that's all. We never got as far as a civil partnership or nothin'.'

'You do miss him, don't you? No, don't shrug like that, yes you do! It's written all over your face.'

'Well. . . alright. A bit. But only cos standing near him made me look even more handsome. Look. Road's empty beyond the junction. You can slam that stiletto down!'

'I'll put my foot down a *bit*, Danny, all right? If we ever get there. Come on, green light. Your turn, your turn.'

'It's, uh, red-amber next, lass. I think you'll find. That Highway Code thingy, an' all?'

'I'll kick you out without slowing. I promise. You don't believe me? Yeah, you might well hang your head in shame. Holy cow, third gear! Anyway, your pal. He might have, like, money problems now, don't you think? I hope he'll be ok.'

'I don't know what Jim's situation is, to be honest. Never have. But he'll be fine, you can bank on that. Always is. You know what he's like, 'ever in some sort of trouble. But, you'll see. Good old Jimmy, he always comes up smelling of trumps.'

Chapter 22

Above an isolated North Devon coastal road, on a tight, dipping bend between Knaps Longpeak and Foreland Point, the night was still and clear but for a few shreds of high cloud, tattered tissues linking constellations. Bats swooped and moths flittered and fled, and on the ground there was no sound louder than a beetle on a leaf.

The young fawn stood still, just twitching his little wet nose and looking down, unsure how well his spindly legs would cope with the strange, new surface beneath him. A shiver ran down his skinny, white-flecked flanks, the starlight glinting in his eyes as they started to moisten. Because Bambi was sad, and confused, and more than a little afraid.

Mummy would know what to do, but wherever could Mummy have gone? One moment, she'd been right by his side, standing tall and proud on the white stripes down the middle of this hard, alien track. Then the two small lights had appeared from behind the hill and, before you could say Walt Disney, Mummy had vanished in a clatter of hoofs and torn undergrowth.

And the lights were bad, Bambi knew that now, from the roar that came with them as they brightened. Scary bad, but where to run? Escape through the hedge had been swallowed by foliage.

Run anywhere! all instincts urged, but his legs wouldn't work and started to buckle. His one bleat was drowned out and all he could do was turn his big, blinky eyes toward the headlights, then close them as the roar became a high-octane scream.

'What the Hell?'

'Aw, look. He's so beautiful!' Annie had braked hard. Very hard. The ABS light had flared orange on the dash but, although they'd both had the breath squeezed out of them, the air-bags had stayed airless and the car had come to rest in a neat, straight line with yards to spare. 'But we've scared him, poor baby!'

Danny scowled at the fawn, frozen in the headlights, a trickle of fear still leaking from its exhaust. 'Damn thing nearly made me spill me swivels.'

'It was stupid, tying rigs in the dark. I told you.' She dipped the car's headlights.

'You should've hit it,' Danny grumbled. 'That's a freezer full of extra-tender steaks you're turning down.'

'If you'd been driving,' she said, 'we wouldn't have had any choice.'

Having found his feet and the gap in the hedgerow, Bambi's cute bob tail disappeared into roadside and he hopped off merrily into the night, his little head filled with dreams of long life and the great antlers he would one day grow, and the terrible, bloody revenge he would wreak upon his mother, with them, when he did.

'A guy in the pub offered me eight legs of venison for fifty quid.'

Annie glanced at him expectantly, picking her moment before ruining it. 'Yeah, I know,' she sighed. 'But you said it was two deer.'

'Oh,' Danny said, his head dropping.

'Done the rounds on e-mail at least twice, that one.' Annie raised the lights and pulled away. 'Maybe three times.'

'Oh,' he repeated. They drove on.

Finally, Annie said, 'I hope you do know where we're going, cos you won't see much with your face in your lap like that!'

She laughed. Danny didn't.

'Yeah, I do,' he said. 'Right here.'

He reached over and grabbed the wheel, one handed, and steered her sharply left into a lay-by of hard, rutted mud. Annie gasped and stamped the middle pedal even harder than before. The car bounced to a stop with its front grill tangled in thin brambles.

'Danny! ' She slammed the wheel with both fists, then Danny's thigh with one of them. 'You-!'

'Got us here?' he interrupted, then patted her on the shoulder. 'Just doin' my job, Ma'am. No thanks necessary. Really.'

She killed the lights, unsettled by weedy, dry-stone wall less than a foot in front of them. 'What if I hadn't stopped in time?' she demanded.

'I already knew you could brake well. For a girl.'

She glowered at him, then got out. Danny did, too, opening up the back to get the gear out while Annie inspected the front of the car, probably itching to find the slightest scratch and an excuse for another good tongue-lashing. Danny pondered the thought of a good tongue-lashing from Annie for a long time, long enough for her to calm down, get bored, and finally give him a nudge.

'Penny for them?'

Danny's hand shot straight to his change pocket but the motion snapped him back to reality and the fixed grin slid from his face. 'Wuh. . . What?

'Daydreaming, weren't you.' she continued. 'A penny for your thoughts.'

'God, no!' he said, then composed himself. 'Just fishing thoughts. Where's best, what bait? You know. Anyway, changing the subject, you're sure you're up to this, aren't you? It's a bit of a climb.'

Annie faked a yawn. 'You said on the way. Five times. Like you were trying to put me off.'

'Of course I wasn't trying to put you off, dear,' he said in a silly voice. 'Else, where would my lift home be if you left early?'

She took the joke this time, without violence. 'Maybe you're not up to it yourself, fatboy.'

'Fatboy? Come on then,' he said, slamming the car boot, hoisting the rucksack over one shoulder and snatching up the bundle of tripod legs and rod sections. 'And remember, you asked for it.'

'I thought you said it would be tough.'

Walking in front, Danny rolled his eyes. The car was only three minutes behind them, and they hadn't even left the road. At least it beat a whiney, 'Are we there yet?'

'This is the easy bit,' he said. 'Great roads, Devonshire motorways.'

It was winding, hilly and lit only by the last trace of dusk and emerging stars. They didn't need extra light to see, yet, but Danny had his headlamp in place, to fire up and prevent them getting mushed if any cars came by. None did.

'Motorways?'

'Devonshire motorways,' Danny corrected. 'You know, roads with those flashy white lines down the middle, 'stead of grass.'

He picked up the pace a little, hoping to turn more of her breath into effort. Yep, he might well be out with the girl of his dreams, on a dark, lonely night - and with a knife in his bag and no witnesses, either - but he felt less and less in the mood for chatting. It was always the same, lately, when he got near the sea. Never knowing what might grab the bait and especially, more recently, knowing there might be something really big out there. Exceptionally big. She kept up with him, though. He was probably slowed down, having to carry all the kit. Thinking about it, though, he'd brought less than usual, so blamed the weight of the fifty pound line he was using for shock-leader.

'So where are we going?'

'In here.'

Danny turned sharp left through a gap in the hedge, then helped Annie down the dry-stone wall beyond. Brambles tugged at her clothing and his skin. They were on a broad, muddy track, almost as wide as the road, and the shade from tall conifers beyond cut out the last hints of light.

Danny turned his on. 'This way. And it's a long way down.'

Annie produced a bright torch and followed closely. The way down hair-pinned back on itself and got stonier underfoot, but as it started to loop the other way, they veered off onto a track between trees and the ground became soft with leaf litter.

'Wait a minute,' Annie said, breathing heavily.

'At last,' Danny thought. He wouldn't mind a rest himself! He turned and smiled. 'Out of puff?'

She put her finger to her lips, switched off her torch and said, 'Listen.'

Danny switched off his headlamp.

There wasn't a sound. Just the night breeze stirring the canopy above, rich with all the scents of summer woodland. The distant, cooing hoot of a tawny owl drifted by.

Small rodents rustled in the undergrowth, and water tinkled faintly somewhere close, draining down the steep slope through a peat-sided stream. And there was the surf, quite close now, sighing along a shoreline of unseen rocks below.

Not a sound. Nothing at all.

Danny broke the silence. 'What?'

She said nothing, just lunged forward, pecked him on the cheek and skipped off along the track. Her torchlight was ten yards ahead before he moved.

'What was that for?' he called. 'And mind those steps!'

'For bringing me here.' She laughed. 'And mind what? *AAAH!*'

Her light went out.

'Annie!' Danny raced forward until his headlamp found her. . . standing against a tree, grinning.

'Yes?' she said, switching on her torch again.

He glared at her but couldn't stop the smile. 'This way. We're almost there.'

The old stone steps stopped abruptly when the trees parted and they stepped out onto a small, steep, sandy beach at the base. They found a gentle breeze blowing and, overhead, astronomy everywhere. Annie turned and craned her neck, taking in the gigantic, vertical silhouette behind them.

'Did we really come all that way down?'

Danny snorted. 'Only as far as we've got to climb back up.'

She let that sink in, then said, 'Cool. So, where are the fish?'

Danny was already at the water's edge, setting up. Just the one rod tonight. Fishing was high on his mind - not to mention Big Silver, the bet and his car - but for once it wasn't the only thing.

He had a new box of frozen squid, plus the front third of a mackerel, re-frozen for the god-knowsth time. A lot of anglers won't re-freeze leftover bait but Danny had never had too much spare cash for gourmet niceties. In the past, he'd caught on mackie and squid that come on so many trips with him he'd begun to regard them as personal friends. However, he'd also learnt that it paid to take fresh along, too, for when the fish were fussier; that a second thaw turns sandeels straight to fish slurry, and that uncleaned crabs become essence of sewage in a shell. The mackerel was past its best, but he'd seen worse on ice in supermarkets, so it would do just fine for Annie's crabbing. He tossed it to her and she caught it out of reflex.

'*Eeew!*' The mackerel plopped onto the sand. 'Cold! Slimy!'

'It's not going to defrost, lying there,' Danny said. 'You'll have to hold it in your hand.'

'I am not touching the bait.'

'Crabs can't eat rock-hard bait, you know. It's either, you hold it, or it's going down your cleavage.'

Annie shrieked and grabbed his unopened tripod, brandishing it like a fighting staff. 'Nothing of yours is getting down there, mister. Not if that's your idea of treating a girl right.'

'Wait, wait,' Danny said quickly. 'No worries. We can always put it in a rock pool and it'll be soft in five minutes.'

'You swine!' she said, clouting his arm with the rod rest, but not hard. 'You'd have let me do it, too, wouldn't you?'

Danny didn't answer - didn't answer, 'Yes', but dug in his rucksack for her crab line, wound up in a plastic bag, and tossed it to her. By the time she had unwoven the barb from the thin nylon rope, Danny was ready to cast.

Skinned down to pure white flesh and impaled on a pair of well-buried 4/0s, an eight inch squid took off into the night, heading across the Bristol Channel; target, Wales. It landed well short, but still a good hundred yards plus out from Devonshire. Danny stopped the spool of his multiplier and lifted the rod tip, tightening the line just enough to feel the lead sinking. The steep beach meant good, deep water and it took a full six seconds before the Danny felt the soundless thud of the six ounce lead finding the sea bed. He bit the new tip light, already taped into place, and as the green glow spread out along its length, propped the rod in his tripod, then gave the reel a couple of turns to put a slight bend in the end.

And waited.

They talked about lots, just stuff, and followed the dropping waves down the beach.

Not driving for once, Danny downed a beer, then another, toasting the memory of his late, lamented, ape-ruined car, and a third to Annie for saving the night with hers. As the tide fell lower than the enclosing walls of rock, the small beach opened into one three times the width. The further they followed it down, the more the shingle shrank, until the beach levelled out into Demerara-fine sand. They weren't hemmed in by the cliffs anymore, with low banks of huge, broken rocks running away on either side, reminding Danny of a crude trial-build of the granite boulder breakwater at Westward Ho!

'There used to be wreckers along here, you know?' he said.

'I thought that was only Cornwall. I grew up on my mum's videos of Poldark, so I know about these things.'

'No, you're confusing it with Cornwall being the only county where it still goes on. It's official cultural heritage. They get grants from Europe for it, as long as they don't exceed the quota.'

She giggled. 'Oh, shut up.'

He did, and they enjoyed a long, easy silence. Then Danny said, 'Not long 'til low.'

'Is that good? Or time to go?'

'Do you want to go?'

'Of course not!'

'Ok. Then it's good.'

She clamped onto his arm and looked up at him. 'Aww, you old romantic, you! I never knew that under the surface-'

'It's good,' he interrupted her loudly, 'because a lot of fish start feeding when the tide turns, if not just before. It's virtually still for an hour, say, which is also good, then suddenly the water's changing direction, and currents reverse and wash food from the weeds. The shore gets re-covered, so they come in close after anything the gulls have missed. And coming in with the flow must be like going downhill, if you're a fish.'

He paused to allow her a chuckle. It didn't come, and he turned to see her torch light bouncing down the beach as she stamped away.

'Romantic, my arse!' she called over her shoulder.

'And mine, darlin'!' Danny called after her, then followed.

Then stopped. Beyond Annie, fifty. . . seventy yards along the rocky ledges, a small, dim headlamp had winked on.

'Stop. Look.'

It took her a moment to find. 'Oh, yeah. Someone else.'

'I know.' Danny trotted up beside her and watched the light bobbing. Then the wearer stood up and it went out. Annie started to speak but he shushed her.

'What?' she hissed, irritated. 'He's miles off. It's not wreckers, for god's sake!'

'Listen.'

She did, to a distant whoosh then hiss of a reel spewing line. The hiss went on and on and she didn't hear the splash.

Under his breath, Danny said, 'Damn!'

'So what? It's someone fishing. Aren't they allowed to?'

He ignored her. 'I wonder how long he's been hiding there.'

Annie laughed. 'Hiding? It's not your coast, you know!'

He looked at her. 'Yes it is.'

She held his eye. Somehow, he meant it, but it wasn't just pride or silly greed. He was edgy, nervous. 'Then why don't you go and find out?' she said cautiously. 'See if he's catching all our fish?'

'No,' he began. 'Because...'

Even in the near-dark, she could see him chewing hard on his lip.

'Because I think I might know who that is.'

'Oh, yeah?' she said brightly, the question implied.

'Let's just call him. . .' Danny chewed again. 'Someone we really don't want to meet.'

Chapter 23

It took just seconds to change his mind. He didn't go straightaway, or explain, but played it cool and led Annie back to the tripod. He slid his knife down the thawing mackerel's side and lashed a good chunk of fillet to the hook on Annie's crab line.

'Come on, then!' he urged, brightly. 'Can't leave me doing all the catching.'

Annie laughed. 'What catching?'

He steered her to the far end of the cove where the rocks were big and smooth but weed-free, well-barnacled and easy to climb. 'There looks good. You can lob it out and leave the spool wedged in that crack, or sit with it for a minute.'

'Great!' Annie smiled and started the small climb out beyond the tide line. She glanced back to see Danny, unmoving, giving her the thumbs up. 'By myself?'

'I'll. . . be up in a minute,' he said. 'Might just pop over there, after all. See how that chap's doing.' Then, just to clinch it, 'That's if you won't be too frightened on your own, of course.' He grinned. He could feel her scowling.

'Don't be stupid,' she said.

'Ok, then. But cop for this.' He dug into his floatation jacket pocket, pulled out his spare headlamp and tossed it up. 'Better than a torch. You'll need both hands to haul upmost of the crabs around here.'

'What?' she exclaimed, but he'd already turned and was trotting to the far side of the beach.

Danny wedged himself into a crack, peeped over the top and scared the bejesus out of a crab trying to wrestle a thumbnail-sized limpet off the rock. Both jumped backward. The crab kept going and skittered down a hole. Danny hoped he hadn't made any noise. He watched the limpet clamp back down, without even a nod of thanks.

The other angler was about thirty yards away, maybe less. It was hard to tell from deep in the jumble of boulders. His light was off, which made it even harder, and also meant he was sat with his eyes glued to the rod tip. So Danny would wait. The other man might not be looking but he would be at his most alert.

'Why the Hell am I hiding?' he thought. What was he going to do? Sit there and watch the guy fish all night? Throw stones to scare his fish? Creep up and garrotte him? Of course, if the guy did happen to catch a gigantic bass, fifty pound mono would do the trick and Danny could be in there, posing for some self-timer trophy pics before he even knew what hit him.

'*Naah,*' he said aloud, then thought, 'No choice, really.'

'Evening, mate.'

The other man's silhouette was bulky. Long arms levered him up as he turned. Caster's arms.

'Alright?' Danny continued, his headlamp tilted down as he approached. 'Catching?'

The other's light came on, the bright one, full blast, no warning.

'Jesus, man!' Danny threw an arm across his eyes. People often forget, though, that a headlamp that can be shone from Morte Point and seen from Baggy is less than comfortable six feet from fully dilated, night-adjusted pupils. He waited for the beam to drop.

It didn't. The man did nothing, said nothing. Didn't move.

'I can't take that light, mate,' said Danny, still keeping it friendly and motioning him to dip it with his other hand.

Nothing, though the shudder in his outline could have been a silent laugh. Danny gave it a few seconds.

'Screw you then, feller. Tight lines.' He turned and left, taking time to find each foothold and hoping it made him look casual. He was ten yards away when the man growled,

'*I hope you brought your car.*'

The adrenaline rush threw Danny off stride and, with the afterburn of the other's lamp still painting his retinas neon-purple, he didn't notice that the flat surface ahead wasn't like normal rock, but a bit more. . . splashy.

Only with the crunch of rough sand underfoot again was he out of range of The Predator's ongoing laughter. What a tit he must have looked, landing - Ba-DOOSH! - thigh-deep in a weedy rock pool. He hadn't even stopped to drain the water from his boot, but sped away across the rocks looking like a spooked mountain goat.

Spooked, though, Danny definitely wasn't. He'd run, alright, but he hadn't been running away. Nearly taking out the tripod's back leg as he skidded to a halt, Danny closed his hand around his rod.

'Alright, feller,' he murmured. 'Game on.'

He remembered Annie, whistling and waving to her, but her headlamp looked busy and didn't turn his way. She must have seen him, though, because he heard her call, 'Hi ya!' then something he couldn't make out, but sounded light-hearted. He'd go over and see her in a minute.

But first the mad dash to get more bait out. He lifted the rod, spared five seconds to feel for any movement, the hauled his surely-bare-by-now hook from the sea bed. It travelled three feet and stuck fast.

Danny swore and yanked hard at the snagged line. From the way it had lodged suddenly, not dragging itself deep into weed, he realised it was more likely that the lead that had got wedged and swore again, this time for not bothering to rotten-bottom. He could have hoped to get his rig back that way but now, if it snapped, all was lost.

It snapped, Danny almost landing on his arse as the tension gave, and a steam of much louder and far more imaginative curses ricocheted around the cliffs. Faintly, The Predator's guffaws echoed back.

Maybe all wasn't lost but a good five minutes would be, measuring new shock leader, fixing to the main line, tying on a... What was the quickest way? Well, he'd be damned if he was going to learn from his mistakes, because he had no time to fiddle with rotten bottoms now. He had bait to get out there, and fast. He would clip a five ounce lead onto a lock-swivel, slide it up the line above a bead, then add another swivel, a hook-length and a chunky, 6/0 Limerick. That ought to hold the bugger. If... When it came.

In darkness, he brought the shock leader and main line together then reached up to his lamp switch before tying the complex knot.

Then he stopped, no reason, couldn't help it, and stood still, just looking and listening, taking it all in.

Tonight was the night. It had to be.

Whether it was something in the air, the tides and currents or the path the moon cut across the stars, Danny could feel it. He drew a deep, slow breath and scanned the dark sea from horizon to shoreline. More than feel it, he knew it, instinctively, as though all his experience, from night after night out alone and mostly blanking, was gelling together into a new sixth sense. He exhaled, heart banging. Yes, tonight was the night. Inevitably, like a destiny already written. Or like being in some shabby novel that's fast running out of pages.

'Hi ya!' Annie called back but she was too busy to look up. She watched another shore crab loom out of the depths, too hungry or too stupid to let go of the scrappy lump of mackerel. Two more of the snappy suckers were already crouching in a saucepan-sized rock pool behind her and she was grinning from ear to ear.

'Come here if you want to get crabs!' she yelled to Danny, then dissolved into laughter once she'd heard it aloud. She expected him to come over but wasn't surprised when he didn't. At least it was the rod coming first and not another woman! Really, she didn't mind at all. In fact, she finally understood why he did it, why he'd so often traipse off into the dark, all alone. Because it was anything but lonely. Nature was everywhere. She glanced at Danny's light. Everywhere, inside and out. Darkness brought another reality, a different world entirely, and one most folk missed out on, unknowing, tucked in beds in boxes, curtains shut. Annie was genuinely grateful that he'd brought her here. She'd pout and nag him ragged when he did come, of course, but that was just down to being female and subject to the laws of nature.

So, true, fishing wasn't just about catching, but she'd picked up a bit of the bug for that, too. She really hoped Danny would catch something, and promised herself to be duly impressed at even the limpest rockling. He must be itching to catch something, Annie thought.

She certainly was - to catch more and bigger crabs! Pointy, spiky legs and pinchy claws? Is that all you got? Bring 'em on! Bring on lobsters for all I care. Then she realised she did care about lobsters, and cared for them deeply. Not exactly in a McCartney way, though. More in a split down the middle and served with salad and a nice glass of white kind of way.

Her biggest challenge was changing the bait, with her third of a mackerel now all but defrosted, oozing blood and the little that remained of its last meal. The thought of a lobster drove her on, though, and she could always bleach her hands when she got home.

'How the Hell do I hook you up?' she asked the white-eyed, partial fish where it lay propped on limpets. Not through the wet end, that was for sure. The hook would probably go straight through the eyes as easy as... Had she really just thought of doing that? She put a hand to her mouth, then wondered how clean it was. She drew a breath, clenched her teeth, snatched up the mackerel and hooked it through the lips in one movement.

'Big bait, big lobster,' she said under her breath as she stood, unwinding about five feet of orange nylon string. Instead of her usual, half-hearted chuck, she began to whirl the weight in a big, vertical circle.

'Big. . . lobster. . . big. . . LOB!' and the fish-head headed for a distant star.

Danny turned on his headlamp, spat a short length of line from between his teeth and looked down. Everything was done: from new shock-leader to baited hook, a simple running ledger rig, all neatly knotted and trimmed, ready to cast. He whirled around, scanning the beach for the magic fishing pixies but, of course, they were too quick.

Obviously, he'd done it all himself, barely aware he'd moved a muscle. He'd been so busy just thinking about fishing that his hands must have got bored and got on with the job. He grinned. It was all coming naturally, everything falling into place. All he had left to do was elastic the squid into a lifelike presentation; at least, as lifelike as it could look with a massive, shiny steel barb protruding from between its eyes. A second, sliding hook at the tail end would have held it better yet, but his fingers had just shown they could work free of his daydreaming brain, so he didn't want to rain on their parade. It was nice for them to have their independence, and if he could take them one step further, training them to work while he slept, he could sell his flat, live to fish and sleep at the office. Talk about working from home!

He shook his head clear of the daylight world and concentrated, seeking fish. All he'd learnt about the habits of bass . . . left him. Danny turned off his headlamp and cranked up a powerful cast.

The bait lay undisturbed. Danny edged along the beach to the nearest rock and sat down. His tip-light was still clearly visible with no need for a constant battery-burning, fish-spooking headlamp to avoid missing bites, plus, he could keep a discrete eye on The Predator's progress, being just about in gloomy line of sight.

Almost immediately, he wished he hadn't bothered. The Predator let out a short, surprised yell and was at his rod in a split second. Danny watched his lamp beam flashing around, glimpsed the rod rise up, strike-ready. . . and the light went out. He hit the fish moments later, without making a sound.

The silence did not last long. The Predator's reel began to scream as the fish broke for freedom. To Danny, it seemed to go on forever and, all the time, half of him wanted to hear the line snap while the other half craved to see the fish. He wouldn't see a damned thing from where he was, though, so he switched off his own light and began to creep forward through the rocks. That fish wasn't coming in any time soon, so he'd get himself a prime viewpoint without giving The Predator the satisfaction of knowing he had an audience.

The Predator was battling the fish hard, much harder than Danny would have dared on his own eighteen pound line, and by the time Danny had got close enough to see, he'd already broken the fish's spirit, however briefly, and brought the first run to an end. And turned the beast, too, it looked like, from the speed at which he was retrieving line. Crouched between two wet rocks, peering through a V-shaped gap at the top, Danny felt sick. It was a huge fish, that was obvious, and certain to smash the long-standing twenty pound record if he landed it. And he would land it, Danny was certain. He might be the most hated man in website-land but his catch record spoke for itself.

The fish began another run but didn't get as far. Resistance, rather than escape, became its tactic then, as it seemed to go twice as heaving in the water, nodding and pulling, but neither giving or taking any line. Danny crept forward just twenty feet away, to where he could hear the other man grunting under the strain. They must have been deadlocked for ten minutes or more, with Danny having to endure the knowledge that The Predator was loving every second. He considered hunting out a few crabs to throw at him but decided to it might void the bet.

Bit by bit, The Predator was getting his line back, with the reel only slipping with the fish's hardest efforts, which were becoming fewer and fewer. He was going to land the fish, win that bet and, abruptly, Danny realised he only had a heap of scrap with which to pay up. Thank goodness Annie had driven tonight, so at least they wouldn't be stranded. He wondered if Annie played poker, because he could always let her win a few hands, build her confidence, then up the stakes to include, say. . . motor vehicles?

Splashing brought him back to reality, just as The Predator's lamp shone into the air like a call for Batman. Danny stretched higher over the rocks and saw the swirling foam in the water just ahead. The Predator had a long gaff in his hand, the steel meat-hook bright in reflected light. For an instant, Danny felt he should go over and help the man, however much he hated him. After all, that was an enormous and unique fish there, and an all-time achieve-ment to catch it. Just being there would be something pret-ty special. An honour. But he knew all that was a load of crap and that, in reality, he couldn't trust himself to stick the gaff in the gob of the right cold-blooded beast.

The Predator's light angled down and Danny's face froze at what he saw. Only for a moment, though, only to make sure. . .

'Yes!' he hissed, clenching both fists in front of him. 'Swee-eee-eet!'

The Predator had caught a great fish, alright, and one that would have smashed the bass record to pulp. But the fish was made of steel, not silver.

More streamlined, athletic, scythe-finned and black-backed, it was clearly a tope, not a bass. A true, toothy, ocean-going shark that sometimes ventures close to shore hunting mackerel and flatfish - not to mention one cracker of a fish, too, Danny thought - high thirties, at least - but nuts to that now cos the bet was still on. He wanted to leap up and laugh but decided on a more discrete response. He'd just slip quietly away, bait up again and catch the fish they were after. Simple as.

He'd gone ten feet when The Predator said - not shouted; just loud enough for Danny to hear - 'Just a warm-up, kid. Run along now, back to your toys.'

Danny sloped back to the beach to a soundtrack of harsh, ringing laughter.

Annie had no feeling in her backside any more. She sat cross-legged on the rock, staring along her orange, half-taut string to where the sea swallowed it, ten yards ahead. When the big lobster came, she'd be ready. Numb bum was becoming a pain in the arse, though, and she shifted a little for comfort. Didn't work. She could still be ready, she decided, while having a short stretch and a clamber about, as long as she didn't stray far. She stood, found a good crevice and wedged the crabbing spool inside, leaving the line semi-tight, then looked around for likely rock pools.

In the first, a deep, triangular one a yard across, she watched a thumbnail-sized, almost-invisible jellyfish pulsating its way nowhere fast. All she could see were pinprick black dots around its edge and faint, rainbow shimmers on the dome, split and bounced back from her light. Tiny shrimp eyes glittered out from the weeds below like Christmas frost. Annie dug out her mobile and tried a photograph, but had to use the flash. She got perfect rocks around a pool of blurry light. She wished she'd got the next phone up, the model with the better camera. It had only been an extra twenty. She sighed, and had to stop it becoming a yawn. Obviously, though, twenty quid was twenty quid, especially when spent on Galaxy chocolate. And where was Danny, anyway? Just across the beach, of course, but why wasn't he here with her? Was this his idea of showing a girl a good time?

With Danny, of course, it was. She was sure he was showing her his very best of times. She managed a smile and hopped down onto the sand to go and get closer to him.

She didn't get far. Annoyingly, just as she stepped away from the rocks she heard her crab-line slip and clatter down between them. The racket it made seemed to go on for ages. She halted, made fists at her side until it stopped, then trudged back to rescue it before the tide came in.

It was nowhere to be seen. The cracks beneath where she'd left it were empty. She wandered around, scratching her head. When, finally, she glimpsed orange plastic and found the spool, it hadn't tumbled down any crack, but was caught on the seaward edge of the rock, an inch from falling into the waves.

'Where d'you think you're going?' she asked it sternly, although, 'How the heck did you get across there?' was the question in her mind. When she rescued it she got her answer. The spool was empty, completely bare, and its orange twine, nowhere to be seen.

Chapter 24

Annie was coming, running and shrieking something about an attack by giant lobsters, but although Danny would have given his left nut to see such a thing, now really was not the time.

'Why d'you think I've been yelling for you, Danny?!'

'You have? Sorry, but I've been busy! That's why I was yelling for you!'

'Oh.' Her disappointment was clear. 'I thought you were just excited for me.'

Danny rolled his eyes, glad she wouldn't notice in the dark.

'Aww,' he said, re-squidding his steel. 'Been having fun with her little crabby-wabs, has she?'

'You tease all you like, mister, but one just pulled my line in.'

'Don't tell me you've lost it already.'

'Only half of it,' she said, producing the empty spool. 'The long, windy half. That had to be a lobster, didn't it? Danny?'

'Never mind that,' he cut in as she got close. Things had changed since he got back from The Predator's mark. 'You've gotta come and watch this. It's … it's unreal!'

'Never mind that? If I'd pulled it in I could have had an arm off!'

'That's why you have a spare.' He was barely listening. 'Come on, come with me. You gotta see this rod to believe it!'

They weren't far from his tripod. Annie directed her head-lamp at it. 'What rod?'

Danny rotated on the spot. 'Ho-leee crap!'

His tip-light glowed green below the water's edge and the rest of the rod was chasing it into the depths! Jolt, jolt, jolt, left and right; only the reel, gouging sand, was slowing it down, stopping it disappearing altogether. Danny sprinted, snatched it up and struck hard. Annie gasped as she saw the rod bend once, then further as the fish on the end went berserk. But then, with a twang, all went quiet. Many silent seconds passed before Danny started swearing.

'It's gone?'

'Gone,' said Danny.

Annie watched him reeling in quickly but calmly, surprised he wasn't angrier. When he looked at her, she saw he was pale and excited.

'That's the third time in ten minutes!' he said breathlessly. 'It's. . . *unbelievable* out there!'

'What are they? Sharks or something?' Annie was only half-joking.

'Huh. Kinda. Maybe.' Danny's fingers flew, checking the rig for damage and rebaiting in seconds. 'That bloke up there just had a tope. They're sharks. Bleedin' monster, too.'

'Wow.' Annie gasped at the prospect. 'I can't wait to see one!'

Danny grunted. 'I'm hoping you won't.' He cast while speaking, a much gentler lob, fifty yards max. 'I'm trying to avoid them.'

'You're what?'

'Hoping it's big silver out there. You know, those-'

'Giant *bass*,' she interrupted. 'Yeah. They're all you've talked about for months.'

He set the rod in the tripod, driving the butt deep into the sand.

'So. . . how will you know what they are? Wait 'til you catch one?'

'Should know from the bite, really. Trouble is, all I've been seeing is the rod crashing down. They're so damned quick! Plus, I'm hoping tope still prefer mackerel to squid. That's how I'm trying to avoid them.' Glancing back at the rod, he laughed. 'I can't believe I'm treating tope as a pest, like dogfish!'

'How can you tell from the bite?' Annie asked. 'Just depends how big the fish is, doesn't it?'

'Not really.' said Danny. 'A bit. But. . . just watch.'

She stood in close to him, both focussed on the chemical tip-light, neither breathing. Eventually, Annie felt faint and things started to spin. She breathed again and recovered. The green glow didn't move.

Danny sighed. 'Ok, then. Most fish have different bites. A tope will pick up the bait and shoot off like they've grabbed a drive-thru burger from a train. Other fish just creep up and swallow it whole, not so much as a by-your-leave. A bass will often hit it first, and that's with the sharp gill covers, not the mouth. They kill their food before they eat it. Far more civilised. You just watch.'

He nodded back to the rod again but Annie knew what to expect, now, and secretly continued breathing. The night breeze slowed and died. Young foxes barked harshly, laughing as they fought in the woods beyond the top of the cliff. Six-inch surf broke diagonally, whispering along the beach. The rod tip bounced like the crack of a whip.

Annie screeched. Danny's hand flew up to her chest, holding her back, not that she'd been going anywhere.

'Now watch!' He'd tried to sound cool but it adrenaline turned it into dolphin-language. He coughed and began to repeat it, and the rod went over again.

'That's IT!' He pushed Annie back and leapt for the rod, just as the butt burst out of the sand, scattering it everywhere. 'That's the Goldfinger bite!' he yelled. 'That's what we've been waiting for!'

He struck as the fish put in its first run, slipped his footing and skidded down the beach behind the rod like a non-swimmer water-skier. Feet in the water, he hit it again, and again, setting the hook in the fish's mouth before it had the chance to spit or swallow. Unlike Danny, the tip was shaking only slightly now, but the rod was bent over like the top of a lower-case F. 'It's on there!' he yelled, hauling back. 'Fish on!'

Danny went deaf and tunnel-vision blind. All there was: an inch of green light and burning biceps. The rest of the world was shut out.

The bend travelled down the rod, testing it to the limits of its flexibility, and Danny had to drive his heels into the sand to hang on. But the fish had barely got started, he could feel that from the steady pull and slow, irritable tugging on the line, as though it had only just noticed something slightly amiss with its last meal. It was heading left, toward deeper water, sailing closer and closer to the shore where. . . No! It was heading for the rocks!

Danny cranked up the pressure and the bend got closer to the reel. Being an open-water fish, it probably wouldn't hole up in a reef like a conger might, but the line would chafe to breaking point if it got dragged over the top of one. And that was if the exposed, shoreline rocks, where Annie had been crabbing, didn't snip it clean through first.

He loosened the reel's clutch just slightly, making the fish work to take line while he moved back from it, along the waterline, then splashed out to welly-depth and hauled it away from the rocks. The fish obliged, but only, Danny felt, because the fish wanted to. It took off again for the open sea and he gasped a breath of relief.

'What is it?' Annie asked, just as breathless.

'Bass,' said Danny. 'Big bass. Gotta be.'

He wasn't as positive as he sounded. He wasn't positive at all. The fish was heading toward Ireland now, stripping line smoothly, effortlessly, even though the clutch was now reset as tight as Danny dared. His heart sank as he realised it was running just like a tope. He'd never thought the words would cross his mind but, for once, he hoped desperately that it wasn't one.

Annie was hopping worse than a full-bladdered toddler. 'Then why don't you wind it in, then?'

All sorts of colourful words came to mind then but Danny bit his lip and let grunts of effort answer.

He thought he'd be whooping for joy but his muscles had first call on all the oxygen he could get. Excitement? That had passed within seconds of knowing he'd hooked up securely. Worry, even fear, that was all that remained. Big fish like this just *couldn't* be lost, but they were also classic one-that-got-away tales in the making. He'd used a hook he could trust but that small bend of wire was all he had confidence in. How do you handle a beast like this? What was he *supposed* to do?!

It was like trying to stop a train with a string. Any second, he knew, a knot could give, a swivel snap, or an unseen flaw in the nylon could sever the line. And if that happened. . . well, there was always suicide or a lifetime in the soft room of the asylum. His spool was shrinking fast, the backing line already showing through, and fear was joined by growing panic. Surely, that would be the worst of ways to lose it, watching the last length of mono disappearing through the rod rings, unable to do anything but drown himself on the spot.

But, gradually, the fish began to slow and the clutch brought it to slow, straining a halt.

'It's tiring,' said Danny. Annie said nothing, just stared intently into the dark. The fish gave no slack, though, and as a light breeze picked up the line began to sing under the tension. After many seconds hanging there, it gave one hard tug and took off again, this time curving back along the beach, toward the other end. Danny trotted with it, winding in when he could and covering the backing line again before the fish decided, 'No more.'

Whether this was the moment when it knew it was hooked, Danny would never know. Maybe it had twigged that its squid snack had not reached its stomach or, perhaps, simply tired of teasing the human on the beach. Something had changed, though. Something that had really, *really* pissed it off. Only one thing was certain. It was a moment he'd never forget.

The fish got off. The lead sprang back and the line lay in slack curves on the water.

'Damn, DAMN, *DAMN!*'

There was a long silence. 'Aw,' Annie began. 'I'm so sor-'

'Arse!' Danny drove the rod butt through the shallows and into the sand. 'I was sure! *Certain!*'

'It's ok,' she murmured, paddling up next to him and squeezing his free arm. 'There'll be another one. They were biting all the time a few minutes ago.'

Danny was ahead of her. 'Get us another squid, would you?'

Annie didn't move. 'I draw the line at touching squid, mister.'

'Here, then. Wind this in and I'll get it.'

She took the rod like it was an alien artefact. 'The reel's stuck.'

Danny sighed. 'Try turning it the other way.'

'Wow, how clever!' she said, trying to cheer him up. That didn't work. 'There's nothing on here, you know.'

Danny wondered where she'd studied for her degree in the bleeding obvious. 'I do know,' he grunted, skinning squid. 'That's what I found most irritating.'

'I mean, there's nothing at all. I can't even feel the weight. I think you've lost that, too.'

It was unlikely. He'd cast onto clean ground so snags were unlikely and, anyway, the fish had been high up in clear water. Maybe it had been a tope, after all, and had managed to bite through the shock-leader, severing everything. Tope had the teeth to do it, too, while bass swallowed everything whole. She wasn't spreading the line on the spool as she wound in, either.

'Here, I'll do it.'

'It's heavy, isn't it?' Annie said, handing over the rod.

'Not half as heavy as a moment ago.' Danny hoped The Predator hadn't been watching. Surely, he couldn't have been, or there would have been a loads of laughs at his slack-liner. Danny flicked on his headlamp, winding and laying the line properly, ready to recast.

Slack-liner. . .

Slack-line bites. He'd read it, on line. Where the fish picked up the bait and carried it in, not pulling seaward and tugging at the rod tip, giving themselves away.

He knew.

'It's still on.'

'What?'

Danny wound furiously until the floating coils of line began to straighten. 'It's still there! Coming at us, not away!'

Annie leapt back from the water like she expected to be attacked but he had no chance to chuckle. The line lifted clear of the water, went tight, and adrenaline at once washed every drop of blood from Danny's veins.

'*It's on!*' he tried to shout, but his throat was so dry and tight that he sounded like a bishop-goosed choirboy. '*Fish on!*'

It certainly was, and that fish didn't like it one bit. As soon as it felt the hook again it yanked the rod tip a yard down, twice, then hit the gas again as hard as before.

Danny let out a yell and his voice broke back to normal. Annie was screeching encouragement behind him but her words blurred as he put everything he had into staying in touch with the force on the end of the thin strand of nylon. He braced the butt into his hip and reached up to switch off his lamp, fingers shaking like a drying out drunk's.

The fish changed tactics, and started playing Danny with a series of long, incredibly hard pulls, all the time towing back left again and coaxing him into clear of the rocks again, each time it let him have a little line.

And line was what Danny needed most. He'd buried the yellow backing line again but the spool still looked mighty thin. And if it was a tope, it was certain to power off into the distance again and swim til it wanted to stop. Danny couldn't let it do that, but couldn't spare the line to let it run. He hoped it hadn't swallowed the bait, hoped it was still starving hungry, and weakened, just so he could get the damned thing in.

And its short, hard runs did tire it. They slowed and stopped and so did the line, the fish hanging in the water like a fallen tree. Danny heaved the rod back slowly but just increased the bend, regaining just a few short inches of line. And god, he wished he eaten more himself as his shoulders were starting to cramp. It had anchored itself in clear water. It was like trying to haul in a drowning tourist parascender, except Danny could actually be bovvered.

Well, if it was resting, so would he. Keeping the line singing-taut, Danny eased off the pressure and got some blood flow back into his aching arms. He drew a deep, slower breath, then another, before turning to Annie to say-

The fish must have been watching. It saw its chance and bolted, almost pulling the rod from Danny's grasp. He stumbled forward into the surf, took another couple of steps for balance and flooded his wellies again. He barely noticed but swore under his breath: he couldn't let the fish run or he'd lose it. The backing was showing. Too much pressure and the line snaps. Do nothing and it's shredded on rocks or you're water-skiing.

It was going like a submarine and, again, Danny caught himself dreading a tope. He gave himself a mental slap, then a real one to hammer it home when he realised just how stupid that thinking was. Even if it wasn't a huge bass, there was no better consolation prize than a beast like the one he had a hook in right then. It was a fish, and it was a monster, 'nuff said, whatever name-tags the scientists stuck on their specimens.

And a fish he really, *really* had to catch. There'd be other casts and other bass, and plenty more Goldfinger bites.

But that bite. . .

It's not a tope.

So *hit it.*

Danny did, striking as hard as a cast in reverse, then again, and again, bullying and beating the great fish into a turn. The hook held firm. No teeth cut the line. The fish wasn't panicked, though, and wheeled around in its own good time, but Danny knew he'd made sure it knew who it was dealing with, and whizzed a good ten yards back onto the reel before the line went tight again. Dropping the rod tip, he took two small steps back, then started to haul.

The fish reacted but didn't bolt, sending a heavy vibration down the rod as it seemed to shake its head. Danny could almost see it, hacking and coughing and trying to spit the hook, so he knew he had it worried. He wound hard and when the handle refused to turn hauled the rod up, slower than a strike but just as powerful.

'Come on,' he growled, teeth gritted, 'super-size me.'

And the fish came with him. Just a rod's length, and it was like hauling a sack of potatoes through treacle, but it did come. So, nearly, did Danny, at the first real idea he might actually beat this baby and get it in. The fish object-ed almost instantly and the fight was resumed but, straightaway, Danny could tell it had lost something, bat-tering wildly like a more conventional fish, albeit a damned big one. And he wasn't about to let the fish forget it.

He glanced around. Annie had fallen silent, hands to her mouth, fixated on the bobbing, horizontal tip light. She looked pale but when he caught her eye she broke into a huge smile and clapped her hands in encouragement. Perhaps it didn't matter if he lost the fish now, he thought, being the only angler around with his own groupie. But

Perhaps it didn't matter?

'My arse!' he yelled and heaved against the fish again, and the fish fought back with just a little less force. 'It's tiring,' he said. 'You'll see. I'll be hauling it out any minute.'

Annie's hands dropped to her sides. 'Your arse is tiring and what?'

But the fish wasn't tiring. It was just taxiing.

The line began loosening and Danny wound fast but couldn't keep up. 'What the Hell is it doing?'

The answer blew in on the light breeze, a small splash, a gap, then a huge one, and a cascade of pattering droplets.

'Did you see that?'

'Yeah, I heard it. It jumped, right? Do tope jump?'

Danny didn't answer for a moment, just retrieved line quickly until the rod tip bent over again. 'No they don't,' he said. 'And neither should bass, not like that. But. . . no, I meant really see it.'

Annie shook her head.

Danny swallowed. 'I did. Just. . . just a dim shape but . . .'

It had only been a glimpse, a shape, the palest smear of movement in the black. But Danny had seen it. And it wasn't a tope.

It was a bass, no question.

And it was *immense.*

The shock-leader knot broke the surface.

The beast was beaten, being towed in, flinching feebly, just twenty yards of fifty-pound mono beyond the end of his vision. From the effort he still had to put in to his ponderous haul-and-wind retrieve, he imagined he'd see the fish's bow-wave first, a fair while before the head appeared.

'Danny, you're shivering.' Annie's voice was just as shaky.

It was excitement, not cold, and in Danny's case, too much exertion and a post-adrenaline crash. His muscles - arms, shoulders, back and hamstrings, were completely spent and close to cramping. The leap from the water had been the last of the fish's serious effort, leaving it almost as drained as Danny, although it had continued to twitch and protest for most of the long, slow drag toward the shore. What had been the biggest sea creature he'd ever seen without a David Attenborough commentary in the background, now felt like the world's largest kelp-afro being hauled through setting concrete. Mentally, Danny pushed aside mild feelings of disappointment, even anticlimax, then filled his lungs and heaved again. Seconds later a spreading wave washed in ahead of the fish. He shot a glance back at Annie, who was staring into the blackness behind him, open-mouthed and wide eyed.

'I see it!' She leapt a full foot in the air. 'There it is!'

A ghostly, shiny shape loomed low out of the night, drifting in like a limbless swimmer beaching after a tow across the channel. And it really was as big as a person, Danny realised. As big as Annie, anyway. Annie without any limbs. Pushing away the inevitable amputation fantasies, he drew a deep breath and, winding slowly now, simply watched it come. Annie clapped once and scrambled for her phone, determined to catch the moment of capture on camera.

The only light came from a sky full of stars but it was enough, every one of their reflections glinting back from the scales of the colossal bass as it glided, on its side, toward the rod tip. Four feet of silver broke the surface, sparkling, and that was with the whole tail section still submerged!

Just beyond arm's reach, he saw it match the length of the far section of his beachcaster.

Danny stretched out a hand, closed it around the shockleader and. . .

Its gold-rimmed, deep black eye rolled toward him. . .

And a beam like the Eddystone Light blasted out from the shoreline, blinding both hunter and quarry and sending both into their own kind of frenzy. Yelling as he threw up an arm to protect his eyes, Danny glimpsed The Predator jumping up from the rocks - he knew he'd be *there!* - but where the Hell was the fish?

Spooked stupid, it was, just like the schoolies in the estuary. The glare galvanised it, giving it the strength for one last, massive leap for freedom and in the split-second it took Danny to whirl around, it twisted, thrashed its great oar of a tail and launched clear of the water again.

Another, re-blinding flare of light caught Danny on the turn and he barely saw a thing. But this was no ordinary fish jumping, no over-skittish mullet breaching a still, quiet backwater. This was a large wild animal, scared and angry, on a solo seagoing stampede. Danny glimpsed a blurry, silver column rising, just inches behind his shoulder, and ducked instinctively, sure he could feel the air move as it passed. Light flashed again and a huge splash split the water just ahead of him, soaking his face and hair and pouring a pint of water down his spine. He staggered back, scrambling for the reel and struck out of reflex.

Bad move. This fish's leap had looped the line around the rod's final ring and the line snapped like a Christmas cracker. Short yards away, the huge fish submerged and was gone.

Danny's heart sank so far it knocked his legs from under him, and he flopped down on his backside in a foot of sea. Annie said nothing. Something looped around Danny's neck dragged across his shoulder, hissing under the collar of his jacket, then flicked up and stung his ear as it passed. Orange string.

Orange string?

Annie spotted it, too. 'My crab line!' she screeched at the fish. 'You ate my lobster, you pig!'

The string lay still, curving away and disappearing beneath the last, round ripples. Annie darted forward, splashed into the water and grabbed at the free end but just as her fingers closed, the slack began to tighten and it began to slip away. She lunged again, stumbled, and was thigh-deep by the time she grabbed it. 'Give it back!'

Danny joined her as she started to pull, dragging in the slack string. It felt snagged on a rock, but the rock was drifting slowly out to sea. Annie looked back, the fixed worry and concentration on her face shattering into a smile as soon as she met his eye. She knew they'd got it. Danny knew, too, and together, they heaved it in.

The fish barely objected. It had nothing left. Pulling slowly, hand over hand, they eased the great weight to the surface. The Predator was babbling something from the shoreline; the desperate sarcasm of the defeated, Danny hoped, and pushed him from his mind with a quick smile.

The huge, pale shape loomed up from the depths.

'Is it ok?' Annie asked.

The fish was floating on its side, motionless apart from weak, reflex twitches from it fins. 'Just knackered,' Danny said. 'It'll be fine in a minute.'

'Look at the size of that mouth! I could get my head in there!'

Danny considered the idea but decided to stick to squid for future baits. There were two hooks in there. One, through the side of the top lip trailed Annie's crab line and a bluish flash of mackerel skin. The second hook was Danny's, shiny-bare and neatly puncturing the bloodless membrane on the floor of the mouth, but still tied tightly to his lost shock leader. Danny snatched up the line, wound it around his wrist and hauled the bass the last few feet to shore.

The Predator was waiting.

The fish was so heavy that it ground to a halt as soon as it was out of the water, and Danny had to do his best to lift it, just to get it away from the waves for unhooking. The Predator didn't help. Danny wondered if he was purposely trying to blind them both with his headlamp, or just transfixed by the sight of the fish, but Danny didn't care. He was lighting the scene better than Danny's dim, non-spooking lamp ever could have. The unhooking was easy, and Danny knelt back and studied his prize.

If the Silver Surfer had a mated with a whale, this would be their love-child. The animal could have been carved from diamond. Five feet of diamond. Clad in scales as big as Danny's thumbnail, each finely blue-edged and reflecting its share of the million overhead stars and varnished with the finest layer of clear slime, like a glossy photograph of polished chain mail. Translucent fins stood proud along its back, their rays as thick as swan-feather quills and needle sharp at the tip. It was as though the fish had its own aura, and being so close Danny felt on the edge of a panic attack, but a good one, all thrill, like the last inch of a plane before a sky-dive.

He knelt, reached out and hesitated, then ran a wetted hand along it's flank. 'This thing could feed the five thousand for a month, loaves or no.'

'Danny! You're not. . .?'

He looked up. 'What?'

'You've got to let it go. You can't kill it!'

She was right, that he couldn't kill it. He'd have needed a shotgun. And it would never fit in his freezer, four small drawers under a boxy fridge, not without a liquidiser and some waterproof sacks. Danny grinned. He'd never even considered it for real.

'C'mon,' he said, 'gimme a hand. And mind the gill covers or it'll get bloody.'

The fish was so heavy that, kneeling side by side, they had to roll it back to the water's edge. As the first, small waves washed over its head its great mouth opened like a garage door, funnelling the sea in and over its gills. Annie cupped her hands and threw water over it, as if trying to rouse a comatose drunk.

Danny looked back at The Predator who stood watching, saying nothing. 'You going to give us a hand?'

The Predator pulled one hand from his jacket pocket and extended it. Danny hesitated, grinned and stood to shake it but, before they made contact, the big man spread his fingers and something dropped onto the sand. Still without a word, he turned his back and walked off into the night, headlamp beam fixed on his feet as he went.

'Danny, quick!'

The fish was reviving, twitching and trying to turn itself upright while still half on the sand. He dropped down beside it, slid an arm around its middle and grabbed the open, lower jaw to lift and drag it forward. Annie took the weight of its tail and, together, they eased it back into the sea. It righted again, took three or four slow gulps of the Bristol Channel and, with one violent thrash of its tail, was gone like a platinum torpedo.

Danny stood stiffly and blew out an enormous sigh. Already up, Annie was frozen, watching the blackness where the fish had disappeared, beaming fit to split her face. He patted her arm. 'Thanks for the help.'

She didn't even notice.

Whatever the unholy hour, it was time to go. There'd be no beating that, ever, most likely. Not unless *The Beast*

From 20,000 Fathoms got a taste for Devonshire calamari.

He picked up his rod and began to dismantle, then remembered The Predator dropping something on the sand. He scanned about him until his light picked out a small metallic glint.

It was a key on a fob.

A car key.

On a chrome and plastic fob in the shape of a rifle.

Chapter 25

Danny meshed his fingers, cracked his knuckles above his head and stretched back in the swivel chair, his half smile reflected in the cold, black monitor on his desk. No one else was in the building yet, nor would be for a while, and the peace and low light gave him the brief, alien feeling that this wasn't such a bad place to be working, after all.

He coughed, shook the idea away like poison and powered up his computer, hoping to jolt himself back into the real world. Any more thoughts like that and he'd be the one taking lithium.

The real world was fishing now, and days at Barum Fixings didn't feel so wasted any more. They were just the means to several ends, namely equipment, end tackle, and bait. So he pushed thoughts of Jim aside with the other depressing details of the working day and headed straight for *The Goldfinger Bite.*

Even at this early hour, the site was alive. Every county forum in the south west, and right along the south coast to The Solent, had four, five. . . six or seven brand new, buzzing threads with 'HUGE bass' or 'Big silver' in the title. Danny clicked through them, lingering on the photographs but barely registering the bait or tactics detail in the reports. After all, he thought, anyone can catch bass, when they're there.

His grin broadened, seeing the first angler posting in each forum thinking they'd smashed the British record. . . until the next report came in, and the next, and the next.

There had never been a night like it.

There were some fine fish on display, too; some blurry, some dimly lit, but all massive. Danny drew the longest, slowest sigh he could. None of them was as big as his own.

Nowhere near.

It was a shame he had no pictures of his own but, although he might regret that later, he was still so high on the thrill of catching. . . no, just touching such a creature, that just for now he didn't give a damn. It meant he couldn't prove he'd caught the biggest of all but so what? He doubted any records would stand long, as these were only the first fish to arrive in what seemed to be a gigantic shoal coming in from the Atlantic. Of course, he could always have smashed its head in and hauled it back to town for an official weigh-in.

He spoke aloud. 'Proof? *Pfff.'*

There was no one there to hear, of course, or see him tap the side of his head with one finger. All the proof Danny needed was locked inside.

Actually, it didn't look like a single, freak shoal, going by the distribution of catches. It looked more like a full-scale migration. . . or invasion! Perhaps they'd return every year! Maybe they were moving in permanently! He brought up *Google Earth*, stopping the auto-zoom long before the virtual camera found Devonshire, while most of the whole planet was still visible. The Atlantic Ocean filled most of the screen, with the British Isles smaller than a thumb-print, top right. It was mind-boggling, wondering what other incredible specimens and species were drifting those depths, so vast it took even sound itself could take five hours to cross them! And what microscopic shifts of current might bring them close to land?

He looked again at the spread of reports. The Isle of Wight boasted the best of the rest, so far. The catch report told of grown men shrieking like schoolgirls when a huge bass took a tiny sand eel and tipped the scales at ten ounces over the twenty pound record.

And *then* they caught the big one.

The best photograph was scale-perfect, and the first fish, laid out alongside something the size of a silver sea lion, looked small enough to have been the winning bait. Thirty six pounds, more than a full stone heavier.

But it wasn't as big as Danny's. The guy used the same reel that he did, and a shot of the fish and the rod on the sand showed the size. Danny closed his eyes. The Compton

Bay fish would have needed a crash helmet, to have a head the size of the one he had caught. He scrolled down through several more snapshots; they'd taken plenty, obviously. The last two were his favourites, with the beaming angler cradling his catch, half-submerged in still water, then catching a great, arching splash of English Channel across the face as the fish lunged for its chance at freedom.

But photographs, kudos or seafood worth spit-roasting weren't the only prizes. Freezers full of floorboard-size fillets were a pretty good reward for some, it had to be said, but Danny was in early to collect two much finer trophies of his own. He checked the clocks on the wall and his computer.

Where was Slade, anyway? He was usually the first one in, which Danny *knew* was just so he could watch his workers' faces fall as the door swung shut behind them. The tables were turned today, though, and Danny was there first to savour the view of a lifetime when Slade finally crept through the door.

The door opened.

'What the. . .? You, of all people, in *early?*'

Sheepishly, Danny popped his head out from behind the monitor. He forced a toothy smile, cleared his throat and said, 'Don't tell anyone, will you? I'll never live it down.'

Annie tossed her hair and sniffed. 'Becoming a proper little Employee of the Month, aren't we?'

'Well,' he admitted, 'sometimes, you've just gotta chase the dream.'

Cocking her head to one side she stared at him, then a smile spread. 'Aww, Mr Company-Man's embarrassed!'

Perhaps he was, just a little, but from that point he wouldn't let it show.

'Embarrassed? How can I ever be embarrassed again, in front of you?'

'Me?'

He held her stare. 'I've seen your bum, now. Remember?'

'Danny!'

'I have, and several times!' He relished her reddening. '*Aaand* I've seen your-'

'*DANIEL!*'

Anger, now. Fake, of course. Danny loved it. She kept up the pretence, though, clutching the bundle of post she'd brought up with her to her chest and stamping off across the room in a huff. She only made it to the photocopiers before wheeling around, now all smiles.

Beautiful, gleaming smiles. For once, Danny wanted the clock to slow time, just so he could look at her longer.

'Well, I've seen yours, too.' She perched her own, perfectly, on the edge of his desk. 'Which explains a lot. I was wondering where the phrase 'rotten bottom' came from.'

Danny glanced past her, from Slade's empty office, to the clock, to the door. 'He is due in today, isn't he?'

'Oh, yes.' She rolled her eyes. 'He'll be in.'

He reached out a hand and she took it instinctively, but all he did was tap her watch and say, 'I wouldn't be so sure. He's normally on his second coffee by now.'

'Slade's late and you're disappointed?' It dawned, and she threw back her head. 'That's why you're in first, isn't it! You want to rub his nose in it!'

'I. . .' he began. Damn, she knew him too well already.

'No, no,' Annie stopped him. 'I like that.'

'Good. You know, you've got to give the man credit, you know?'

'Slade?' Annie feigned shock. 'I'd rather give him an uppercut!'

'That tope,' said Danny. 'That was a damned fine fish in its own right. He did bloody well to land it. You don't get many tope that size from the shore.'

Danny hoped Slade had taken pictures. He'd ask him, in a week or so. Things would settle down.

'Ach! Anyone can catch a big fish,' said Annie. 'We did!'

Danny nodded, smiling. 'He didn't just give me the key, though.'

'Jim's key.'

'Yeah, I know. But he chucked a spring balance down, too. Right after. I'd never have got it weighed, otherwise.'

'Well, it was a sporting gesture, I suppose,' she conceded.

'Yeah,' said Danny, nodding. He hadn't kicked up over the unconventional way the winning fish was landed, either.

Danny wondered if he'd have been as generous himself, with positions reversed. 'Yeah, you know, I think it was.'

'So how much did it weigh, exactly, your fish?' Annie asked. 'I was too busy snapping it!'

Danny couldn't bring himself to say, not exactly. He held up a fist, palm forwards, and opened four fingers in order. Then a fifth.

She shared his huge smile for a moment, then leant around his monitor. 'The Goldfinger Bite?'

'Course.'

'Bet you can't wait for a good brag.' She grinned. 'Hey, you never did tell me why they call the web site that.'

'I did! It's how the fish hits. The first jolt, pause, then Bang!' He mimed a rod tipping over with his arm. 'It's typical. You know what the fish is before you strike.'

'Yes, but why a Goldfinger bite.'

Danny looked at her blankly. 'Because it's Shurely Bassey.'

'Oh.'

'And a lot of people saw 'em last night,' Danny went on. 'I'm just reading all the other reports. Haven't posted my own yet.' He sat higher in his chair. 'They're everywhere! It's amazing! They're pulling them out from Land's End to Littlehampton, now. No, wait. Look. *Twenty six pound* silver whale! it says!' He clicked the link. 'That's Eastbourne!'

'Wow,' said Annie, trying to keep up with his enthusiasm. 'They'll be around to John o' Groats, next.'

Danny clicked through a few more reports, then couldn't resist a good smirk. 'None as big as ours, though.'

She smiled back. 'I'm glad it got away, though.'

'Got away?!' He thumped the desk silently. 'I'll have you know that's called catch and release, young lady.'

'Whatever,' she said brightly. 'It's still breathing sea.'

One of those mildly awkward, new-friends silences followed. One of the last, Danny felt. Annie broke it with a laugh.

'And at least we're breathing cleaner air.'

'Sorry?'

'You know. Going to feel strange without himself here, isn't it?'

'Who?'

Annie snorted. 'Your civil partner, that's who.' She crossed the room and perched on the desk beside him. 'Jim, of course.'

Danny stared at her, expressionless. 'He's not my civil partner,' he said eventually, then looked down at his desk, at nothing. 'Government paperwork, so formal. So sterile. You can't just rubber stamp free love and boy-boy romance.'

She hit his arm. 'Have you spoken to him?'

'Jim? No. No mobile, has he? He used to, but he said every time he answered it he heard voices in his head.'

'But surely you've got his home number?'

Danny shook his head.

'So. . . that's it?'

He shrugged.

'How long have you known him?'

'I dunno. A couple of years.'

Two years. But how well?

He did feel sorry for him, in some ways, but Jim was always talking about leaving Barum Fixings, and it wouldn't have surprised Danny to discover that all Jim's recent time off had been spent chasing jobs. And he certainly came prepared for his grand exit. 'Good god,' he recalled. All that licorice!'

Stupid idiot. Danny had to admit one thing, though. He would miss all the fun. With Jim gone, time would grind close to a standstill.

It must have shown on his face.

'Poor old Lithium Jim,' Annie sighed psychically.

Danny snorted. 'You wouldn't have got away with that name if he was here.'

'I know.' She smiled, knowing Danny knew she'd meant no harm. 'He wasn't. . . I mean, he was a bit strange, though. Don't you think?'

'Ha. Just a bit. But you were going to ask, *'He wasn't really mad, was he?''* He grinned. 'I know you were.'

She reddened, just a shade. 'Jocelyn swears he is. Like, properly nuts.'

Danny shrugged and shook his head. 'Jocelyn swears all the time. She'd be a fishwife, but no fish ever gets that desperate for a quick spawn.'

'She says that Lithium thing's for real, you know. Says she was behind him in the chemist, once.'

'Don't believe a word of it. If Jocelyn ever set foot in a chemist she'd be too busy bulk-shoplifting Immac to notice anything.'

'Come on, admit it, Danny. You love her really.'

'That's a joke too far, that really is.' Danny didn't even want to follow that one up. 'You know, he um, he used to come in on Sunday nights, sometimes. Jim, I mean.'

'What, in here, to work?'

'Yeah, back when I first started, before the new alarm systems went in and everyone got a key.'

Annie pulled a face. 'I can't imagine Jim putting in extra hours for free. I mean, he was never a single minute early in the mornings.'

Danny shook his head. 'He used to sneak in here to draw crop circles in the dust on Slade's desk.'

'Crop circles?' She laughed, beaming. 'That's brilliant!'

Danny joined her smile, nodding patiently before dropping his gaze. 'A bit weird, though.'

'Weird? Why?'

'The contract cleaners come in on Saturdays, and leave the place clean enough for surgery. Jimmy used to bring in his own dust.'

She stared at him, wondering if he were serious. It took just seconds to realise that he was. 'Here,' she said, sighing and shaking her head. She tossed down her three inch pile of white and manilla envelopes, of varying thickness. 'Now do some work!'

The door swung shut behind her and it was quiet again. Soon the traffic built outside, though, then more drones filtered into the building. Chappell was the first through the office, nodding a silent, blind Good morning from the doorway aimed at anyone who might be in, not even noticing if anyone was. Danny nodded back but he had already walked away. Jocelyn was next, also pleasingly mute and scowling like a Vietnamese pig chewing tinfoil.

Excellent. She vanished straight into the staff room, shortly followed by Charlotte Langtree, also looking pretty haggard, and definitely less than happy over something.

Danny understood, though. Monday mornings must be such a drag, for anyone who hadn't caught an elephant of a bass! He rubbed his hands with glee, then turned them to the incoming mail.

A postcard? Danny studied the picture, the view of an exotic, palm-lined marina with a cruise liner the size of a toppled skyscraper anchored just offshore. He tuned it over. The stamp was garish, a small lizard on an alien flower.

'To all at BF&A,' said the big, short message. 'Reaping the benefits of all your friendship. Sincerest thanks to the bad boys.' It was signed with an enormous flourish, 'Joanie.'

Danny snorted. Should he take that as sarcasm or a compliment? Good on old Joanie, though, partying away her constructive dismissal compensation before the award was even made. He smiled. Amazing how different people were, away from work.

Picking his way through the most routine-looking stuff first, Danny watched the others start to trickle in, leaving their selves in the car park and heading for another day the same as all other days. A nameless temp, Joan's locum, crept in with a look of keen blankness on her face, then retreated the way she had come. Two drips from the typing pool followed in sad silence, then Janice Bodley arrived, a small, personal rain-cloud hovering over her head.

No Slade yet, though. Danny still couldn't get over it, that smarmy, fat slug being the biggest loudmouth ever to pick up a fishing rod! Talk about a dark horse! But he was a dead horse, now, given the good flogging he so richly deserved. Maybe he'd gone into hiding, licking his wounds, or been so distraught at defeat that he'd thrown himself down the throat of his own tope. But no problem. Danny could wait.

He had a car, at least. A crappy one, maybe, but a crappy estate car was still perfect as a fishing wagon, and definitely an improvement, room-wise, on his last little *Matchbox* thing. He wasn't *quite* sure he'd got exactly what he'd bet for, but not sure he could or should object, either. He'd probably gone up in the fixings and attachment world, too, becoming a company car driver. He'd have to remember to raise it at his next annual assessment. Which was another good reason for not rubbing Slade's nose in it too much.

He heard Jocelyn shrieking and cackling somewhere downstairs, probably complaining again about problems finding space to park her broomstick, then Joe Stibb was the last to beat the clock into the room. Danny and Stibb never liked looking at each other at all if they could help it, but something about the geek caught Danny's eye, which accidentally caught Stibb's.

Stibb looked ill, pale enough anyway, and panda-eyed as though he hadn't slept. No, not panda's eyes. . . they were more like a bad boxer's! Both were black but edged with purples and browns, and there was a fresh scab across the bridge of his nose. There were scratch marks on his face and neck, too, some pretty deep.

Marvellous! The day just got better and better. Stibb saw Danny's broad smile, got a rush of colour back into his deathly cheeks and seemed to mouth the word Vacuum, before storming off to the staff room. Charlie-otte had arrived by herself today, and Danny wondered if Stibb was simply what her men looked like when she'd finished with them. Or maybe he'd met someone who'd done what everyone who ever met him wanted to.

Maybe Jim. . .?

Danny hoped so, but the idea made him shudder. Jimbo didn't have it in him, did he? Whatever. It should have been Jim, Danny decided; first because he had more reason than most and, second, because Danny would have sold his Grandma to buy tickets to watch.

Still, it would make a nice little mystery to ponder, whiling away the pre-fishing hours. He reached for his in-tray again. The first envelope had just 'Danny' on the front. It still took him a few seconds to recognise her handwriting. He untucked the flap and slid out three A4 sheets. Pictures.

They were a little grainy and the colours on them none too true, but the focus was perfect, better than many posted on the forums.

It was the fish. Danny's own. There were a dozen in all, shots of it from beaching to release. The conventional, perfectly-posed trophy snap was missing but these were far better, true all-action wildlife photography, not some smug bloke kneeling with a knackered lump of fishmeat. One held his eye for a long time, taken just as he'd gone to unhook it. As he'd tightened the line, the great head had swung up, and it looked like it was trying to swallow Danny's hand. It's great, black gob took up half the paper. His whole arm would only have been a quick snack!

Annie.

He leafed through the rest, grinning until his face ached. Then he found one she'd tucked one away at the back, out of sequence. She'd saved the best for last.

It looked too good to have been true, but too real to have been faked in any way. Annie, bless her cotton socks, had hit the button on her phone at the very moment the huge fish had leapt from the shallows, just before snapping the line. Danny - clearly Danny - was crouched beneath it, reaching up, showered in a trail of glittering droplets.

It made him gasp.

'Underneath it!'

'They're only draft copies. I didn't have any printer photo-paper at home.' She'd been waiting out of sight, just inside Slade's empty office. 'They'll come out much better than that when we print them up here.'

For a moment, Danny was speechless. 'They're. . . amazing. Thank you!' He flicked slowly through them again. 'You had these all the time? Why didn't you tell me over the weekend?'

'Well,' she purred, resettling herself on the end of his desk. 'We were busy over the weekend, weren't we?'

'How can I ever thank you?'

'Ooh, I don't know.' She chewed her little fingernail, eyeing him over her knuckles. 'Busily, perhaps?'

He laughed and picked up the next the first of the day's proper business mail, a chunky, padded envelope.

'Wow,' Annie said, 'I must have shocked you.'

'Why?' he asked, slitting the stuck-on, transparent delivery note pocket open with a pencil. 'I mean, yeah, maybe the first time. And again with that thing on Sunday morning, but. . .'

'No, you. . . fool!' She scowled and smiled at the same

time. 'Shocked you into working before lunch! Looks like a return. Send someone the wrong box of widgets, did we?'

'I don't know.' It was a little odd. Returns never came to the sales office. This was specifically addressed to Danny, too, and had Personal rubber-stamped at an angle near his name. He held it to his ear and shook it. The sound wasn't one of rattling widgets. Not fixings or attachments, either.

'There's a box but it sounds like, I dunno, something with . . . *liquid* in it?'

'Who's it from?'

Danny unfolded the delivery note and saw the logo at the top.

'Aagh!' He tossed it onto the desk like it was burning.

'What is it?'

He spat the name like it was the product of a heavy cold.

'The Pasty Boys!'

He retrieved the note. 'I wonder what this is. A peace offering?'

'Oh, I doubt it.' Half-smiling, Annie picked up the package and began poking at the corners with Danny's scissors. 'But I'm sure it's just another childish game. Let's see, shall we?'

Danny studied the rest of the delivery note.

The details were irrelevant.

It was signed in red ink: *James Molton, Regional Manager.*

'*Annie, don't open it!*'

But it was too late.

THE END

About the Author

Colin Roberts is wanted by police on six continents and yearned for by women worldwide. After captaining Manchester United to European Champions Cup glory in 1999, then a stint in SAS covert operations overseas and in space, he retired to his palatial twenty-bedroomed mansion overlooking England to pursue a lifelong passion for compulsive lying. His fabulous wealth and legendary physical prowess have, for many years, allowed him to keep a string of beautiful actresses and pop starlets as mistresses, unbeknown to his wife and two children until the publication of this book.

Writing fiction was the only apparent legal vent for his drive to deceive and his first published novel was Samhain, in which he made up some crazy, horrific story about fierce Celtic demons from the past and expected people to believe it.

Many didn't, so two other efforts are rumoured to be close to release or escape: The Severed Garden, a really big, gruesome one with people wandering about, getting nasty and bitey after they've died - yeah, right - and Seleniazomai, more demon-based tosh blending horror and comedy with sickeningly laughable results. A book about sea fishing was, of course, the obvious progression. People don't just expect a fisherman to lie, they demand it, and rightly so.

While The Goldfinger Bite contains none of his trademark supernatural drivel, and only glimpses of the perverse orgies and maniacally sadistic violence so characteristic of his earlier work, it does provide him with the opportunity to falsify to his heart's content, which he does on every page except this one.

Surprisingly, Colin Roberts really has caught a handful of fairly good fish. Nothing to get too excited about, though, and as he doesn't believe a word he writes about devils and stuff, either, all his work is best avoided unless desperate. Consequently, this biography appears at the back, not the front, of the book that you have bought and paid for, which he sincerely hopes that you have enjoyed but, in all likelihood, you haven't.

Please address all complaints to his web site:

www.thegoldfingerbite.net

Yersinia Press